CREATIVE WRITER

By

Tom Fynn

First Published 2015 by Abyssopelagic Publishing

"Writing is finally about one thing: going into a room alone and doing it ... The haunting demon never leaves you ... that demon being the knowledge of your own terrible limitations, your hopeless inadequacy, the impossibility of your ever getting it right."

William Goldman

"Writing a book is a horrible, exhausting struggle, like a long bout of some painful illness. One would never undertake such a thing if one were not driven on by some demon whom one can neither resist nor understand."

George Orwell

For all aspiring writers

The alibi

'WHERE'S THE DEVICE, son? It's better if you tell us now.'

'The device?' I feel sobriety struggling to the forefront of consciousness. 'The device? What, like a tin opener? A PC? Or do you mean an emblem of some kind — a family crest? Is it a police euphemism? Give me a clue.'

My interrogator looks at his colleague behind me, presumably for permission to brutalise the suspect. He receives a shake of the head.

'I don't think you appreciate what trouble you're in,' he says.

We're sitting in the back of a police van a safe distance from the venue of the York Literary Festival. A sniffer dog has been invited to sample my extremities but been unimpressed. A blank-faced man wearing a pistol on his belt has frisked me, finding nothing worthy of comment. My hands are handcuffed behind my back. It seems I'm in some trouble.

'Police state,' I mumble, beginning to regret the last four rums. 'Is heckling an arrestable offence now?'

'Where's your phone?' he says.

I nod towards my left breast pocket. 'No international calls, please.'

He checks my number and recently sent texts, apparently not finding what he's looking for.

The guy behind me hands a piece of notepaper to the interrogator, who holds it up for me to read.

Death to Avery Johns! I, Thomas Flynn of Manchester Gallagher University vow to destroy myself and my enemy today with a bang during his talk at the York Literary Festival. Long live literature!

'Seen that before?' he says. 'Not the paper. Just the message.'

'Nope. But any one of my students could tell you I wouldn't have written such crap. Look at those clanging clichés that bookend it. And the exclamation points? No. I won't even mention the piss-poor word order; I would have put *today* after *with a bang*. And why would I send such a note anyway? What would be the point? None of it makes sense.'

'We're checking under your seat for a grenade or other missile.'

'A grenade? Where would I get a grenade? I can't even get a whiteboard marker at work.'

'Have you served in the forces?'

'What do you think?'

'I'd say not. Have you a grudge against the writer Avery Johns?'

'He's not a writer. But . . . yes, I suppose so.'

'Would you like to tell me why?'

There's a "code knock" at the back door and it's opened to reveal a man I recognise: Avery Johns' PR man.

'Yes, that's him,' says the PR. 'Tom Fynn, or TG Harkett if you prefer.'

The policeman turns to me. 'It seems you've been sending abusive emails to Mister Johns for some time. Anything to say about that?'

'Is it illegal?'

'It depends if Mister Johns wishes to press charges.'

The PR stares at me, more pitying than contemptuous. 'Mister Johns is willing to overlook past abuse provided it ends today. If any further instances occur, all previous evidence will be used to prosecute.'

My interrogator looks to me for agreement.

'Yeah, OK.'

Another policeman arrives from the hotel. He's wearing a giant padded vest like a military baseball catcher. No missiles have been found under my chair.

'Look,' I say. 'I think I know what's happened here.'

Faces turn to me.

'I think it's my stalker . . . or my hacker. Both. I mean, it's the same person.'

'Your hacker?'

'Well, I suppose it started with Lexxi Cummins.'

The interrogator shows utter incomprehension.

'Porn star,' says the guy behind me. 'Adult performer. American. *Game of Bones? Ass Crash II?*'

'That's her,' I say. 'Well, not her exactly. A copy of her. Biologically accurate. But I'm forgetting the note from the student Janet seduced ... only it wasn't from a student. Or for Janet.'

'Would you consent to a drugs test?' asks the policeman.

'I'm not on drugs. I'm a writer.'

He leans forward and pins me with his best interrogator stare. 'I think you'd better tell us the whole story, Mister Fynn. From the beginning, and as coherently as you can manage.'

'Right. Good. That's what I do. Listen ... '

Creative writer

FENELLA GASPED as Thad's turgescent member tumbled from his boxers. It throbbed and swelled, swelled and throbbed, twitching perpendicularly pythonic: a monstrous proboscis of purple-headed majesty. It was a club. It was a truncheon. She was rapt at the spectacle. 'Oh God, Thad! she moaned. 'Wield it!'

Fantastic word, *turgescent*. A better phrasing would be *Thad's avid turgor tumbled*, but there's something ugly and even more arcane about *turgor*. How about that *gasped*? A bit too sibilant for the context? *Groaned* is more bestial; it complements the later *moaned*. *Monstrous proboscis*? A lovely euphonic pairing – alliterative and assonant simultaneously – if a little too entomological. *Protuberance? Appendage?* No. They minimise the music.

There are too many metaphors, true. The snake (and let's face it: no editor at G-Spot Books is going to let me get away with *pythonic*), the insect nose, the phallic armoury ... too many conflicting images. Too much for the one-handed reader to grasp. Have to keep the focus clear. Those repetitions'll have to go as well. They might possibly let me keep the two *it was*'s.

But no. No they won't. Who am I kidding? There's no place for style at G-Spot books. If I don't edit out all the good stuff, they will. Got to keep it banal. Got to keep it the Wordsworth side of graphic. Stick to clanging clichés and hackneyed formulae. *He plunged his massive tool. She rode the tsunami of* ... Can we still use *tsunami*? Have to check that.

It's all disposable shit anyway. This third book in the series (*The Fenella Ardent Chronicles*) will be bought by the same half-wits who bought the first two, sweatily keen to follow the fortunes of young Fenella as she proceeds through her degree in Advanced Sexual Techniques at the absurd and absurdly prestigious Aphrodite Finishing School outside Zurich. This year, Fenella gets to grips (ooh!)

with a huge (aah!) dissertation (um?) on fellatio or frotting or some other glistening perversion.

It nauseates me even to describe such things. Not the sex, but the books and their market. I do it only for the money, which isn't bad at all: £2000 for a full-length (70,000-word) novel. No royalties, of course. And I have to pay British tax on it. But I can knock one of these out in a single draft every six months. G-Spot seem to want a limitless supply. The market is mostly American (a copyeditor turns all my *colours* to *colors*) and mostly downloads. Low overheads. They must be selling about 5000-10,000 copies of each book. More than I ever sold of my own.

See, I'm a proper writer, though you won't have heard of me under any of my pen names. I write the *Fenella Chronicles* as Jed Tyler, while my three legitimate novels — the last of which was published three or four years ago — were by TG Harkett. Pseudonyms are useful, merciful. When the books fail, as they almost inevitably do, the failure is more easily shrugged off by the fabricated identity. It wasn't me; it was Jed Tyler, TG Harkett. Hacks. Losers. The next book will be better and by a different writer. There's just the minor irritation of having to start all over again, prove oneself all over again ... go right back to the beginning each time as if no novels had ever been written.

My real name is Thomas Fynn. Tom. I'm not sure there'll ever be a novel in his name.

A proper writer, anyway. Meaning my books (plural) were legitimately selected by a genuine publisher, printed, distributed to bookshops and libraries, and reviewed by professional reviewers in actual newspapers ("Harkett offers a flavour of the modern Kafka", *Times Literary Supplement*). My books were on the shelves. I had actual fans (at least four) who were not my friends or relatives. But this is all past tense. Over. Welcome to the publishing industry.

I should also say that I teach on the MA Creative Writing Course at Manchester Gallagher University (skip over the name; all the jokes have been told). At MGU, I'm mostly concerned with post-grad novel writing, though I also supervise BA "creative dissertations". The university may be splashing in the dregs of the league tables, but the course is well regarded by those who've heard of it. We produce, on average, one published writer a year (at least, in the sense that they tend to get published a few years after finishing the course). When people ask me whether writing can really be taught, I paraphrase Kurt Vonnegut: you can train athletes who already have ability, but winning gold is up to the individual.

Creative writing. I've never liked the term. Professional novelists aren't "creative writers". Journalists and copywriters aren't "creative writers". It's a patronising term redolent of hobbyism. Go into WH Smith and look where the creative writing magazines are shelved: near the woodworking and scale-model-building magazines, the thimble-collecting and the angling magazines. There's a taint of amateurism to the term. The *creative* is tentative and tremulous, underlined with a pitiable yearning. I am creative. I really am! It's implicitly the kind of "creativity" that children engage in at kindergarten: coloured safety scissors, pots of primary-coloured poster paint, glitter. It's the indistinguishable swirl held to the fridge door with magnets. Pat the child on the head. It's beautiful! What is it? A particle-accelerator? Well, I'll be! Wait 'til grandma sees it.

Real writing is work. It's backache and stiff necks and not speaking to anyone all day. It's forcing yourself to meet the daily word count even as snot drips on the keyboard. If it's fun at all, it's fun in the sense drug addiction is fun. Writing is a cerebral narcotic: the zen zone, alpha-wave activity, dopamine. It's the one place in your brain you want to be instead of in the real world, but a part of the brain that has to be exercised and developed over years of acutely self-conscious writing practice.

Still, none of this — the porn, the teaching — is proper writing. That's something I don't do much of these days. And not because I'm blocked. "Block" doesn't exist. If you can write, you can write. What *might* be lacking is ideas, or planning or preparation or the sufficient willpower, all of which a proper writer should have. No, I've sworn specifically *not* to write anything else until my masterpiece is published.

The masterpiece took me six months to research and two years to write. It's 250,000 words. Unlike any of my published books, it takes risks with style and structure. It's *brave*. Writing it, I allowed myself no restraint, no fear, no second-guessing of how the market might respond to it. The only consideration was the world of the book, its style, its themes, its rhythms. I was Melville shunning dinner as he wrote *Moby Dick*. I was Rabelais scratching blasphemies on vellum in his monastic robes. I was Joyce squinting at the birth of the twentieth century. I had nothing to lose and nothing to gain but some ineffable breakthrough to a higher plane of literary ability. No thought of publication. No consideration of genre or market or readership. It was pure writing. Writing as it should be: as Nabokov or Burgess or Miller (Henry) would have recognised it.

My masterpiece was to be my monument and my epitaph: a statement of ability after which I could die. But first it needed to be read, which meant tossing it into the gladiatorial arena of the publishing industry and letting the lions gnaw on it, the *retiarii* jab at it, the crowd cast a wave of descending thumbs at it.

It's been rejected by about twenty agents and/or publishers so far. I'm not keeping count. That's a normal figure. The main thing is that each one of them has given a different reason: too long, too weird, too episodic, too unlike anything else on their list, too *like* something else on their list, too literary, not literary enough. Of course, the majority of these people don't even read the thing. One agent replied that they don't publish children's fiction. Another agent later told me that he typically takes less than an hour to skim through a novel – like listening to the first twenty seconds of "Stairway to Heaven" and dismissing it as a bit slow. Great books cannot be skimmed. They're read and then re-read. That's how they're designed and written.

So. Not another serious word from me until the masterpiece is accepted. I have to believe it will be. We'll see. I know I can write publishable stuff. I have been published. I've been employed by a university as some kind of authority on the subject. I've written articles on novel-writing for magazines. Everything I know tells me that the masterpiece is publishable. All it needs is for someone to actually read it properly and see what I was trying to do . . . and for the market to be amenable . . . and for a committee of editors to agree.

I'd say I'm hopeful, but hope is a poison to the writer. Hope of success. Hope of acknowledgment and praise. Empty promises. Better to just get on with things. Best not to think about the masterpiece out there in the Coliseum, in the bloody maw of the hyena. It'll come home if it can, maimed and limping, the victor's laurels askew on its temples.

Until then, I'll sit here in my cold flat writing poor-quality porn, reading never-to-be-published manuscripts by my students and bashing out the occasional article for one of those Creative Writing magazines. I also write a blog, more of which later. This is my world: the mouse knocking occasionally against a cold cup of tea, the trusty Chambers dictionary (*turgescent, turgor*) by my left hand; the keyboard opaque with dust and speckled with croissant flakes; yesterday's bolognaise now a sanguineous pattern on white ceramic; a shot glass with the sweet-sticky stain of a premium rum; the metallic-glaze vase that Lara bought, now dry and empty. She always wondered why I couldn't or wouldn't buy some flowers occasionally.

Back to Fenella, then. She of the ample breasts, lissom legs and voracious tonsils. Another 1000 words before I turn on the heating.

Pipe smoke and pickled onions

MANCHESTER Gallagher University in week one, semester one: Fresher's Week. The undergraduates swarm. They look younger than I ever felt as a Fresher, and they're definitely more fashion-conscious.

Students on my first degree looked like refugees or the homeless. That was back when mobile phones and the Internet didn't exist. Back when the proto-laptops had screens the size of a post-box slot (has anyone under the age of twenty even used a post-box, I wonder?). These young MGU students all seem to be dressed alike: baggy grey tracksuit trousers for him, black leggings for her; the faux-fur-lined hoods and the ludicrous woollen hats that droop off the back of their heads like some encephalitic growth; the tatty Converse All Stars that are so prevalent as to be almost a uniform.

What do I look like to them? I'm 40 – older than most of them can imagine ever being. My hair is thinning and greying at the sides. I'm wearing a sensible GoreTex waterproof jacket they won't be able to afford, and wouldn't want to wear, until they hit their thirties. I've got a bulbous gut I'll never lose because I like food more than I like exercise. In short, I'm invisible to them. Probably a lecturer. Possibly a member of the public caught up in the youthful crowd. They don't know I'm a published author. Once on the shelves. One day, perhaps, they'll buy the masterpiece and never know they'd walked beside me here. Such thoughts are necessary.

I'm carried through reception, where people in coloured t-shirts are handing out leaflets/packs about study skills, mental health counselling and safe sex. Nobody offers me anything. I pass through swarming juveniles to the English department and my office.

I say *office*. As a part-time lecturer, I share a "hot-desk" with an unspecified number of other part-timers whom I almost never meet. I can gauge their quantity and characters only by the clues they leave: a lip-sticked (lip-*stuck*?) cup, a scrawled Post-It note, a freebie hotel Biro, a review copy of a book, a smear of

13

something that might be chutney on the right-hand shift key. My donation is a dusting from some M&S mini-poppadums. A full-time historian sits at the other desk, casting occasional dismissive glances at us interchangeable dilettantes without doctorates. I don't mind. I've published more books than he has.

There's a curling Post-It for me on the monitor: a reminder from reception that I have a meeting today with Percy, one of my novel supervisees. There are three of them – long-term students working on full-length novels that represent their final MA submission. Percy is the only one who can write. He's 80 and has been working on his book for about thirty years, currently on its eighteenth or nineteenth draft. He uses a manual typewriter, which I admire. I learned to type on one and there's pleasure in pages dimpled by percussive keys. Still, a computer is faster and easier on the carpal tunnel syndrome.

But first there's the departmental meeting that kicks off every academic year.

I arrive to an empty room and take the opportunity to stuff my mouth and pockets with biscuits laid on by the university. The coffee is toxic but hot and free. An overhead projector has been left on in the room, illuminating the whiteboard with a heavily-branded scene of laughing multi-ethnic students in a park somewhere, no doubt manifesting the joy of their excellent educational decision. I turn this off. I'm not alone in yearning for a blackboard and chalk.

Jerry comes next. He's the Creative Writing programme leader, a novelist whose single book came out in 1987 to no fanfare and few sales. I haven't read it. Silver-haired of head and beard, he seems to care about nothing at all. Why would he? He's full-time. He's published. MGU is his silk-lined sarcophagus.

'Tom,' he says, filling his mouth and pockets with free biscuits. 'Good summer?'

'The masterpiece was rejected eight times.'

'Excellent.' He pops an oat crunch. 'What'd they say?' A Viennese shortbread.

'Too episodic. Doesn't suit the market. Too many big words. No boy wizards.'

'Ah.' A fruit square.

'You?'

'Saw one of mine in a charity shop in Austin, Texas. Someone had written "Couldn't get past page seventeen" inside the front cover. One dollar.'

'D'you buy it?'

'No. I've tried to read it. I couldn't get past page seventeen either.' Another oat crunch. 'Did you get the message about Percy?'

'Yeah. He forgets things and reminds others to help him remember.'

'Think he'll make it to submission?'

'50/50. His wheezing is getting worse.'

'Talking about me?' says a voice from the doorway.

It's our poet, Gwynn Palmer, reeking of fresh cigarette smoke, beer and the mints he's eaten to disguise them. He looks like one of the Thompson twins from the Tintin comics, but without the bowler hat and with occasional lapses into substance abuse. His last collection came out twelve years ago, but it won the TS Eliot Prize so he never has to publish again.

'Everyone glad to be back?' says Gwynn, grinning. He sniffs the coffee and grimaces.

'Joyous,' says Jerry.

'Never happier,' I say.

And finally there's Janet, the screenwriter. She wears thick-framed rectangular glasses, a hoodie and a pair of grubby Converse, though she's in her late thirties. She wrote a couple of episodes of a TV drama four years ago and was a co-writer on a film that nearly won something at Sundance once. She's known to sleep with at least one of her (female) students each year, but that's OK because tribadism (interesting etymology) is cool.

It's a tiny sub-department of the English faculty that'll probably be cut soon to free more budget for managers. In the meantime, it's our playroom.

'Top o' the mornin' to yehs,' says Janet, wryly noting the empty biscuit bowl. She's not Irish. It's probably a film quote.

Jerry's printed out an agenda. The first point is admissions for the next intake.

'So I'll just go through the list and you can say 'yay' or 'nay' *etcetera*,' says Jerry. 'Radcliffe Harvey − screenwriting.'

'Nay,' says Janet. 'Not an ounce of talent.'

'Prudence Braithwaite − novel.'

'Yes,' I say. 'She hasn't learned punctuation, but there are apparently books you can buy ... '

'Maria Squillino − poetry.'

'Lovely name,' says Gwynn, 'but it's English-as-a-second-language territory. A no.'

'Yeah, you can cross off Mubuta Yllanga from novel,' I say. 'Same reason.'

'I believe Mubuta has a Cambridge Proficiency certificate in English,' said Jerry, flipping papers. 'From Lagos?'

'Yeah, but did you read her sample? TEFL colleges don't teach novel-grade writing.'

'She's published in Lagos, Tom.'

'Self-published. Photocopied, actually.'

'OK. Fine. Your decision. Less students for you.'

'*Fewer*, not *less*,' coughs Gwynn.

'Fuck off,' says Jerry, matter-of-fact.

The list goes on. Most students are accepted on the courses they've applied for − not necessarily because they have any ability, but because we won't have jobs if the courses fall below the quotas. Since the university has no budget for marketing and publicity, the course is always in danger of being under-subscribed and cancelled. You'd have to be pretty much illiterate not to get on.

But not dyslexic; that's different. It's a recognised complaint with budget set aside for support and counselling. I've had a few self-diagnosed dyslexic students, not one of whom has shown the slightest difficulty with spelling or reading. My feeling is that some use it as a shield for their fears of inadequacy, and others – whisper it – because of the extra 10% slapped on their final mark. The bigger issue is that of 'Special Circumstances'.

'Special Circumstances,' says Jerry.

We groan theatrically.

'Come on. You know we've got to do this. You've seen the reports from Student Welfare. Any questions?'

'There's a guy in my group who can't sit down,' says Gwynn. 'He has to stand all the time. Not just stand, but walk around as I'm teaching.'

'And your question?'

'Does anyone else find that funny?'

Jerry looks sternly over the top of his glasses.

'I've got a girl with a nervous condition,' said Janet, clearly building up to an outburst. 'I'm not supposed to raise my voice, move unexpectedly or use bright colours in my lessons.'

'Yes ... ?'

'So my question is: "What the fucking fuck?"'

[Definitely a quote: *Stepbrothers* (2008)]

'It's a difficult case ... '

'We're learning screenplays, Jerry. I'm showing films. I'm screening *Die Hard* this semester. What's going to happen to her? Seriously?'

'Yippee ki yay!' says Gwynn.

'Couldn't she watch something else?' says Jerry. 'There must be other films.'

'*Silent Running*?' says Gwynn.

'*Stand by Me*?' I suggest, sending Gwynn into an emphysemic paroxysm.

'Look,' says Jerry. 'You know how it is. Just try your best. The worse that'll happen is she drops out. I've got two dyslexics, a chronic fatigue syndrome and a diabetic myself this semester. I've got to take a course in how to inject emergency insulin or something. You just have to turn the volume down.'

'Someone should do a study,' says Janet, folding her arms. 'What is it about writing courses that attracts them? You know I've got three undergrads this semester who claim to be bi-polar. Three. When I was at uni, *bi-polar* was a down jacket.'

'I thought you liked the bi- ones,' says Gwynn. 'Bi-curious, isn't it?'

Janet sticks her tongue out, but smiles.

'Speaking of the BAs,' says Jerry,' have you all got your supervisee lists?'

We mumble assent. Each year, increasing numbers of undergrads opt to do their dissertation in Creative Writing as the easy option. No reading. Just make it up. Most receive very low grades.

'They're supposed to contact you and arrange meetings—' says Jerry.

'In the final week before submission,' says Janet.

'—But you might want to remind them that their dissertation is going to take longer than they think. I'm nearly done.'

Gwynn's cigarette packet has appeared on the table. Janet is fiddling with her watch.

'There's a late application for your novel course, Tom,' says Jerry, pulling a stapled sheaf of papers from his pile. 'Mohini Aboulia.'

'Is she the Indian girl I saw in your office this morning?' says Gwynn.

'That's her. Anglo-Indian. Home Counties, actually.'

Gwynn offers a *Carry On* leer and winks at me. 'Lucky Tom!'

'She was lovely,' says Janet.

'She's actually a transfer from Brunel,' says Jerry. 'Accepted on their MA but had to move up here at short notice. I've accepted her. Hope you don't mind, Tom.'

'As long as her English is up to scratch.'

'It's wonderful. Lead crystal, in fact. Her sample submission was quite ... spicy. I've put it in your pigeonhole.'

I nod, thinking only that Jerry has now obliged me to mark another 20,000 word piece. In fact, his decision has set in motion much, much more.

'Here endeth the meeting,' says Jerry.

'Be careful out there,' says Janet. Probably a quote.

I SMELL PERCY before I see him: a granddad aroma of pipe smoke, pickled onions, mildew and boiled sweets. He's waiting for me outside the meeting room, bent over his aluminium walking frame. His old leather briefcase hangs from it. He's wearing a flat cap and a tweedy jacket with leather-patched elbows. He's wheezing.

Percy's novel is (as are most first novels) a thinly-disguised autobiography: the story of how he met his wife, their travels and her slow death. It doesn't sound like a page-turner and it isn't. But it is remarkably frank, unadorned and honest. Think Charles Bukowski in *Ham on Rye*, but more English. The major challenge − as always − has been structure. A book like his needs to move.

'Morning, Percy.'

'Ah, Tom. Tom . . . Good summer?'

'Fine. You know, you can go into the room if I'm not here. No need to wait outside.'

'I was just . . . catching my breath.'

'Are the lifts not working?'

'Yes . . . yes. But full of . . . chinks, you know. Full of 'em.'

'We don't say that anymore.'

'Oh. Yes. That's right, isn't it? You can't say things.'

The Racist's Charter. His book has already been purged of its various brown, black and yellow epithets.

We sit and Percy dithers for a while, laboriously taking the typewritten manuscript out of the briefcase. Other supervisees email me their work so I can read it at home between bouts of distractive self abuse and Internet surfing, but Percy's twentieth-century methods are different.

'So this is my rewritten last four chapters,' he says. 'I followed all of your suggestions. Cut out the excessive description of the coffin and the embalming process. Expanded the bit where I stand by the grave. For the "pathos".'

'Good. I know it feels artificial to you, but it's a great scene to tie your themes together and the reader will want it by that point.'

He harrumphs – a sound I've got to know well over the months. Every writer finds his own ways of responding to editorial criticism.

I glance absently through the pages. 'Good, good … I'll have a read through this … but I think we're probably done. You're ready to submit. How do you feel?'

When I look up, I see his eyes are wet. He's fumbling for his hanky.

'Silly old bastard!' he says, avoiding my eyes. 'Don't mind me.'

And suddenly I get it. His wife died thirty years ago and he's spent most of that time writing about her. What does he do now the book's finished?

It gets me thinking about Lara.

The escritorial embryo

THE FIRST BOOK is the hardest. You write with a wilfully blind hope that what you're producing is good: publishable. Nobody has asked for your book. Nobody is waiting for it. You have done nothing in your life until that point to support or justify the idea that you can write a novel. Who are *you* to write a novel? To attempt such a feat is surely a path to failure, which is why you've spent decades making excuses for not even trying. Not trying means not failing.

Lara made me try.

Or rather, she got sick of hearing me whine about how I couldn't possibly achieve such a thing. She'd been listening to it since we'd met and got together at university. I'd written thousands of words explaining to myself and others why I would never produce a novel. I had well worn monologues on why the task was beyond me. Of course, I'd tried. Five thousand, ten thousand, even twenty-thousand words on a typewriter or written with an expensive fountain pen bought for the purpose. But I'd always been writing, from the very outset, with an expectation of failure. That made the failure acceptable. Inevitable. Natural.

Lara made me really try. She was the conscience I'd never been able to develop.

'Just do it,' she'd said. 'Write a whole novel, however long that is, and then see if it's good. You're always saying how everything in the shops is shit. I'm sure you can write shit, too.'

'Thanks.'

'I'm serious. You don't have to write *Ulysses*, do you? Just write a novel just to prove you can. It'll probably be shit, but at least you'll know you can do it. Then you can write another, better, one. And if you give up — if you just can't write one — then that's the end of it. Don't even talk about it anymore. Don't even try. Are you going to spend the rest of your life regretting not even trying?'

She was right, of course. She usually was, with her no-nonsense mind. And that was my breakthrough: the knowledge that I had nothing to lose except my doubts and fears. I just needed to know if I *could* write a novel. Knowing that would make things better. I could live with myself if I genuinely proved I couldn't produce the book. And if I *could* ... well, that was too much to hope for.

Being serious meant I would need rules. I realised I had to approach it the same way I had approached long essays as a student (the only successful pieces of writing I'd ever produced). That didn't mean writing it the night before, sky-high on coffee and Red Bull (I was never one of those). It meant having a process, a goal, a deadline. Plus, preparation might conceivably last for years and still count as "writing a novel".

The first challenge, then: do a lot of preparation. Research into the subject area, research into novel structures, research into the market. I started to reread my favourite books as a writer might: counting how many scenes, how many chapters, how many storylines and how they interwove. I asked myself why I liked these books and tried to list their common characteristics. I started to sketch a rough plot, then scenes, then character arcs. I'd never done anything like it before, though it had all been right in front of my face for years. I'd been reading my whole life, but I'd just been inhaling it unthinkingly like TV.

I felt more confidence than on any previous attempt when I actually began writing. I felt I knew – nebulously, notionally, with a kind of religious faith – where I was going. Still, it was like walking a tightrope over an abyss through impenetrable mist. All I could see were my feet taking small, tentative steps: the daily word count of 500-700 words. I learned not to look back at the accumulating words or down into the billowing void of my presumption. Either glance would have caused crippling vertigo and toppled me. The only view was forwards into the white blankness, step by 500-word step.

Such focus leads to obsession. My life was taken over by the book. I was working in a normal job back then and the book was like a DVD playing constantly in my head. I'd pause it when more immediate cerebration was required, but play it at every other opportunity: cycling to work, sitting on the toilet, in a meeting, in the pauses of a conversation, as I walked from one place to another. Pause. Play. Pause. Play. My entire day and everything in it was nothing but a placenta for my escritorial embryo. I realised at one point that I was pressing the lever on the toaster at exactly 7.28 each morning because that was a conscious step in the next twelve hours before I could start writing again. It *had* to be this way. I had no idea if I would reach the end, but reaching it would be my nirvana, my ascension, my apotheosis.

I actually thought of it in those terms. Committing completely to something is a risk seldom taken by anyone. It breeds maniacs and fundamentalists. It destroys reason in the name of self-belief. Finishing the book − not even getting it published − was something I'd yearned for since I'd first learned to love reading. The writer had always been my astronaut or fireman or stuntman. The writer was a god. Producing a book would make me a writer. Soon, like Macbeth, I'd gone so far that going forward was no worse than going back. I was closer to the dream than I had ever come.

Of course, Lara supported me all the way. She'd occasionally make story suggestions (style interested her not at all). She seemed to understand when I came home from work, rushed a meal and went straight to the spare room and the computer. There I'd sit for two or three hours − or until I hit the word count − before falling into bed. I'd read her extracts as she tried to fall asleep (sometimes while she *was* asleep) and then I'd dream about the book. Often, I'd wake with the precise word I'd been looking for, or a plot development that had been evading me. I kept a pad and pencil handy.

I'd write at the weekends, too, or talk about the book as we did the shopping. There was no other topic of conversation. The book was my life. I was responding to her challenge. I was taking it seriously − more seriously than I had ever taken anything else. It was more important than anything or anyone else. If I'd been diagnosed with a fatal illness and given mere days to live, I would have spent my dying breaths on the book. *It* would be my gravestone and my epitaph.

Perhaps this is what it takes for everyone to complete a first book. Not just a piece of work, but a wilful rebirth. A restatement of being. Orwell went through it. Nietzsche went through it. Rousseau, too. Henry Miller wrote in *Cancer* that one must be destroyed as a person to be remade as an artist. One must lose in order to gain.

In the agora

THE DAY of my first MA seminar. The university is less busy (most of the undergrads in bed or watching daytime TV) and I'm able to find a photocopying machine that isn't broken and/or jammed. My pigeonhole at first appears to be empty as usual but then I notice the thin sheaf of papers that is the late application by the Indian girl. No need to read it now that she's already been accepted. I stuff it in my bag and notice a single sheet of yellow notepaper curling within the pigeonhole, its perforations ragged where it was torn out of a spiral pad. A handwritten note.

Think you can get away with what you do? I'm going to show you!

There's no name and no other indication of who might have left it there. The copying room is accessible only with a MGU pass card. Then I realise what must have happened. Janet's pigeonhole is directly below mine. No doubt one of her disgruntled student conquests handed in the note, folded, at reception and it was put in the wrong hole by mistake. I drop it into Janet's and get to work on the photocopier before someone else comes to break it.

I know the names of my class today but have no idea what they look like or who they are. It's possible I saw their applications a year ago, but such things vanish instantly from memory. As always, though, I worry about who I'll get. My greatest fear is that they'll be good. People who can already write have no need of this course. There's very little I can teach them except some rudiments of structure and planning that they might not have picked up. The whole workshop process depends on their prose being sufficiently raw that a semester of feedback will definitely improve it.

Actually, no. My greatest fear is that they'll be better than I am. The thought of having to teach someone who is manifestly more intelligent, knows more about literature and who's a better writer is a nagging dread. I won't know for sure until I see their first workshop samples. Then I usually feel the vast relief of seeing all those old familiar flaws. It doesn't matter if the person is twice my age, a professor of literature or a government minister, a flawed prose style puts them safely under my tutelage. Submissive. Teachable. If nothing else, I still have the holy and apostolic seal of genuine publication.

Checking emails, I see that a number of my assigned BA supervisees have contacted me in order to arrange a meeting. Here is a generation born to emails without ever having written a paper letter. Their messages are ragged, illiterate, presumptuously informal and polluted with smiley faces or emoticons. They have evidently embraced the notion that, as customers rather than students, they may regard me as an educational serf.

> *Hi!*
>
> *Someone told me your my superviser for the dissertation ;-). I can meet you at 12.00 on Friday. I'm interested in writing a novel about a Russian prisoner who has tattoos after seeing that programme on Channel 4. Cheers*

Last year, one of them asked me how he could get his novel published: a novel he had yet to write about an assassin with telepathic powers. He believed that a six-figure advance was inevitable on the basis of this premise and in respect of his experience as a twenty-year-old undergraduate with zero writing knowledge. I told him to send a letter to Penguin. He probably got his advance.

I suppose I should have given him credit for having his own idea. Every other student is writing a pastiche of *Game of Thrones* or Harry Potter or Terry Pratchett. They've not read anything else. Or nothing else has penetrated their minds. The books on their reading lists – the finest and most renowned titles of world literature – have evidently had no impact on them. Despite their wide-web worldliness, they remain infantilised: soft targets for children's writing.

Wasn't I the same? Not at all. At their age, I was blown away by Scott Fitzgerald and Eugene O'Neill and Sam Shepherd and Nathaniel Hawthorne. Even by Shakespeare and Milton. Even by Chaucer and Rabelais when I learned to understand what they were doing. But that was in the days of attention spans, when a long train or bus journey was a chance to read. When learning to write meant a decade's apprenticeship of reading rather than a single premature ejaculation of *X-Factor* "talent" into the TV-anaesthetised face of the world.

That's the problem. Nothing deep and essential can be immediate. Creativity requires some development of the self, transformation through growth and realisation. Nobody just sits down and writes a novel. Not a novel worth reading, anyway.

That's why I've asked my MA group to come today with an extract to read out: a few paragraphs of a book they've found inspiring − the kind of prose they aspire to write. You can tell a lot about someone by the writing they (claim to) revere.

So I walk among the sterile and commercially-carpeted corridors of MGU, through multiple wheezing fire doors, to my classroom, where I peer through the vertical glass window to get a surreptitious glimpse of them. A dreadlocked youth in a camouflage jacket. An elderly man with a yellowed Panama hat on the desk beside him. A pale young man with home-cut hair and an Adam's apple like a swallowed iron. A tired-looking middle-aged woman who manifests exactly my concept of a mature student. No sign of the Anglo-Indian girl Jerry mentioned. My class.

Can you tell a writer by appearance only? A certain dishevelled cast, perhaps? A piercing eye that takes in more than you realise? A frank and uncompromising stare? An autistic shyness, maybe. I don't think so. It's like asking if you can tell who's going to win the gold medal. They all look fit; they're all wearing shorts and running shoes. The winner is the one who crosses the line. That's how you know.

I introduce myself. I tell them about my published books (the alpha monkey climbing to the top of the tree) and outline the course. I give them my speech about becoming a novelist: that they should dismiss immediately any fantasy of the muse or of imagination and "talent". There's nothing innate. There's no mind for writing as there's supposedly an eye for drawing or an ear for music. Writing is work. It's practice, reading, failing, application, failing and reapplication. It is, inescapably, who you are as a person and learning to express that as naturally as you can. It is technique and structure. Punctuation and grammar are absolute rules that you must learn before you think about breaking them. Deadlines are serious and necessary − if you can't provide a few thousand words each week for the workshops, you'll never be a writer. Your kids and your job and your spouse and your disability and your imminent death are all lesser priorities than writing . . . if you are serious.

They look serious. Or terrified. Statistically, 0.5% of them might get to the level where they might be able to write a publishable book. About the same percentage of that 0.5% might actually get published. It's important to be upfront about such things. The spectres of Disappointment and Frustration will accompany them every day of their writing lives. Do they still want to continue?

They do. They're fresh. Also, they've paid about £3000 each to do this course (some of them in the mistaken belief that any publisher or agent will give a shit . . . as if having a certificate of immortality will halt a speeding bullet.)

And so to their introductions. I sit and listen, hearing what they say, what they mean and − God help them − who they probably are beneath the carapace they've built around themselves:

'My name is Gerald. I wear a Panama hat because it lends me a spurious sense of authority and, simultaneously, of frivolity. It's the kind of thing a writer wears − a hallmark, if you like. A commissioning editor at Random House or Transworld would recognise immediately that I'm a writer if I was wearing my battered old Panama. I am a stalwart of my local book club and writers' circle, where my stridently sententious monologues are dreaded by all, and where my reputation is that of a tiresome pedant more concerned with talking up his talent than with demonstrating it. I have chosen to read my extract from the Book of Ecclesiastes (King James Bible) not because it is a piece of powerful and compelling poetry, but because it is the Bible and an indication that my tastes are not just unimpeachable but also rubber-stamped by God Almighty. I am writing a novel about a man in his early sixties who wears a battered Panama hat and who overcomes the mediocrity of his peers to become the greatest artist of his generation. It is a work of fiction. I am also mildly racist and disappointed to discover that my tutor on this course, Tom Fynn, does not conform to my own fanciful notions of what a great writer is. I'd prefer to be taught by James Joyce (whose *Ulysses* I have never managed to finish, but which is commonly thought to be the best book ever written.)'

Gerald seems disappointed not to receive a round of applause when he finishes. As is my habit, I bestow a first-seminar mnemonic on each student. Henceforth, he'll be known as Stalwart.

'Hi everyone! I'm Margaret. I'm married to Dave and have two young sons called James and John. I've been keeping journals all my life and I've always wanted to write a novel. I've read a load of books about writing but none of them has ever really helped. I suppose, if I'm honest, I've just never had the discipline. I need someone to give me deadlines and I'm hoping this course will sort me out. I've brought an extract from the book that's being serialised on Radio 4 at the moment: the one by the woman with the twinkly, just-so prose style in which every sentence is wrought with a chocolate-box aesthetic that becomes nauseating after a page and in which even dogs or insects have their own thoughtful narrative point of view. I've brought this because it's my idea of what good writing must be, though personally I find it a bit nauseating and I'd rather read one of those crime thrillers with the author's cover name printed in shiny foil. I'm afraid that everyone is going to judge me and that I'm not really good enough to be here (although I already feel superior to this Gerald bloke, who's clearly an utter tit). I don't think I'll be able to meet Tom's expectations, but I'm going to have a damn good go. If I don't make a breakthrough on this course, I might as well give up.'

I nod. A husband and two kids. Little self-discipline. The odds are not great. But her self-deprecation is appealing and I enjoyed her rolling eyes as Stalwart held forth. She'll be called Mum.

'Yo, I'm Damian and I've got dreadlocks. I've just, like, come off the BA in Combined Studies and I've been allowed on this course despite only having a 2:2 because there was a quota for MGU undergrads doing postgrad degrees. I dress like a tramp, but my dad owns a company that makes frozen ready meals for Tesco. I've never really written anything and I don't read much, but I really love the sound of my own voice and my friends think I'm hilarious because I engage in the glib inanities that sub-educational people find amusing. Everything I know is a post-modern patchwork of movies, TV and YouTube music videos – a chaotic melange of images and sound bites that these days masquerades as culture. Like many of my generation, I adopt an arch sardonic tone that pretends to be knowing but which is its polar opposite. I am a cipher who believes Kurt Cobain is a hero for killing himself aged 27 (I was a one-year-old at the time). I have chosen to read from Burrough's *Naked Lunch*, which is, like, shocking to some people but not to me because I smoke joints (don't tell mum!) and that's pretty near to being a junkie. I've not actually read the book all the way through (has anyone, actually?), but I carry a copy of it. I'm here to shake up this course, so hold on to your Panama hats!'

I christen him Dreadlock Twat.

'Hello. I'm Toby. I'm afraid I haven't got anything interesting to tell you about myself. I haven't got a TV, by which I mean you to understand that I'm a serious person. I work at a local so-called creative consultancy where my job is to write Twitter feeds, Facebook updates and other social media pap for companies stupid enough to believe that their customers look at such things. I hate the job, though I love writing and want to write a novel just to prove to myself that I can. I love reading, which is just as well because I haven't got a girlfriend or many friends. I'm secretly a bit of snob because I got a first-class degree from a better university than this one. At the same time, I recognise that I've achieved nothing and can't call myself a writer based only on my excremental 140-word effluvia. This course is probably my last chance at maintaining the illusion that I might one day write a book. I've chosen to read from Cormac McCarthy's *The Crossing* because it's literary dynamite. The real deal. If you don't agree (you with the idiotic Panama hat; you with the dreadlocks), you shouldn't be in this class. I might have an Adam's apple like I've swallowed an iron, but I'm serious about writing. Watch me.'

Toby has enough disdain to be a writer. He'll be Earnest Youth.

I'm just about to start on the photocopied extract I've prepared (a piece of bad writing for us to practice on) when the door sighs open and my brain floods with hormones.

'Hi? Is this the MA Novel group?' she says, a lead-crystal English voice with a lilting sub-continent inflection.

I stare.

'I'm Mohini Aboulia?' she says. 'My train was cancelled and . . . '

They said she was attractive, but she is something more.

Her face is an abyss of dark, pitiless beauty. She has almost black eyes, made glinting wells with an expert chiaroscuro of powder and mascara. Her eyebrows are thick and artfully shaped. Her hair is a cataract of night around her shoulders. Her lips are full and shaded a dark red. Her skin has that permanently healthy hue of a foreign sun. She smiles, pausing there at the open door with one manicured hand holding it open. Waiting for permission.

I realise that I am staring and that the rest of the class are staring at me. She, too − Mohini − is staring at me with a sly, amused expression: the look of a woman who knows the effect she has on men.

'May I come in?' she says.

'Yes, yes. Come in,' I say. 'You've missed the introductions, but . . . ah . . . did you get an email about bringing an extract of something you like?'

'Yes. I have it here.' She pats her large handbag and enters.

The rest of the class watch her as she takes a seat immediately to my right. Are they, as I am, watching her body as she moves? She's wearing black leggings that adhere to her like skin and, beneath her black leather biker's jacket, a burgundy top of some silky material that's just as form-fitting across her breasts. Her presence brings with it a perfume of exotic and expensive provenance: an earthy concoction of frankincense, sandalwood, myrrh and ambergris. An ancient aroma. The perfume of Cleopatra or Aphrodite. The Fenella part of my brain awakes: *Her gravity-defying orbs . . . legs parting with wanton abandon . . . the moist mouth a welcoming dell . . .*

'Would you like me to introduce myself?' she says.

'Yes . . . er, yes. Please do.'

I glance around the other faces to see if anyone has been as affected as I am. Dreadlock Twat is leering at her; Stalwart is pursing his lips (not only is the impertinent girl late, she's also a darky!); Mum has that subtly destroying look women reserve for other, thinner, more attractive women; Earnest Youth is attempting, vainly, to avoid drinking in her image. He's enough of a feminist to know that outright ogling is unacceptable.

'I'm Mohini. Hi. I was on the MA at Brunel but I had to come up here on a project for work so I transferred and MGU was kind enough to accept me. I've brought an extract of *Lolita* because I think it's the best novel ever written − a novel about infatuation with a girl and with language itself. In it, Nabokov makes love to his mistress: the English language. You only have to look at the opening lines to see that he writes with his tongue and his mouth. He's French-kissing the language. That's what I'm going to do to you, Tom. I'm going to become your mistress. I'm going to seduce you. I've already started. Look at me. You'll see, in time, that I'm no magazine pin-up. Not vacuous or painted or PhotoShopped. I am abundance. I am a voluptuary. I am total satiation. Follow me with your eyes, smell my perfume, imagine me naked and staring into your eyes as you climax. Get lost in me, Tom. Forget everything else. I am everything you want and I'm going to give it to you. Give me everything, Tom. Give until you have nothing left.'

She holds my gaze throughout. For a second, I feel that we are the only two in the room, yet I have heard barely a word of what she actually said. *Lolita* is probably my favourite book. Has somebody told her that? She read the extract like a professional actor, her voice so precisely moderated, so textured with meaning. An almost hypnotic voice. She sounds more like a writer than any student I've taught on this course. I'm going to call her Mohini. She is nothing else.

The rest of the seminar is supposed to be a discussion of their literary intentions and answering their questions about the course, the market, writing in general. It's a good opportunity for me to learn more about them and for them to understand exactly what's required. It plays out with a surreal, otherworldly atmosphere — as if Mohini's late arrival has brought an astronomical force into the classroom. A black hole drawing my attention. A satellite exerting its own pull. A sense of denser gravity. I try to remain professional, even as Stalwart predictably veers like an idiotic dog down the sewage outlet of banality. *Her* eyes goad me to be the alpha writer, the Great Teacher.

'You say that you don't believe in inspiration, Tom ...' says Stalwart, chuckling smugly, explaining to a grandchild that open-heart surgery cannot be conducted using a spade.

'Let's be clear,' I say. 'I don't believe one can sit and write a novel using just the Divine Spark of inspiration. Ideas will come and surprise us. But those flashes appear out of preparedness: a plot, character arcs, the hard discipline of routine and ritual. A cathedral is not built on a whim.'

'Ah, but [*self-satisfied smirk*], Gaudi's Sagrada Familia—'

'Still isn't finished after 130 years. And is a building rather than book. I was speaking figuratively.'

Mohini's dark eyes flash with humour. *His trembling turgor throbbed ...*

'Yah, but what about Kerouac?' says Dreadlock Twat. 'He, like, wrote *On the Road* on a long piece of toilet paper while he was travelling across America on drugs.'

'Have you read it?'

'Yeah.'

'All of it? To the end?'

'Well ...'

'Save yourself the trouble. Nobody has ever finished it. Even after a hefty publisher's edit, it's still unreadable. People read it when they're stoned because there's no other way to endure it. And I'll tell you someone else who wrote on toilet paper: the Marquis de Sade. *120 Days of Sodom*. Here was a man who sat on custom-made dildos the size of fire-extinguishers for his inspiration.'

Dreadlock Twat giggles because I said dildo. Stalwart purses his lips. Mum makes a note: "de Sade, sodomy, extinguisher."

Mohini gazes at me darkly. I know so much about literature! *His cisterns filled with pulsing passion to be unleashed as geysers ...*

'So, we're going to cover all this on the course?' says Earnest Youth, pen poised. 'The preparation and plotting.'

'All of it. That's the main difference between this course and others. Elsewhere, they get you to read a handful of books and encourage you, somehow, to extrapolate how to write from them. If it were that easy, no such course would be necessary. We'd all learn it just from reading.'

'Can I ask ...' says Mum. 'I mean ... I've always wondered ...'

'Why is it that we can all recognise good writing without necessarily being able to do it ourselves?' says Mohini.

They all nod: sagely, energetically, thoughtfully. She's caught the collective haze of thoughts and grounded them in a flash through the lightning rod of her dark beauty.

'Interesting question. And an essential one for anyone wanting to be a writer. It's a paradox. In fact, it's like teaching. Almost everyone has been taught at some point in his life, but becoming a teacher is something else. As a student, you feel that the teacher is simply telling you things, but what's really happening is that the teacher is preparing a framework on which you learn. *You* do the learning; the teacher does the teaching. As readers, we feel that one thing simply follows another, but it doesn't happen automatically when we sit to write. Why? Because writing is the process of preparing a framework that directs the reader. Suspense, humour, pace, story – they don't just happen. They're set up by the writer for the reader to respond to. Such mechanisms are – and should be – invisible to the reader. That's why we think we can write because we can read. No. Reading and writing are two entirely different skills.'

I watch them frenziedly scribbling. Not her. She's looking at me like we're already secret lovers. Her smile is carnal. Those delicate incisors . . . I actually feel afraid.

'Could you . . . ?' she says.

Strip me? Kiss me? Wind me in your sheets until my flesh glistens and my hair sticks in black tendrils to my skin? Until I gasp for breath and my mascara runs?

'Could you,' she says, 'say something about style and voice?'

It was exactly the point I was going to raise next. This stuff is pure literary aphrodisiac. Their pens twitch, ready.

'Style and voice,' I say, [*Pericles on the Parthenon platform, Socrates in the agora, Christ winding up for the Sermon on the Mount*] 'constitute your goals as writers. They have no especial mystery. They come to you through long practice of writing and close reading, during which your written expression comes to match perfectly, seamlessly, the voice in your head. First you learn the tools, then you learn to use them. We'll be covering some of this in later classes . . . '

I rattle on for my audience of one. She seems to write nothing. When a question needs to be asked, she asks it or helps one of the others to shape a nascent opinion. By the end of the seminar, she has me.

Mise en abyme

IT'S ONLY AFTER the seminar, on the train home, that I remember the slim sheaf of papers from my pigeonhole: Mohini's application submission. The one that Jerry called ". . . spicy" (the ellipsis was clearly audible). But I don't read it on the train. I'm afraid to. I feel like an adolescent bringing home his first pornographic magazine found under a hedge or inside a hollow tree stump, terrified that his mum is going to say something like, 'Why are you hugging your Adidas bag like that, Tom? Is it stiff with hardcore German pornography?' Today's lads are spared such stress. Just log on and whack away (not that I condone pornography, which is exploitative and which objectifies women *etc*).

No. It has to be saved and savoured. Is it not, after all, a formal application for the course? As the tutor, it's my duty to examine the work closely for stylistic content. Perhaps in the bath with an aromatic candle burning and the door double-locked.

In the end, I can't wait for the bath. I start reading it as soon as I'm out of the train station and walking the fifteen minutes home. It's a short piece — maybe 1000 printed words — describing a dream in which the female narrator is visited in her sleep by a spectral lover. The names and prose style seem to be borrowed from Indian mythology — a clever distancing technique. These are not *her* fantasies *per se*, but the tropes of an ancient literary tradition.

I read with such febrile urgency that I can barely follow the narrative. I feel that there must be some personal message within: something she wrote specifically for my eyes. She must have been told who the tutor was this semester. This is a coded letter to me. It even seems to carry a faint scent of myrrh, of sandalwood. I skip through phrases like: *My lover comes to me as cloud and rain, drenching my skin.* Phrases like: *We intertwine as waves, becoming one, crashing, foaming.* Phrases like: *I inhale him. I swallow him. He is my sustenance.*

The rational part of me is impressed. She has a sense of rhythm and a way with punctuation. She's captured the mythological idiom well, if a little too slavishly. It'd be interesting to hear her own voice. The rest of me — the majority — swells with synaesthetic arousal. These typographic marks evoke fresh memories of her perfume, her eyes and the face-slapping corporeality of her limbs, her torso, her neck. She *is* her writing.

I'm reading the piece again as a light drizzle begins to fall, looking for my name hidden within a word or acrostically or palindromically. I must be in here somewhere. I just feel it. She intended this for me. The paper becomes damp and the letters seem to blur. Surely the writing is waterproof? Photocopy toner is. Laser print? But no — even as I realise it's too late, the words have begun to seep and dissolve as if the page had been doused with water. The letters vanish implausibly quickly, fading to leave only an unintelligible grey static on the page. The text might never have existed at all.

Can I remember it? Could I try to type it from memory as soon as I get through the door? Only 1000 words. I try to recall the phrases. Waves. The rain. What the hell kind of printer was that? It's like the writing was actually designed to vanish. I'm going to have to talk to her about this. Some cheapo printing ink or something.

Once through the front door, I turn on the laptop and then the kettle. There's three days of dirty pots cluttering the kitchen and I search for a clean cup, eventually sluicing the scummy tea out of a recently used one. If Lara was still living here, I'd probably cook something. A chilli. A nice cauliflower cheese with macaroni and turmeric. Any excuse to use the fantastic Sheffield-made Damascus-steel chef's knife she bought me (rosewood handle, brass rivets). Instead, I pull a ready meal from the freezer and post it into the microwave. The pale light of the laptop is already calling me to the desk.

Sitting there in my ergonomic chair, I feel like a Formula 1 driver must as he straps in. The keyboard and the screen are my conduits to another world, a more real world than the one I'm about to leave.

There are more emails from BA students arranging, or re-arranging, tutorials. They very often forget to turn up for their sessions, offering quasi-apologies like 'I'm rubbish at checking my email!' (they check their email every five seconds) or 'My bus was late' (they live two minutes' walk from the campus) or simply 'I was ill' (apparently twenty-year-olds are the sickliest members of society). I wouldn't mind if they managed to come up with better lies. It would at least show some imagination.

I open the *Fenella Chronicles* document, but the microwave's *ping!* takes me from the desk. By the time I return, carrying the steaming carcinogenic rectangle on a tray, another email has popped into my inbox. Its subject is the title of the masterpiece.

I put the tray down and stare at the unopened message. It is either a rejection or an acceptance, the former being more likely. The limbo of not knowing is actually preferable to rejection, but I prepare myself for another failure. As an unpublished writer, I'd always get the single-sentence rebuttal sent in to every unsuccessful submission. These days, I tend to get a personal note. It's just a question of how many words they waste before they drop the axe. There's usually something like "Thank you for submitting your fascinating novel [title]", followed by some platitudes about its strengths and finally a meek, vaguely apologetic reason for saying no. The praise is certainly welcome, but it makes me think of some absurdist firing squad in which the sergeant yells: 'Ready! Aim! (Lovely suit, by the way). Fire!' I think I preferred the single-sentence shiv to the kidneys.

I click on it.

Dear Tom [the familiarity!]

Thank you for letting us read [nice touch] *your novel* [insert title]. *I found it a fascinating journey and a very accomplished achievement* ["accomplished" – that old stand-by]. *You are a terrific writer* [but not terrific enough to publish, evidently] *and an impressive stylist* [a stylist being akin to a performing poodle in today's market]. *However,* [note the decision not to give this a new para in order to minimise its impact], *we* [no longer "I"] *believe* [!] *that your book would be difficult to place* [but not impossible?] *in the current market. You say that you are influenced by late nineteenth* [missing hyphen here] *and early twentieth-century fiction, but we are now in the twenty-first century and we are looking for books for the modern reader. Congratulations* [fuck you!] *on a remarkable* [but unpublishable, yes?] *piece of writing and we would welcome any further submissions more suited to the current market.* [I'll be submitting a gift-wrapped box of my own excrement!]

Seriously? *Seriously?* Doesn't the modern reader buy Dickens, Collins, Melville, Conan Doyle, Conrad, Kafka? The modern reader has continued buying these authors for hundreds of years. Is Defoe not still in print? Eliot? Austen? Chaucer? Homer? Who *is* this modern reader who checks the date on his novel to see how recently it was written? Who's the reviewer who writes, "Great news for readers who like something written about the last fifteen minutes . . ."? The current market is everything that's ever been written. All of it. These ephemeral trends that marketing teams fetishise are ludicrous. Good writing is what sells. That's what's always sold. Let the readers decide!

I spoon in a dollop of toxic ready-meal. Mousaka? Lasagna? Placenta? Could be anything.

I delete the email.

Fenella's void waits patiently to be filled, but I can't face her or her delicate swellings now. They repulse me. She'll have to diddle herself until tomorrow. I know from experience that I can't write the porn if I'm bilious. I just write even more vindictive parody.

No. What I need is some therapeutic work on my blog

I'd be affecting modesty if I said it's become very popular in the last six months — sufficiently popular that I may soon be able to host lucrative adverts. In fact, I'm appearing on local radio to talk about it this week. It's called Penthesilea (a classical allusion; look it up) and I use it to review bad self-published books in a brutally uncompromising manner — not senselessly insulting, but applying the same criteria that would be applied to a conventionally published book. True, I do enjoy the opportunity to mock and sneer, but these people have left themselves open to it by uploading a seething mound of dreck. My criticism may be cruel, but it's also highly constructive. If they can stomach my advice and take it, they'll become better (proper) writers.

The bad books are easy to differentiate from the better ones. They're usually free, usually genre, usually part of a series and almost always with a heinous self-made cover featuring abysmal design: cheesy pictures, muddy colours and clangingly incongruous fonts. I'm no designer, but I know enough to recognise rank amateurism when I see it. A bad cover invariably equates with a bad novel.

They all share the same kind of prose faults, too. Execrable punctuation, dodgy grammar, sloppy description with imprecise vocab, a fatal addiction to flashbacks, grossly obvious exposition, clunky dialogue, erratic narrative flow, a profound love of the cliché, and a penchant for formulaic writing of all kinds. In summary: all the classic hallmarks of not being able to write.

I've been reading a romance novel — *Happiest Days* by Margot Schulbaum (volume two in the *Blessed Isles* trilogy) — a novel so contrived and saccharine that I have risked diabetes merely by reading it. I start typing:

> *Putting aside Ms Shulbaum's interchangeable use of semi-colons and commas as decorative confetti, her major mistake in the opening chapter is the inadvertent mise en abyme of multiple flashbacks that take us from a car, to a church, to a first date within 200 words. Which is the main narrative thread? It's not clear that the author has considered this. She does, however, seem to own a cliché*

thesaurus. In just one paragraph, the heroine (Pettigrew Harper) has
her heart "going like the clappers", a memory of being "knee-high to
a grasshopper" and her father being "proud as punch". It made me
as sick as a parrot. Clichés are not writing; they're substitutes for
writing.

The ready-meal has gone and I have the urge for a proper coffee, meaning whole beans ground with cardamom seeds and made in a moka. As the water farts and mutters in its pressure chamber, the subject of cliché makes me think automatically of Avery Johns.

I take my coffee back to the laptop and go to Avery Johns' website. The URL is saved in my browser. There he is, the smug, grinning bastard, with his cravat and hound's-tooth jacket. You'd think he was seventy and the heir to the Duchy of Cornwall, but he's my age. He was first published in the same year I was first published, and by the same publisher. The difference is that he's now rich and famous. But still a terrible writer.

I know I shouldn't, but I click on the News tab. The latest headline is a hammer to my forehead.

SCARLETT JOHANSSON TO PLAY MIMI
The Hollywood actress has agreed to play the role of Mimi in Steven
Spielberg's production of Avery's worldwide bestseller Home. The
actress said, "I loved the book and really identified with the character
of Mimi. I am Mimi!" Filming is set to begin in the autumn. For
more information, click here . . .

I stare at the screen. A void has opened in my bowels. Johansson. Spielberg. Hollywood. Is my ready-meal going to rush back into its tray?

I've read some of *Home*, his second novel: a cynical, box-ticking exercise that some people (me) have suggested was brainstormed by a committee. It's got everything you need these days: a character with some ambiguous mental issue that gives him an unusual take on the world, a charming family setting, a quirky jigsaw-style structure (the chapters can be read in any order) and a contemporary theme (does social media complement, or substitute, our identities?). The prose is so banal that I started to drool as I read it. His use of cliché is prodigious. You can hear the plot mechanisms creaking and see the character arcs as clearly as if a child had scrawled them in crayon (Mimi: "I feel I've really grown as a person since my cancer scare last week!")

But the sales figures are undeniable. People love the bloody thing. Translated into forty languages. Sold in supermarkets. European signing tour. And now the film. Now the film.

I watch my hand move the cursor to the Forum tab. I'm already signed in as HomeIsShit69 and my previous period of being blocked from commenting has expired. The caption says, 'Avery cares what every reader thinks. Please tell him, or ask a question.' So.

> *Avery — I am an aspiring writer. May I ask you how you achieve your distinctive voice? I find that your writing is quite devoid of any style or personality. Rather, it is a loose smear of platitudes, predictable allegories and hackneyed stock characters. I have asked my writing teacher how to achieve this effect and he answered: "Become a moron."*

I send this before checking it through. It'll be deleted almost immediately and I'll be blocked again. But perhaps he'll see it. Perhaps it will shake his foundations. Then I feel the usual guilt for my outburst. It's the public I should be attacking — the same public I expect to buy my own books.

It's the familiar conundrum and fear. Your writing is ultimately limited by who you are. Regardless of reading and practice and technique, your writing is you: your personality. There's nothing you can do to change that. People actually like Avery. He's amiable. Reminds me of my late grandma (fishbone, gullet) who would vote for whichever politician had the nicest TV manner. (I make no apology for that filched Nabokovian parenthesis in the previous sentence.)

I know I shouldn't, but I Google TG Harkett and limit my search to the last week. Nothing. A German site offering illegal downloads. A lingering blog post in which someone put one of my books on their *To read* list. I am invisible.

It's now cold in the flat. The ready meal (cottage pie? Cat food?) is gurgling into my intestines. I should really do a thousand words on Fenella whether I want to or not. Perhaps if I think of Mohini … Some libidinous energy might be found there.

I look around for some item of clothing and see the folded shawl on the arm of the sofa. Lara's shawl − the one I bought her in Italy that she never really liked. She wore it, but only for my sake. I reach for it and drape it round my shoulders. And the smell of her flows over me: her perfume, her shampoo. Soap. She might as well be here in the room, her arms around me, her hair tickling my neck as I sit at the keyboard. But the room is empty.

Ice

PUBLICATION meant vindication. Until that breakthrough, I was just another one of the countless millions who dream of being a writer but who hardly dare adopt the term for fear of ridicule. I'd tell people I was writing a novel and they'd offer a variation on Peter Cook's response to the man at the party: "Yes. Neither am I'. Or they'd just smirk. Another self-deluder. Another fantasist.

Publication meant I had reached a certain standard. I could write. Officially. A company was prepared to give me money and risk more in printing, marketing and distributing my book. They weren't just being kind. They saw hard commercial potential in it. All my years of hoping and trying and yearning had been rewarded. My greatest ambition achieved. It was the highlight of my entire existence. It changed my life.

For thirty-odd years, I'd lived as a failure. Whenever the plane shuddered through the turbulence, or the speeding truck veered too close to the car, my instant thought had always been, 'So this is how it ends: unpublished.' It had always been my single indicator of existential purpose. Achieving it made me happy as I'd never been before. No negativity could touch me. House destroyed by a lightning strike? Doesn't matter; I'm published. Bowel cancer diagnosed? Don't forget to buy my book; it's on the shelves.

Lara was the one who broke it to me.

Lara was the one who pushed me to send out the manuscript in the first place. I'd initially been happy enough to finish the thing. I might have just let it curl in a cupboard somewhere if she hadn't harassed me and even taken packages to the post office. She seemed to feel as much hope as I did. It had never been her dream, but she knew it was mine.

The news came in an email. My inbox was open as she was surfing the Net and she saw the novel's title. She opened it. The first I knew was when she started crying.

My first thoughts: a family member dead or injured. A redundancy notice.

'What is it? What's happened? ... Lara?'

'Your ... book ... '

'What?'

'They're going to publish your book!'

That wasn't the moment. Such news cannot be processed at once. It's like being told, 'Yes, Tom, you *are* the Risen Christ.' Too enormous. Too unreal.

I sat beside her at the computer and read the short email too quickly to take it in. *It is my great pleasure ... accomplished piece of writing ... hopeful ... three-book deal ... contract ... meet you in person at our London office.*

There was mention of a small advance, but that seemed unimportant. I would have done it for a Kit Kat. There was mention of some editing process — *just clearing up a few things* — but, again, I would have gladly bled for it.

We hugged. I strutted. But it didn't really, fully, sink in. I daren't believe it. Might it be a hoax? The email address seemed legitimate. I replied, thanking the guy, and he replied back with a date to meet. It all seemed real enough. Still, I told few people. Only after I'd signed the terrifying contract did I allow myself to accept it (I asked my boss to countersign, proving beyond all doubt that I was a better writer than he would ever be).

The impact came shortly after. I was taking my lunchtime stroll by some fields where I'd spent many months thinking about the book, plotting the book, imagining the success of the book. It had been my daily waking dream, the book. And now it was going to be published. I was immortal.

Or so Icarus thought as he soared into solar annihilation.

'I'm so glad for you,' she said. 'It's your dream. But you need this more than you need me.'

'That's not true ... '

'It's true. We're already separated; you just haven't realised. Every night for all these months ... would you have even noticed if I wasn't here? I've become invisible.'

'Lara ... '

'*Your* dream, Tom. And now they want two more books. Two more years for me sitting alone in front of the TV, listening to the keyboard drumming upstairs? I don't want that.'

'We can work something out. I'll—'

'You'll devote yourself one-hundred per cent to these next two books. One-hundred per cent, Tom. You have to. That's what makes you a writer.'

'I'm a writer because of you.'

'Too late ... it's too late. I told myself if you got published ... You don't need me.'

'Lara ... I need you.'

But I didn't. Not then. She knew it. I would have killed to get those next two books written. Part of me was even glad. Just me and the books. Unlimited time for writing. I was the embodiment of Graham Greene's shard of ice in every writer's heart.

I had won everything I ever wanted. And lost her.

Achilles and Penthesilea

THE OFFICES of MGU Student Radio. Lots of plate glass, contract carpet, strip lighting and posters featuring the nauseating DJ line-up, all of whom look like the stereotypical regional radio presenters they'll probably become. Thumbs up, cheeky grins, winks. Names like Dave and Jed and TJ – famous in their own bathroom mirrors. Bullied at school.

The live feed comes through speakers in every part of the building, even the toilets (*and that was* plop! *Duran Duran with* plop! *their 1982 smash 'Hungry like a Wolf'* frrrrrb!) Right now, Jed or TJ is interviewing a local man who's self-published an "epic poem" incorporating every street name in Greater Manchester.

> *I Mosely'd down the avenue,*
> *A curry smell like Palatine,*
> *I've never been too Savio,*
> *Nil-nil the Scaw(ton) in my mind.*

'Interesting,' says Jed or TJ, a youth in a baseball cap. 'I suppose you mean *Palestine* when you say *Palatine?*'

'That's right,' says the poet. 'But there isn't a Palestine Road in Manchester.'

'Not tempted to pop a sneaky '*s*' in there?'

'It's a different spelling. And there is no Palestine Road in—'

'OK,' says Dave or Jed. 'Welcome to the '80s Lit Half-Hour here on MGU Student Digital. We've got some more literature for you now in the form of our own Creative Writing lecturer Tom Fynn, who's been ruffling a few feathers with his blog: Penth . . . Penthes . . . I think we'll get *him* to pronounce it . . . '

A girl with straightened blonde hair and heavy make-up has beckoned me to the studio door and is now gently pushing me inside. I have been instructed not to crowd the microphone and to avoid obscenity or blasphemy.

'How *do* you say it, Tom?' says Jed or Dave.

'Penthesilea. It's Greek.'

'But you're not Greek, are you, Tom?'

'Not that I'm aware. It's the name of a mythological queen who was killed by Achilles.'

'She was also an Amazon, isn't that right?'

'Indeed. That's kind of the point.'

'So you're killing Amazon? Is that it? Tell us what the blog's about.'

'I review self-published books.'

Jed or TJ makes a circling, beckoning motion with his hand.

'Why are you doing that with your hand?'

'Ah, *ahem* . . . first time on radio, Tom?'

'No. I've been on BBC Radio 4.'

'Well, could you tell us a bit more? Why are a lot of people getting a bit shirty about your blog?'

'Because I tell the truth. Look – some people think they're a writer if they just cough up some illiterate gobbet of ill-conceived pastiche, fan fiction or quasi-plagiarism and upload it. No need to bother with correct grammar, punctuation, style or structure. No need to design a proper cover. These people aren't writers; they just want the same instant success that YouTube and Vine and Instagram and Twitter have granted to a few talentless nonentities.'

'Er, I can see that those attitudes might upset some people who've taken a lot of trouble to write a whole novel . . . '

'Come on. Let's be honest. The majority of these so-called writers have taken no trouble to learn how to write. They're often delusional. They've proved nothing. The only measure of their literary worth is their belief in themselves – invariably misguided to a sociopathic degree. Why not just leave them alone to their little fantasies, you might ask? Why get upset about it? Because this is the English language they're mutilating.'

'So you're . . . what . . . punishing them?'

'Educating. I'm an educator. I'm doing this for their own good. It's free criticism.'

'So's throwing a stone, Tom.'

'No it isn't. Not unless you're some kind of Neanderthal that hasn't yet learned human speech.'

'Right ... some, er, forthright opinions from MGU lecturer Tom Fynn. Let's go to Culture Club with "Karma Chameleon" and we'll be right back with a response from self-styled street poet Derek Crabbs and some callers.'

The song plays. Dave-or-Jed's face is dark. 'How about lightening it up a bit, Tom?'

'I can't. It's not just a hobby for me ... er, Dave.'

'TJ.'

'This is our language and our literature. People get upset by my blog because they're looking for a pat on the head, a "writer's badge", a one-album deal with Simon Cowell. They should want more. Being a writer means being able to write.'

'I agree,' says street poet Derek Crabbs.

I snort derisively, immediately regretting it.

'What was that?' says Derek.

Boy George is singing that loving would be easy if your colours were like his dreams. TJ is making broadcasting semaphore signals to his producer on the other side of the glass.

'Nothing. A sneeze.'

'Aaaaand we're back,' says TJ, 'with MGU lecturer Tom Fynn and street poet Derek Crabbs. Derek — you're an artist. What's your take on Tom's opinions?'

'I think he's a prannock, as my old dad used to say.'

'Devastating critique,' I say.

'Could you be a bit more specific ... ' says TJ.

'He's jealous,' says Crabbs. 'His last book was out years ago – he writes as TG Harkett if you didn't know – and he's on the scrapheap. So he takes it out on others.'

'Are you saying my criticism isn't accurate or relevant?' I say.

'It's bitter and twisted.'

'It's correct. And useful. You might benefit from a bit of it yourself.'

'Oh ho!' says TJ. 'What do you say to that, Derek? Could your poetry use some of Tom's criticism?'

'First of all,' I say, 'it isn't poetry. It's not even verse. It's doggerel. I wrote the same kind of stuff when I was about seven. *A curry smell like Palatine?* What does that even mean? The Palatine is a hill in Rome. No, this is nothing more than a strange, possibly autistic, folly: forcing street names into the straightjacket of irregular metre, poor rhyme, garbled meaning and no rhythm.'

'You calling me disabled?' says Crabbs.

'Your writing has learning difficulties.'

'I'm gonna fuckin' lamp you!'

'So speaks the poet,' I mutter.

Crabbs lurches from his seat and TJ attempts to restrain him while making urgent throat-cutting gestures through the glass.

Bryan Adams' "Summer of '69" begins playing and a security guard is obliged to escort the apoplectic street poet to the street, where, presumably, he can Mosely home at his leisure.

'No more of that,' says TJ, rearranging his clothing. 'We're going to take some calls after this song and I hope you're going to be polite. People want encouragement.'

'What they need is guidance.'

He glares.

'Great playlist, by the way,' I say, sarcasm clotting on my tongue. An alarm in my head sounds distantly – *careful!* – but I find myself borne on a wave of indifference. It's an almost willed immolation. A faint smell of myrrh causes me to turn, but nobody has entered the studio.

'Caller one,' says TJ. 'What's your name and your question for Tom?'

'My name's Angie. I'm a first-year at MGU and I want to know why he has to be so rude. I'm a writer myself and my friends are always really nice about my stuff.'

'Hello, Angie,' I say. 'Let me answer your question with a question. Let's say you go to the doctor with some . . . oh, I don't know, some intimate oozing. It's cancer for sure, but the doctor gives you a cream and says it's yet another STD. Wouldn't you feel cheated? Wouldn't you demand that the doctor tell you the truth even if it's bad news? Your friends aren't doctors, Angie. Would you ask them about your intimate oozing? You ask them about writing, so I guess they must be writers or publishers or lecturers. It's not enough that they can read. They need advanced critical tools. My granddad can read, but I wouldn't ask him his opinion on how chapter four balances the pace in the first twenty per cent of the book. Or whether he'd advise a dash or colon.'

Silence on the line.

'Er, I guess what Angie's saying,' says TJ, 'is that, er, if she did have the ooz-. . . if she had a medical condition, the doctor would be kinder about it.'

'Like that would make a difference? Lovely day today, Ange! You've got the Big C!'

'Wanker!' shouts Angie. She hangs up.

TJ sighs, shakes his head, looks through the glass and receives some kind of signal.

'Caller two. Some thoughts for Tom?'

'Yeah. John here. I wanna ask Tom what qualifies him to dump on other people's books.'

'I've been published,' I say. 'That means I have reached a particular standard. That standard means I've been employed by this university as a specialist in writing.'

'But your books are shit, mate.'

'Language, John!' says TJ, a nervous tic beginning to flicker at his left eye.

'Wrong,' I say. 'You can say that you don't like my books. That's entirely up to your personal taste, which I imagine extends no further than those by-numbers laureates of violence McNab and Patterson [*Careful!*]. But if you say my books are ... poorly written, then you have to justify that with some critical analysis. What makes them poor?'

'You're not selling any, are you? I've just looked at your Amazon rank — in the toilet, mate. I've seen 'em in Poundland.'

'So you're implying there's a direct correlation between sales and writing ability,' I say. 'Is that right, John? That would make Dan Brown the greatest writer in the history of literature. Is that what you're saying, John? A quantity theory of quality? You should write a book yourself. Are you literate, John?' [*Careful!*]

TJ snaps off a switch and glares. His eye flickers. The producer signals one more caller then cut it.

'Strong words from our MGU lecturer Tom Fynn. I wonder if his boss is listening. Caller three — you're live!'

'Yes. I've read Mister Flynn's blog.' An elderly, male patrician voice. A student? 'I wonder if Mister Flynn knows the full myth of Penthesilea: that as Achilles plunged his sword into her exposed breast to kill her, he fell in love with her at that instant. He fell in love with his enemy, the Amazon.'

TJ looks to me with an interrogative eyebrow.

'Yes. I did know that.'

'I find it very interesting,' says Caller Three. 'Indeed, I have to hand a review of your first novel that was very recently posted on Amazon. It says, "Harkett tries too hard, stretching for a depth of style that he does not possess, and emulating too clearly his literary heroes. His is a minor talent: imitative, unimpressive, and evidently already diminished — no new titles have followed in these last few years.'

I haven't seen this review. I've seen all the (handful of) reviews. It must have appeared in the last couple of days.

'Tom?' says TJ, who appears to be smiling. 'That sounds like the kind of structured criticism you were just talking about. Have you an answer for … sorry, sir, what's your name?'

'Fair criticism is, er, fair criticism,' I say. 'A genuine writer already knows his flaws.'

'I'm going to get you, Tom,' says the caller's voice, suddenly lower and dryer. 'You can't get away with what you do.'

The line goes dead.

'Er, thanks to the mysterious caller three!' says TJ, looking at me with a shrug. He flicks a switch and talks over the entire one-minute-thirteen-second guitar intro of The Stone Roses' "Love Spreads". The '80s are over.

I allow myself to be led from the room by the painted blonde. What did I just do in there? It was like I was briefly … possessed with some self-destructive urge. I just didn't care. Thank God only about twenty three people listen to this station.

I hope street poet Derek Crabbs isn't waiting for me outside.

LATER, back at home, I go online and listen again to the show. The expletives have been edited out with a comical bicycle bell effect (a nice touch − *someone* at the station is creative) and I'm appalled, as always, by the sound of my recorded voice. Nasal. More regional than I imagine. Not a writer's voice. I remember recording *Hamlet* soliloquies as an A-level student, the better to memorise them, and hearing Shakespeare's language spoken back to me by a flu-ridden labourer. Aye, there's the Vicks VapoRub.

What shocks me more than my voice is the forthrightness of my opinions. Yes, I actually believe what I said, but I'm normally able to control and dilute such opinions. I'm a teacher after all. That voice telling me to be careful … I'm hearing voices now? Perhaps Derek Crabbs street poet was right. Perhaps I am being poisoned by my own bitterness. Too much time alone at the keyboard; not enough time with real people. The people I meet speak only within speech marks, their ellipses and dashes always visible.

I look for that review on Amazon and it's there just as the man said: a new one by 'MrSmith'. Quite literate. Quite incisive. I probably agree with most of it, but that was my first book. Is anybody's first book their best? Henry Miller, maybe. Harper Lee. I can handle adverse criticism when it's about old stuff because I don't like most of it myself. Any serious writer should expect always to be improving. Still. Reviews never used to matter that much when they were on newsprint. Now, your star rating can be reduced by a few nutters with a grudge and it remains online for eternity. This 'MrSmith' has given a two-star review when there were only three reviews in the first place. I'm not a fan of the stars. In my experience, the low-star reviews are typically by people who clearly didn't understand the books or just didn't like them. They bought the wrong book and blamed me. Would I give a one-star review to bacon because I don't like it? Does my personal taste for bacon say anything about the essential nature of bacon? My liking or disliking it is irrelevant. The question should be whether it's organic, lean, smoked or fresh.

The room is silent. The only light is the pale glare of the screen.

I reach for my phone and scroll to the contacts. Will Trewitt: my old university housemate, now married, breeding, and incarcerated in a respectable London job. We used to meet up a couple of times a year but communication of late has been mostly phone and email.

'Hello?' he says. Tense. Harried. The sound of a wailing child in the background.

'It's Tom . . . is now not a good time?'

'*Dottore!*'

'I told you: I'm not a PhD . . . '

'Tom . . . just a minute, OK? Carol? *Carol!*'

'*What?* [*Carol in the background. Child still wailing.*]'

'Can you clean this up? I've got Tom on the phone.'

'Like I've got nothing better to do? [*Her voice getting louder*]. Hi, Tom!'

'Hi, Carol.'

'I've not spoken to him for *ages*, honey ... and Jack's puked his turnip — it's like the *Exorcist*.'

That's for my benefit. Bring the scene to life. Bit of humour. Will always wanted to write. He now works in Internal Communications, which is to writing what house-painting is to Picasso.

'Oh ... talk to Tom then. Go on. Tell him about the competition.'

The wailing fades. A door closes.

'OK, I'm free.'

'Turnip?' I say. 'That's very middle class.'

'And he's called Jack. How's it going? Long time, no cliché.'

'Oh, you know: went on a radio station and accused a woman of having an STD, a guy of being illiterate.'

'Great. So this is your breakdown. Any news on the masterpiece?'

'It's accomplished, remarkable, thought-provoking ... '

'The usual, eh? Screw 'em. They've got no idea what they're looking at. You should write something new. Why not do something really commercial like Brown? You know it'd be easy for you. Make a bit of money and then sell 'em the good stuff.'

'I've told you that doesn't work. They'd just want more of the same. They don't care about the writing. It's just about the story.'

'Hey, I bought one of those Fenella books online. Hot stuff!'

'Oh God.'

'Yeah, I showed it to Carol and she said it was obscene.'

'Wonderful. Just remember not to tell people that I'm the author.'

'Of course. Anyway, it worked for me.'

'Thanks. Knowing that will help me write the next part.'

'Does she get together with that professor with the ten-inch—'

'Inevitably. Did Carol say something about a competition?'

'Oh yeah, I've got another one for you. It was in the *Guardian* I think. Four-hundred words about a travel experience by the end of this month. Think you can manage it?'

'Send me the link. What's the prize?'

'A holiday. I really don't mind if you enter it for yourself. Do you know how much I've won off your writing? I added it up.'

'Don't tell me.'

'Almost two grand, and that weekend away of course.'

'Well, anyway. How's work?'

'It's hell. They've got me working on a hundred-page PowerPoint presentation about comms policy for the next quarter. It doesn't need a hundred pages. I could say it in three minutes, but the presentation makes it look like there's some skill or depth to what I do, so we all play the game.'

'Still writing that internal magazine?'

'Yep. I did a feature today about Jeff in the warehouse at Luton. He won an egg-and-spoon race or some inane shit. *"I've always been a fan of the egg-and-spoon" said Jeff (53). "I use an eleven-inch spoon that belonged to my dad."*'

'Ha!'

'Yeah, so count yourself lucky, Tommo. You're writing stuff that you really care about.'

'Not really . . . not at the moment.'

'Yeah, you are. Even the Fenella stuff. It's creative. Not like Jeff and his fucking spoon. Any hot students in your class? It's the new semester, isn't it?'

'There's an Indian girl: Mohini.'

'Yeah? You gonna pork her?'

'Will . . . '

'Come on! Everyone else is doing it there. That lesbotic film woman . . . '

'I hope you've not told anyone about tha—'

'Treat yourself. How hot is she?'

'About as hot as it gets.'

'Lucky Tom!' His voice quietens. 'If I was in your position, I'd be banging myself lame. I can't remember the last time—'

'Will?' calls a muffled Carol. 'Are you still on the phone?'

'Got to go,' says Will. 'Look, we should meet up sometime soon. You can tell me about Mo-hottie — all the dirt. Right?'

'Yeah, right. Send me that compet—'

He's gone.

The mention of Mohini starts me thinking of her. That perfume, like something out of ancient history . . . Perhaps I can wring a few thousand words out of Fenella.

Biologically accurate

'TOM. Can I have a word?'

Jerry is sticking his head out the door of his office. I go in.

'How are things?' he says.

'Fine.'

'Good students this semester?'

'They're OK. We'll see. I'm seeing a supervisee in two minutes . . . Is there a problem?'

'I'll be quick. The '80s Lit Half-Hour on Student Radio.'

'Ah.'

'I didn't listen. I've been told that almost nobody does. But I've heard a few comments . . . and someone sent an email to the vice-chancellor. I wouldn't care, but they introduced you as an MGU lecturer . . . '

'Yeah. I get it. Lower profile.'

'Yes. Please. If you need some time off for any reason . . . '

'Why would I? I'm perfectly fine.'

'OK. I have to ask. It's just that . . . well, there's also a delivery for you at reception and it's a little inappropriate. I'd imagine you'd have something like that sent to your home address.'

'I haven't ordered anything . . . '

'Well. Just saying.'

'Thanks, Jerry.'

I walk quickly to reception. I'm sure I've ordered nothing recently. I never have anything delivered here.

'Tom Fynn. I'm a lecturer. There's a delivery for me, apparently.'

The receptionist is a doughy woman with a pubic thatch of greying hair. She turns her mouth down and examines me as she might a dog turd on her sole.

'Sorry. Do you speak English?' I say. 'I'm in a bit of a hurry.' My supervisee is already in the meeting room. I saw her as I rushed by.

Somebody giggles unseen in the office area behind reception and a young man lumbers from behind a bank of filing cabinets carrying a luridly-coloured cardboard box the size of a medium coffin. There's a flash of transparent plastic: evidently a window in the box. I focus on the gaudy font and feel the blood drain into my shoes.

It's a sex doll. Not one of the cheap inflatable ones, but a silicone model designed to replicate the authentic texture and weight of real human limbs. Expensive. Very expensive. The writing says, "Lexxi Cummins Doll: modeled on the exact dimensions of America's favorite XXX adult performer." Bullet points say: "Three-speed biologically-accurate pussy, vibrating ass, auto-grip hands, lube-reservoir mouth cavity. Wipe clean." The filmy window shows the face, presumably, of Lexxi Cummins: a heavily painted slut with wide-open mouth (lube reservoir not immediately obvious) and bounteous blonde hair.

'I didn't order this.'

The doughy-pube woman jabs a finger at the address label, whereupon my name is clearly printed.

'There's no other Tom Fynn at the university?' I say.

She shakes her head.

'Well, it's not mine. I didn't order it. Can't you just throw it out … give it to charity?'

'University policy,' says the young man with his arm round Lexxi Cummins. 'You have to take your own mail. We can't dispose of it. Recycling issues.'

'You realise that even if I had ordered this doll, I wouldn't have had it delivered to MGU unwrapped like this? Why would I do something like that?'

The young man shrugs. The minge-maned Cerberus maintains her sour expression.

'OK. Just give it to me. *I'll* throw it away.'

'It's heavy,' says the young man, tipping it over the top of reception.

And it is. It must weigh about fifteen kilograms. I balance it on my shoulder and walk back towards the meeting room, passing the severe looking woman who teaches feminist theory. Can I pass this off as irony? Is she going to spit at me? No. Not yet.

How many people already know about this? Probably as many as know about Janet and her bi-curious conquests. If this is someone's idea of a joke . . . Might it be a message? Has someone found out that I'm the author of the *Fenella Chronicles*? I've kept that pseudonym secret from everyone except Will. I feel suddenly sick.

My female supervisee waves as I manoeuvre Lexxi Cummins into the room, her smile dropping when she realises what the box contains.

'It's not mine,' I say. 'Some sort of joke. Just ignore it.'

Lexxi Cummins goggles open-mouthed at us through her plastic film window. I turn her to the wall, revealing the bullet points. Wipe clean. Lube reservoir.

I sit and start shuffling papers out of my courier bag. All business. This supervisee is known to me as Radio 4 owing to the kind of writing she produces. It's the kind of writing I loathe, but it's her choice and I have to respect it. My professional concern is only whether it works. And it doesn't.

'So I've read your latest draft . . . ' I say.

'Oh, it's too long and flowery isn't it? The scene where the woman looks at the dewy spider's web and describes it—'

'For a page and a half. Yes. The description is OK, as it goes, but there's no purpose to the scene at all. It exists purely so you can describe the spider's web. No plot purpose. No characterisation. But it seems you already know this . . . '

'Yes. I suppose so.'

'You have to write for the reader, not for yourself.'

'I know, but . . . did you see that piece in the *Guardian* by Will Self? He says he doesn't care about his readers at all.'

'He's Will Self; you're not. Besides, I've never met a person who finished one of his books — certainly none I'd want to be trapped in a lift with. Self has a brilliant mind, but you shouldn't take him as a guide for your work.'

'I'm never going to please you, am I?'

'Not with that attitude. And it's not about pleasing me; it's about writing well. You have the tools; you just need to use them. OK, look at page thirty-four. Read that a moment. I'll wait.'

She reads. Lexxi Cummins stands facing the wall. Biologically-accurate. Designed for your pleasure. Who? Who sent this? Nobody but Will knows about Fenella … unless there's some other meaning to the doll. That I myself am some kind of literary whore? It's a bit of a stretch …

'Done,' says Radio 4.

'Right. So let's look again at this passage.'

> *Henley lovingly stroked the owl's feathers: gossamer remiges of silvered shaft and tender vane; barbules proximal and distal; rachis, calamus and hooklet. A poem of filament softness. A fluttering sonnet, a downy elegy. Whither came thee, jewel-eyed wisdom-symbol and nocturnal terror? What tiny mammals have you killed in your time? What pellets extruded of bone and delicate gristle? Grounded now, and stuffed on a plinth.*

'It's the ornithological vocab, isn't it?' she says. 'Too obscure.'

'A bit of obscure vocab never hurt anyone, though this is clearly a haemorrhage of research material. The words themselves are nicely juxtaposed. No, it's more a matter of scale, tone and purpose. Henley has gone into the shop to buy a pot of glue and she's seen the stuffed owl. OK. But that amount of description for something she sees only in passing? And let's remember that Henley is an uneducated chambermaid. Would she think like this? Would she know these words? That's you, the author, contaminating the narrative world you're trying to evoke.'

Radio 4 nods solemnly. I see her gaze drift to the upright box. Her eyes trace the bullets.

Vibrating ass. Three-speed pussy.

'What if Henley had taken a course?' she says. 'Then she'd know the bird words.'

'What if Henley was an omniscient empath from Alpha Centauri? What if she was a visiting demi-god from the future? She's a chambermaid.'

'I suppose so.'

'Forgive me, but Henley is essentially a bit of a moron. She gets murdered in chapter seven. Does she need such depth? We need only enough to pity her slaughter.'

'I suppose so.'

'Good. Let's talk about the scene where Lord Fortescue spends three pages polishing the brass door knob.'

I talk, but she's really not listening. The door knob business isn't even a euphemism, alas. Like many of my full-novel supervisees, Radio 4 has undergone the fatal metamorphosis from trusting student, through affronted "artist", to obstinate fantasist. She's probably the best one in her Thursday-night writers' circle; her peers on the course tell her she's good (because they want to hear the same); she's heard something very similar to her book on Radio 4, and she's now decided that I'm essentially wrong in everything I tell her. She will resist. She will filibuster. She'll hand in a terribly flawed manuscript that'll earn a mid-2:2 and never be published. Then the blame game, the bitching and the official complaint. There's nothing I can do. The process seems inevitable.

So I talk mechanically and she pretends to listen. Lexxi Cummins leans up against the wall, her perfect silicone buttocks no doubt proffered for immediate invasion. Whoever sent it was very shrewd. Nothing else would provoke as much offence in the right-on corridors of MGU. Unless it was a black version of Lexxi. Then I'd be dead.

I leave Radio 4 indignant in the meeting room and lug Lexxi to my office, attracting baleful stares as I go. There's a fresh Post-It on the monitor. Jerry's handwriting.

Sorry to report: Percy dead. See my email. Jerry

I fire up the computer and go straight to my inbox, where Jerry has pasted a link to the *Manchester Evening News*.

Salford man found dead in home after neighbours report closed curtains

Retired train-driver Percy Braithwaite has been found dead in his home after his neighbours did not see him for four days. They alerted police, who discovered the 81-year-old in his armchair in front of the TV. No cause of death has yet been announced ...

Percy dead. I barely knew him, although I've spent the last year or so reading and re-reading his life story. He leaves no living relatives as far as I'm aware. No kids. Just his manuscript, of which I have the final (and only?) draft. He told me he disposed of earlier versions. Like any good writer, he'd learned that the best writing is always the *next* piece.

The decision is instant: I'm going to get his book published. Retype it or scan it or whatever's necessary. It's good enough. And his death is the perfect marketing angle as long I act quickly. Did he know this? Did he plan it? Suicide, then. Nothing else to live for. Cynical old Percy. I'd been his teacher long enough for him to absorb my views on the market. The book is his epitaph. If only I can get it in front of an agent or publisher.

But right now I've got another seminar with the MA group. And Mohini.

I leave Lexxi facing the wall and scuttle down the corridor. As I go past Gwynn's office, he shouts, 'Tommy Fynn killed the radio star!' followed by a rasping laugh.

Not bad. For a TS Eliot Prize-winner.

His urgent ardour swells

MY CLASS is waiting. I peer at them through the door pane. Mum looks nervous; it's her work in front of our first workshop this week and she has a face full of imminent martyrdom. Stalwart is wearing a tweed bow-tie and leaning indulgently in his chair like a sedentary cricket umpire. Dreadlock Twat is wearing a vast beanie in Caribbean colours. Earnest Youth is diligently reading through his notes on Mum's piece. They've not yet gelled as a class. These first workshops are always a slog.

Then there's *her*. Her beauty lifts her above and beyond the other mere mortals in the room: a golden apple in a sack of potatoes. But it's a dark beauty, absorbing light. That impossible hair. Those eyes. Does she sense me there outside the door? She looks straight at me and smiles with a look that I feel in my hip pocket (credit: Raymond Chandler).

I go in.

'Afternoon, everyone. Ready for the first workshop?'

'No!' says Mum, hand in hair, feeling absently for the crown of thorns.

'Relax. This is part of becoming a writer. The criticism isn't aimed at you. It's aimed at your work.'

'But my work *is* me,' says Mum.

'No. Your work is a device . . . a machine for engaging a reader. Criticism is an MOT. We're looking for the dull spark plug, the loose wire, the oil that needs changing. It's is not about character assassination. If your work's flawed, you fix it.'

'And if our work isn't flawed?' says Stalwart, fingers interlaced and steepled.

'Don't worry; it will be. Everybody's is.'

'Yours included?' says Dreadlock Twat. A cocky wink.

'Mine included. Everybody's. Nabokov said, rightly, that certain parts of *Ulysses* can be safely skipped. I think most people now accept that many of Shakespeare's characters are expedients: slaves to plot. Hamlet's procrastination?

The play would be over in an instant otherwise. Iago's destruction of Othello? Essentially motiveless — conflict for its own sake. So . . . '

'Shakespeare was, and is, our greatest writer,' says Stalwart.

'I agree. But not perfect. That's my point. At the same time, we might want to consider him the consummate writer's writer. Unlike his contemporaries, he had little interest in fame or posterity. Just the words, and putting money in his purse.'

Earnest Youth smiles to himself. Mohini giggles and I feel a spark — a jab — of affection for her. Affection and insensate lust. Those black, black eyes. I'm drawn towards her as Hamlet towards the void at Elsinore. Poe's "Imp of the Perverse" flashes to mind: *There is no passion in nature so demoniacally impatient as that of him, who shuddering upon that edge of precipice, thus meditates a plunge.*

'Anyway,' I say. 'Let's not get distracted. We've all read, er, Margaret's work. What I want to hear first is what we think of it in general, in its broadest sense. What parameters has it set for itself? Does it succeed in what it aims to achieve? Does it know its aims? Who'll go first?'

Silence.

Silence like eternity.

'Drea- . . . Damian — why don't you kick off?' I say.

'Er, I liked it. I thought it was good.'

'Good how?'

'You know . . . the car journey with the two kids and that. It seemed realistic.'

'Realistic. OK. Let's have some other opinions.'

'The semi-colon in the second line is misused,' says Stalwart.

Mum pales and searches for the winking mark. Out, damned spot!

'That's . . . not terribly helpful in the larger scheme of things,' I say.

'Correct punctuation is important,' says Stalwart.

'It is. But changing that semi-colon will not affect the overall success of the piece by even a fraction of one per cent. Let's focus on the big things for now.'

Stalwart purses his lips and noisily scores a circle round the errant semi-colon.

'I thought the flashbacks were a bit ... intrusive,' says Earnest Youth. 'You just start to get into the car journey and then we're back at the house again. Three times, in fact.'

'Good point. If we're beginning with the car journey, that's our primary narrative and it needs time to develop before we leave it. We need to become engaged. Otherwise, you set up a conflict in the reader's mind. Where should their focus be? There's time later for any back-story.'

They all write. Then she raises a languid hand.

'Yes, Mohini. No need to put your hand up ... '

Because it tautens the material across your chest and lifts it to reveal that café crème abdomen. That skin. I can feel its smoothness on my tongue.

'Sorry.' Giggle. 'I don't want to contradict you, but might not the flashbacks work if we were trying to build tension?'

It's a not a challenge. It's a prompt. She's identified a point I was going to make but discarded as being irrelevant at this stage. Her smile intimates a conspiracy between us — just we two have had this thought. Her eyes confirm it.

'Well ... that's exactly right. Mohini is right. Let's say the mother character had left the iron on and was worrying about it. A few, short, well spaced flashbacks to the house would emphasise her concern. But only short ones so as not to disrupt the primary narrative.'

They write. And so it goes, with me attempting to move their critical reactions from "a bit boring" towards "lacking in pace", from "confusing" towards "conflicted narrative perspective." It's not about jargon or labels, but learning to identify textual mechanisms behind the gut feelings we experience as readers. Thereafter, it's about understanding and using these techniques actively to manipulate reader response. This is writing: deciding how (and when, and why) to move the reader, then using the necessary craft to effect it.

Throughout, she watches me like my greatest fan. She nods encouragingly when I make a decisive point. She smiles when she senses my frustration with a facile comment. She rolls her eyes when Stalwart goes off on a tedious monologue. When there's a minor breakthrough of understanding, she reinforces it, all the while colluding with glances and gazes – my unofficial co-teacher and co-conspirator. The abyss into which I yearn to leap.

Her beauty is hypnotic – the kind seldom seen in common life. Only in adverts or galleries. Here in dull, puddled Manchester, she seems otherworldly. She's not of this one. And her body ... voluptuous, abundant, ripe, languid. A curvilinear sweep of hip, a straining breast, an arc of buttock, her legs parting as she leans back in the creaking plastic seat. Lucky seat. Enviable seat. I curse thy privileged proximity! *His urgent ardour swelled ... his cisterns pulsed with roiling lust ...* Her every posture and gesture is a provocation. A teasing upward glance and I visualise myself upon her, inside her. I believe I'd deplete myself entirely – I'd wither and die – to satisfy her. I *am* possessed.

Have the others noticed all of this? Am I trying too hard to disguise it, neglecting her with my questions and addressing her with forced formality? Do they see my surreptitious glances? I'm grandstanding even more than usual to impress her. Must stay focused.

'Ultimately,' I say, 'everybody's writing can be improved at a stroke. Most beginners make the same few mistakes. Eradicate them and you immediately reach a new level. I'll list them.'

Pens poise. Even Stalwart's.

1. Punctuation. Most people never learn it properly, and even fewer understand that mastering it turns prose into music. The dash, the colon, the comma, the semi, the full stop ... even the tiny hyphen – their permutations are endless.

2. Clichés. Avoid them. They prevent you from using your own words. Find the precise way to evoke something.

3. Paragraphs. Most people — especially those with academic backgrounds — tend to write in long, blocky paragraphs that slow pace and clog the prose. Break them up. Use longer paras only for dense focus.

4. Vocabulary. An approximate word is never good enough. English has the largest vocabulary of any language so learn it. *Smell, scent, perfume, aroma* — there's a world of meaning between these words, much of which cannot be delineated solely in a dictionary. A word is more than its definition.

5. Showing and telling. Most of what the reader perceives in good writing is not written at all. It's implied, suggested, alluded to. What the reader believes they've cleverly inferred has purposefully been implanted by you. Sometimes we tell; sometimes we show. The reader should never notice either.

6. Dialogue. It's criminally underused, especially by those who see it as a hallmark of genre. Good dialogue is pure narrative. Shakespeare used virtually nothing else in his plays.

7. Make 'em wait. There's no need to give everything at once. You want your reader to want to get to the end, not to want the end at the beginning. Promise constantly; deliver slowly.

'That's pretty much it. Beyond this basic list, we're into voice, style and ideas. That's where the great writers pull ahead.'

They're still scribbling, she with a beatific grin that's one measure art, three measures lasciviousness. Lucky pen. Enviable pen caught in that web of fingers.

'Now, you're all entitled to a one-to-one this semester,' I say. 'Either email me or arrange something at the end of the class.'

'If you don't mind . . . ' says Mohini.

Don't mind inhaling me, tasting me, consuming me, washing ashore on my body a drowned and passion-wrecked man.

'. . . I'd like to arrange one now.'

'Of course. Great. No problem. When's good for you?' The junkie flicking his syringe, tying off, tapping the vein, twitching for the fix.

Publication, publication, publication

A FIRST BOOK is like a first heroin shot. Every successive book is just a vain attempt to replicate the original high. Addiction follows. Then overdose.

It took a year for book one to go through the editorial, proofing and marketing process, during which time I made very few changes to the manuscript – just minor finessing of plot points or description. The structural edit took me an afternoon. Then I was straight on to the second book.

The sequel was effortless. Some authors exhaust their creativity in a first novel that gestates for years and is drawn from some dank, primal source. I'd made mine up from scratch, teaching myself along the way how I might repeat the research-ideas-structure process indefinitely. So the second book was easier and actually much better, jettisoning the gauche tentativeness of the first and racing ahead with the new confidence of publication. I was on fire. An editor was waiting for this one.

I felt I ought to miss Lara. I dissimulated a sense of loss. I tried to force some pain. I fetishised the few possessions she'd left behind – more out of a sense of required guilt than of genuine grief. That would all come later. Sitting at the keyboard, however, I thought of nothing but the second book. I wrote it in nine months, delivering it to my editor's fulsome praise even before the first had been released. I made plans to start the third.

Pausing in that endeavour was a mistake. It gave me time to take an interest in my imminent debut.

The first warning sign was the cover artwork for the hardback. Not only was it amateurish, it was also worryingly naïve. It looked like a children's book, which it definitely wasn't. 'No time,' they said. 'We need to rush it on to the shelves.' How could I argue with that?

Then I saw the paperback design and it was worse. It screamed fantasy or whimsical magic realism, neither of which it remotely resembled. Had anyone actually read the thing? My opinion counted for nothing. I was not a graphic designer. I was merely the person who had created every character, scene and concept in the 100,000-word novel I'd dreamed of writing since I was nine years old.

I began to understand – slowly, and in depressing increments – that they didn't see it as a book at all. They saw it as a package consisting of strap line, some blurb and a cover. Not a reading experience (clearly, nobody responsible for selling it had read further than the first three or four pages), but a product. A product needed placing in a market, and so they were dressing it up in the stockings and sequined bustier of a genre it didn't belong to. It might as well have been toothpaste. Beans. Haemorrhoid treatment.

Still. Publication! And in hardback, too. There was a kind of party in London where I met some of the others being published that week. Avery Johns was one of them – no cravat or tweed at that point. I remember being given a goody bag containing our first books and finding his style so laughably bad that I purposefully left it on the train going home that night. The Publicity department was at the party, too, but nobody from the media, no readers … in fact no discernible purpose for the party other than giving the writers a collective pat on the head. Well done. You must be very proud. Oh yes, I absolutely loved your first page. Here, have some stale nibbles and a (plastic) glass of very cheap wine. Next!

Meeting the other writers that night was an anti-climax. I expected to feel a profound kinship, but every one of them – Avery included – gave the impression of being there as a winner of some trivial competition. As if they'd had their book published by collecting coupons from margarine tubs. They grinned, they shuffled, they became flushed with too much cheap wine and they wittered on about their agents (I've never had one; couldn't get one) or their day jobs. Where were the furrowed brows? Where was the fire of creation? Were these people writers like me? Was writing, for them, the essential purpose of being? Had they sacrificed a relationship for it? Looking around at them and their books, I realised that every one of them had produced something solidly generic. Mine was merely genre-influenced. Hubris rose like bile. I … I was better than them.

It was the same at the first few mass signings I attended. I tried to start conversations with other writers about thematic structures or stylistic influences, but they seemed to care nothing for the actual prose. They, too, thought solely in terms of product and market. 'I'm putting a Chinese character in my next one. Big market over there.' Perhaps they were right. They're all still in print.

The first review was very short, but good: a high-brow weekend broadsheet and just a minor quibble about a historical point. But that was it for the first book. No more reviews. Avery Johns, meanwhile, was in every paper and magazine for the next month. Interviews. Features. A renegotiated six-figure advance on his next two books.

Still. Publication! I was in my local Waterstones almost every day looking for it on the shelves, then asking the assistants when it would arrive. On order, they said, having to look it up on the system. Avery Johns' books were on the shelves. They were on tables. They were by the checkout in supermarkets. They were being given away with magazines. It seemed weeks before the two copies of my book finally arrived on the shelves. Two copies with that awful faux-fantasy cover. And they stayed on the shelves as if glued there. Nobody had heard of the book.

I wrote to the publicity people and suggested articles I might write, things I might do, talks I might give. I didn't realise – and wasn't told – that my five minutes had passed. That was last week, last month. New books were being published every day. That one review was the sole extent of the publicity I could expect in return for yielding 93% of the cover price of the book I had written.

Perhaps the second book would be the breakthrough. I followed the process from a disembodied perspective: a kind of near death experience. The same misleading cover (this time featuring the wrong character name – they hadn't even read the first page), the same shoe-horning of the book into a market segment it didn't, and wouldn't, fit. The same lacklustre attempt to actually get some copies into shops. And this time no review at all – or, at least, no professional review. By this stage, they'd found it was easier to send review copies out to housebound bloggers, Twitterers, OCD Facebookers whose tastes and literary education barely extended beyond Hogwarts. These people seemed not to mind the book, but then they seemed not to mind everything they were sent for free. They all knew each other and their opinions swarmed uniformly like starlings around the rotting ribs of the print publishing industry.

The third book vanished into a hole. I no longer enquired about publicity or why there were no copies of my books in shops. Even on Amazon, the first two titles had gone entirely unreviewed for almost two years. Great job, Publicity. Well done. Have another glass of very cheap wine and pat the new writers on the head. Loved your first page. Next! Avery Johns, meanwhile, had over a thousand reviews on Amazon (some of them hilariously spiteful, and some of those by me). The publisher now had a six-figure advance they needed to reclaim through sales, so Avery was priority number one.

I thought about getting a few friends to write me some great reviews as everyone else does (note how many very literate five-star reviews appear in the first week or so of publication, even before the book is generally available), but a stubborn sense of fairness prevented me. I wanted genuine readers to respond. I also realised had no friends.

This wasn't the end of it, though. The final indignity was soon to come. I failed totally to anticipate how they'd break me.

Testeronal

I'M AT HOME listening to an instrumental version of Backstreet Boys' "Quit Playing Games with My Heart". I've been listening to it on a loop for about nine minutes now and am reaching the stage where I'm planning to unleash a maelstrom of passive-aggressiveness on whoever picks up the phone. Unless it's a pretty-sounding girl, obviously.

'Good afternoon you're talking to Ahmed at NatWest card services. How may I help you?'

'Sorry . . . What did you say?'

'You're talking to Ahmed at—'

'Right. Finally. I think I've been the victim of fraud. There's a payment I don't recognise on my card.'

'OK. Let's see what we can see. Can you tell me your card number?'

'The one I typed into the phone about fifteen minutes ago?'

'That's the one.'

'So why did I type it if I have to tell you again now?'

'It's just procedure.'

'Should I read it again at the end of the call, just to make sure?'

'That's not part of the procedure, sir. Could you tell me your card number?'

Sir? The inflection is unambiguous. *Sir* is code for *wanker*. I sigh and read out the number, along with all the other details I thought I'd just given.

'OK, sir. I'm going to read out the most recent transactions. Tell me if you don't recognise any.'

'I can tell you right now. This call is probably costing me about £1.00 a minute.'

'Please bear with me, sir. Right . . . £2.50 at MGU Coffee Time . . .'

'Yes, that's me.'

'£17.50 at Hildebrand Rarity?'

'A second-hand bookshop. Yes. Me again.'

'£1120 at Sexx Foxx Industries?'

'Yes ... I mean no. That's not me.'

'A silicone likeness of Lexxi Star? The deluxe model with vibrating, er, anus?'

'What ...? The purchase is actually detailed? It's not mine.'

'Auto-grip hands?'

'Will you stop reading that stuff out loud! That's the fraudulent purchase.'

'Have you lent your card to anybody?'

'No.'

'Do you always cover the pin pad when typing out—'

'Of course.'

'Well, this is a significant amount and there are no other fraudulent charges. We tend to see numerous smaller purchases ...'

'Are you saying I've bought this doll and then gone so far in my denial as to actually call the bank and report it as a fraud?'

'That would be a crime, sir.'

'Which is why I haven't done it. I've been robbed.'

'I'm going to have to pass this up to our fraud investigators—'

'What?'

'And in the meantime, you might want to check the security of your computer if you're making purchases online. Your system may have been hacked. Is your anti-virus software up to date?'

'Hacked?'

'It's becoming increasingly common, sir.'

'Could you stop calling me *sir*?'

'I'm sorry, Mister Fynn.'

Mister Fynn! He says it like it rhymes with *Dickhead*.

'Is there anything else I can help you with today, Mister Fynn.'

'You haven't even helped me with this, *sir*!'

I hang up and feel immediately guilty. The guy was just doing his job. Never rely on a writer for incisive argument or snappy repartee (unless he's Irish). Such things come solely through the keyboard. Was it Vonnegut who agreed to his *Paris Review* interview only on the condition he could write the whole thing?

Hacked.

Does that mean someone has access to all my files? The *Fenella Chronicles*? Is someone reading my emails? The same person who'd sent me the doll . . . ?

Must think. If someone has my card details, they could have cleaned me out . . . but they've chosen not to. Not yet. They were sending a message. Perhaps they knew that a single transaction would look more incriminating. But what message? Who have I pissed off recently? Most of Amazon. Many of my students. Avery Johns. Ahmed at NatWest card services. The twenty-seven listeners of MGU Student Radio. What about that crusty old caller at the end? What had he said? 'You won't get away with it'? His voice wasn't familiar.

But the phrase is. Seen it somewhere . . . My pigeonhole: the message I thought was intended for Janet. For me, then? Does that mean the hacker's an MGU student? Or a colleague. Maybe I'd better start using the Internet at work instead, though I'm pretty sure my anti-virus is up to date. I must talk to Will about this. He'll know.

There are a few emails in my work inbox. Would it hurt to check them? They're only from students. Nothing worth hacking. An undergraduate called Jared has emailed me a few ideas for his creative writing project.

1. Its set on the earth in the future and humans are like second class citizens because a new race of animals has taken over. Humans are slaves with genetic autism, but they get together and overthrow the new animals in a war.

2. Its set in a fantasy place similar to earth and all the young people have eating disorders and die when they reach sexual maturity. They're sent out into a desert and they

have to fight kind of clone zombies. Some of them don't want to die and they get together to change it.

3. Its set in another galaxy where a demon prince is using dark magic to rule. A young bi-polar man travels across the wilderness with a magic sword that's the only thing that can kill the demon prince. He succeeds.

Jared thinks these projects will be easy to write because he's seen the films. If he'd read any books, he'd know that establishing fantasy or sci-fi worlds is much trickier than it looks. The urge is to forget story and explain all the weird stuff in the opening chapters. Rather, it needs to be absorbed initially as background detail. I choose option two for no other reason than it contains the word *sexual.* Maybe he'll write a smut scene that'll amuse me.

Sex. Smut. I'm lagging behind on Fenella, whom I left spread-eagled on some kind of advanced orgasmic piston a few days ago (. . . *her eyelids fluttered as the apocalyptic climax rushed upon her quivering Fallopians* . . .). Instead, it seems the textual lubricity has slithered off the pages and into my everyday life.

I turn to the sofa and look at Lexxi Cummins. She sits with legs open like a pair of compasses (obtuse angle) and her mouth agape. I'm forced to admit that the aesthetic rendering is well done. She could easily be mistaken for a real person after a few beers, or in low light, or under the influence of any number of testosteronal excuses. As if to tempt me, one of her auto-grip hands holds a bottle of porter.

Her nakedness embarrassed me when she came out of the box so I found some of Lara's abandoned clothes to dress her: a crumpled white blouse, that tartan miniskirt from Edinburgh that Lara always refused to wear (even at home, ideally with heels and too much make-up). The problem is that these few items, with their inadequate veneer of modesty, have made Lexxi seem extraordinarily erotic. Her ludicrous (but pert) breasts now reveal just a coquettish canyon of cleavage. The skirt is hiked up to her hips by the angle of her thighs, turning it into a wilfully revelatory pose whose shadows nevertheless tease. And be certain of it: Lexxi has deigned not to wear underwear this evening. Lexxi is a bad girl. Lexxi needs spanking.

A few times, I've glimpsed her sidelong from the keyboard and felt a rush of lust. If I don't move her to a cupboard soon, I fear that I may lose all dignity and invade her biologically-accurate amenities. Has it really come to this? The auto-grip hands are truly a marvel. That silicone mouth tells no tales.

Blame Mohini. She's stirred something in the stagnant black wells of my libido. This is not just the toddler-insistent impulse to leer and possess that afflicts every man. I've got plenty of that already. No. This is something much more animal. It's barely a conscious understanding. It's nothing that might be rationalised and tamed with a term. It's a rage in the blood: a yearning dredged from the most primitive, atavistic core of manhood. She is the elemental compliment to whatever it is I'm missing. Only by conjoining can we become fully one.

I'm meeting her on Monday at the university for our tutorial and I can barely think. The anticipation of being in a room with only her. And yet ... and yet. Part of me is still sane enough to realise that I'm no Janet. I've never had a relationship with a student. Yes, many of them are attractive, but their minds are typically too unformed to attract me. I'm not so inhuman that I can disassociate the body from the person. Mohini might change everything. Her mind is something else ...

I need to distract myself.

Percy. Poor, dead Percy. I've read through his finished manuscript again and it's as good as I remember it. A few typos here and there, the occasional bit of flabby writing he managed to get past me, but it holds together. It's structurally sound. The only question is whether the market will accept a serious, slow-paced novel by an unknown eighty-year-old Manchester ex-train-driver, who may have killed himself on its completion (no word yet from the police). It's not exactly commercial cat-nip.

What if I submitted it in my name? As TG Harkett.

The thought is a mere flicker, but I snatch after it with a lepidopterist's net. However unsuccessful I've been with the masterpiece, I know that publishers at least give you some kudos for already having been published. It means you might be able to write. It means you've already withstood the cudgels and jackboots of the market, emerging dead or alive (or temperamentally maimed).

If I submitted in my name, would they notice the disparity in style and subject with my published stuff? Probably not – nobody has read my Harkett books. Not even my own publisher. I can't see any editor rushing to read them prior to leafing through Percy's work. That'd come later, after a decision's been made. All it needs is a new cover sheet, a synopsis that makes it sound like a story, and a bitchin' cover letter. No need to mention right now that the writer is dead. Let them accept the book first. In the meantime, this novel is by me. I'm claiming it as one of mine. For Percy.

I bang out a synopsis and cover letter within an hour then lean back in the chair to stretch. Should I send it? If only as an experiment? To see if I can still interest the big publishers? Or whether I'm utterly dead to them after those other books. What have I to lose?

Lexxi Cummins sneaks into my peripheral vision: slack mouthed, unbuttoned, legs akimbo. If you keep on looking at me like that, young lady, I'm going to fill up that lube reservoir and ...

An email drops into the inbox. I vacillate momentarily between Lexxi's silicone inner thighs and the screen. I notice the subject line. The masterpiece.

Right. Here we go again. Deep breath. Let the bile begin to rise. It's one of the big publishers so ... Anticipate rejection. Embrace the rejection. Click.

Dear Tom

Thanks for sending us your book and synopsis etc. We enjoyed your cover letter and your tales of how many people have so far rejected it.

I think it's a marvellous book: accomplished, inventive, humorous and experimental without being too ambitious for the average (intelligent) reader. You are a terrific writer and you have written a book I think people would like to read.

I can't promise you publication in this letter, but I would like to suggest a few edits (see attached doc). If you can make these edits to my satisfaction, I will gladly submit your book to our publishing committee. Please feel free to ask any further questions once you've had time to read through my suggestions . . .

Publishing committee. The phrase sounds like a celestial bell, no matter what the cacophony of other senseless words around it. Sorry, Tom – I'm afraid your entire family has fallen into a tree shredder, but your book may be submitted to the publishing committee. *Fenella arched her back and welcomed the rigid anaconda of the* publishing committee. Never mind that there's no mention of a contract. I could make a year of edits and still get nothing for my work.

I open the attachment with a shivering mouse and scroll through the pages. Three, four, six, ten, fifteen pages of edits (the most I ever had for my published books was a page and a half). And not just the minor things I might expect. Drastic things. Cataclysmic things. Cut the word count by 30%. Scrap the storyline about Jonas Dunkham (one of the main characters). Add more themes. Cut the scenes featuring the matchmakers (more of an entire subplot than scenes). Bolster this character, trim that chapter, introduce this idea, adopt more of a serious tone overall. Sharpen the prose. The main character doesn't work. (The main character!)

He doesn't want the masterpiece. He wants his version of my book. A market version of my book. He ends with: "Ultimately, the novel hesitates between genre and literature. We need to nudge it one way or the other. Genre offers the bigger market but I think your book is better than that. You need to step up and make it into the book I know it can be."

Step up. Literature.

I look through the edits again. The task is monumental. I'd essentially have to rewrite the book that took me two and a half years to write. How? I've never rewritten anything. Once a book is written, it's chiselled in stone. It's taken the only form it can. Additional stone cannot be added to the Parthenon marbles. Chipping back will reduce them, diminish them. Can I pick up the chisel again and use it on this book I considered perfect? My narcissan reflection. Will I yield and carve a new likeness better to suit the mirror of the market?

I can't face it. I can't do it.

I must do it. This is the next step. The step up.

I sit staring at the pages of edits. The fear wallows up from sublimated depths – the doubt that never really leaves you, no matter how much you write or how much you publish.

Am I good enough? Is this when I finally get found out?

Darkness falls

THE PRESSURE was too intolerable. The task too immense. So I did what I used to when I was writing the masterpiece: I went for a walk. A swim, a bike ride, a walk … such things engage a different part of the brain and set the writing mind at rest. At least, it retires to a dark room for a little nap, dreaming and whirring all the while until a breakthrough occurs and leaps irresistibly to consciousness, causing you to gulp water, swerve into a bus or slip off the kerb. It's no accident that Archimedes had his ideas in the bath.

Thus do I find myself in Waterstones, a place I used to visit almost every day when I was an optimist. It was a church in which I thought I communed with the spirit of literature. The books were talismans of fundamental goodness, their shelved concentrations a magnification of that goodness. It was a religion I wanted to be part of.

Getting published changed all that. It gave me a personal place in the holy of holies and began a tortuous process of estrangement leading to inevitable apostasy. On publication, I'd be in the shop every day waiting to see my books on the shelves. When they appeared, I'd stand at an inconspicuous distance and observe as shoppers walked tantalisingly close, their hands hovering just to the right, just to the left. I lurked, waiting for someone to take a copy from the shelf (*hmm, what an interesting looking book* …) whereupon I planned to leap forward with a gushing recommendation. The dialogue was already planned.

Me: Oh, that's a great book!
Customer: Really. Have you read it?
Me: Actually [*self-deprecating laugh*], I wrote it.
Customer: You're an author?
Me: Yes. Yes I am. A writer.
Customer: If I buy all of them, will you sign them for me?
Me: It would be my pleasure.

It never happened. But any time I saw my books, I'd rearrange the shelf so that my covers faced outwards rather than the spines. A lot of new authors do this. I'd also take copies to the checkout and go through the delightful charade of:

Assistant: OK. Would you like a bag?
Me: Actually [*self-deprecating laugh*], I'm the author. Would you like me to sign them?
Assistant: That would be wonderful.

Then you begin to notice that the books are still on the shelves — and not because they're being restocked every week. Nobody has bought them. You know this because they're the same copies you signed three months ago, now yellowing along the top edge. Still, you're glad to see them in the shop at all.

Until you don't. They've not been sold; they've been returned to the publisher as unsellable. Now, when you go into the shop, you scan the shelves nonchalantly but with a quiet desperation, half knowing that you're not going to see any copies. Thereafter, you stop looking on the shelves at all — it's just better not to. Then you just stop going into bookshops altogether. Awful, awful places.

That's not the end of the process, however. In time, you are able to return again and barely even think about your books. They are a vague dream that may have been reality. Finally, the only time you think of the books in any capacity whatsoever is when you come across one by surprise — mis-shelved somewhere, perhaps, and preserved from the cull. Or more likely in a bargain bookstore: three for £5. Then you smile fondly and remember that once you were published and you laugh self-deprecatingly to mask the still-bleeding wound at the heart of your very being.

I'm aware that no accident has brought me here. Some impulse has suggested that I might find inspiration amid the shelves — some burst of positive energy to get me through the masterpiece edit. I walk automatically among my heroes, sensory filaments extended to catch some particle of their talent. Vonnegut, Eco, Melville, Twain. Nabokov. Wolfe and Woolf. The Millers Henry and Arthur. The hardboiled boys: Hammett, Chandler and Ellroy. Burgess and McCarthy. Pale Poe, Rollicking Rabelais. Flaubert, Cendrars, Maupassant, Sartre and Camus. Bukowski. Mostly men. Am I, as Nabokov said of himself, homosexual in my literary tastes? There's Proulx, Oates ... not many more. Men write with their egos, their work a peacock's tail feather or gorilla's chest-beating cry.

Might the masterpiece one day find a permanent place among these greats? (Laughter echoes through hallways of posterity.) The burden of that outrageous hope weighs cripplingly — an asphyxiating force — upon my edit.

And yet I stroll the racks as a recovering alcoholic must pass a pub, inhaling holy odours of hops, of barley. Here, too, are the books I loathe but which outsell mine. Reminders of my failure. Glitzy, gaudy, disposable fiction for the dribbling masses. Piled high on tables, they're repositories of cliché: story filling them like stale breath inflates a balloon. Let the flatus out and what's left? A withered, barren condom. The book as prophylactic — preventing fertility of thought, denying procreative genes their will to nurture minds.

Here's Avery Johns, his latest excretion stacked in ziggurats. Fawning endorsements pock the cover with quote marks — not because anyone genuinely likes the book (should we imagine David Cameron has really read it?) but because it's popular right now. The cover is an intravenous line into the zeitgeist: the best advert around. As I stand there, an assistant arrives with a sheet of golden stickers and begins to apply them: "Soon to be a major Hollywood film featuring Scarlett Johansson!"

'Have you read it?' she says.

'Should I?'

She appraises me. She looks around the mid-week store. 'Honestly? It's a cynical bag of shit.'

'Will you marry me?'

She laughs nervously and goes back to the till, where she appears to talk about me to the other assistant ('Isn't he the one who kept coming in to sign those books that never sold?').

Other books are stacked on other tables — books heavily advertised in the media, books by cricketers and TV presenters and celebrity chefs and that woman who did that thing that earned a nanosecond of fame. These are the books I loathe more than the fart-filled balloons of commercial fiction. They're the kind of books I should be writing, each one a carefully sourced and laboriously marketed gimmick. The postmodern-neo-modernist approach: write it backwards, or from eight points of view, or in chapters that can be read in any order, or in a single paragraph, or without using the word *the* throughout. Such things are literary aphrodisiac to the beard-stroking wannabe aesthete ('Yes, I'm reading the latest Johns. Whole thing done in mirror-writing, you know. I've gone quite cross-eyed . . .')

Just as long as you're not a normal person writing a well written book with a good story and good characters. That's so twentieth-century. Who'd read a book like that? It can't be marketed.

I wander to the crime section, where a woman is sitting at a small table bedecked with posters and piled high with books. She's that famous writer who's sold millions and millions. Giddy fans line up for a signature and a few sacred words with the author. A suited PR woman hovers ominously nearby (got to recoup that massive advance or she's out of a job!). I loiter close to hear what nuggets of wisdom might drop from the lips of this golden goose, but then I'm overtaken by an irresistible urge. I join the queue.

Me:	Love your books! In fact, I'm writing a book myself . . .
Writer:	[*Wince turning into a stiff smile*] Oh really?
Me:	Yes. I wonder . . . could I ask you a writing question?

Writer: Yeees?

Me: Well, it's more a vocab thing. Do you think we should be more influenced by a word's strict etymology or by its syllabic gestalt? I mean, a word is more than a definition isn't it? It's a constellation of context, sound and even appearance: the double consonant, the extended vowel sound – the combination with juxtaposed words to create alliteration or assonance or both.

Writer: I ... er ... [*looking round for the PR woman, flashing the danger sign*].

PR: [*Stepping forth with laser-strobing eyes*] Move along please. There are others who'd like to speak with—

Me: Just a quick answer then. You're such a successful writer.

Writer: Look, I just write stories. I'm more concentrated on the stories.

Me: Even if the writing itself is GCSE level at best?

PR: [*Swooping hawk-like to grab my arm, dragging me out of the queue*] Thank you for your question. Let's give some genuine fans a go, shall we? [*Aside*] If I were you, I'd give up on my book right now. It sounds like you're an awful writer.

Me: Maybe there's a career for me in PR, then ...

That's why I stopped coming into Waterstones.

I wander upstairs to look at the art and cooking books and gravitate almost unconsciously to the photography section, where I pick up the well thumbed (by me) copy of Taschen's *Little Book of Pussy*. The trick is to brass it out rather than lurk round-shouldered. One must adopt a scholarly air and prepare the justification in advance. I'm not a semi-employed literary failure; I'm a photography lecturer sourcing titles for my MGU course on, er, Transgressive Art. My name? Professor Derek Crabbs – yes, the street poet. Why I have been coming in for the last three weeks to paw this book, which is essentially just pornography under the guise of aesthetics? OK, look ... I've got this student called Mohini.

It all comes back to her, the galloping libido. I'll be seeing her on Thursday and I feel like a fifteen-year-old ready to touch his first boobs. Never mind that we'll be meeting in one of those dim MGU meeting rooms with Darth-Vader air-con. Just getting her alone is sure to unleash some hormonal torrent or hot-eyed confession. 'Tom – I've wanted you from the first moment ... Can we go to a hotel right now? I'll pay ... '

'Nice pussy!'

A young female voice at my right shoulder. I snap the book closed, revealing the no-less incriminating front cover. *MGU lecturer ... Crabbs ... Transgressive Art ...* I turn.

It's Mohini.

I feel my face throb chilli-warm. 'I was just ... '

She puts a hand on my arm and squeezes. She leans close so her earthy perfume washes over me and she whispers, 'Don't worry! I've got the *Little Book of Big Penis.*'

'You have?'

'Why not? Are you surprised?'

'I ... what are you doing here?'

'Shopping for books?'

'Of course. Stupid question.'

She's smiling and looking into my eyes. This is the closest I've been to her. Kissing distance. Her hand is still holding my forearm, which has become quite rigid. I force myself to speak.

'Have you, er, seen anything you like?'

'I think I've found something I'd like to take home with me.'

Does she actually wink, or do her eyes just close languidly like a cat's? Her hand's still on my arm. It transmits an erotic power that has my Marks and Spencer briefs trembling.

'I've got an idea,' she says. 'Why don't we do the tutorial now? We're both here. We could go for a coffee.'

'Yes. Let's do that.'

'There's a nice little place just round the corner. Intimate.'

Yes. Yes. In the name of God, yes. But don't let go of my arm.

She doesn't let go of my arm. Indeed, she loops hers around mine as we walk down the steps and out into the street — an innocent, almost girlish gesture that seems to affirm we bear no mutual threat. We're at ease. But as we walk arm in arm and fall into a regular step (as couples do), her shoulder or her hip touches mine, impossibly soft and yielding in contrast to my own bony angles. Her long midnight hair is lifted on a breath of wind and brushes my cheek, a single strand catching between my lips. Her perfume intoxicates. I can barely walk straight from the welling turgidity.

'Don't you live around here?' she says.

'How did you know . . . ?'

'Oh, somebody said. We could just go to your house . . . if you don't mind, I mean. Have you got coffee?'

I think of the bachelor squalor: the unwashed pots, the discarded clothing, the balled tissues, the remnants of a dead relationship . . . Lexxi Cummins bent over the back of the sofa in her tartan slut skirt and wearing Lara's too-large white stilettos (don't ask; I won't tell). At least the bed linen is fresh.

'I don't mind if it's a mess,' she says. 'You should see my place. I swear there's things growing in cups.'

'I've got coffee beans. I grind them with cardamom . . . '

'I love cardamom. That settles it. Lead on.'

But like a returning dog, she seems to know the way and leads me with gentle arm steerings that become gradually firmer the closer we get to my door. Will I have time to rush in before her and hide the evidence of my true self?

No. Mohini stands in the living room with her hands on her hips and takes in the scene with an ironic smile.

'The writer's room,' she says.

'Yes.'

She looks at Lexxi and shakes her head slowly. She wags a mocking finger at me: naughty Tom. Dirty Tom.

'It's not mine. It was some kind of joke . . . '

'Is that your position of choice?'

'I . . . er . . . they're all good for me. With real women, I mean. Coffee?'

'Yes, please.'

I unscrew the moka with shaking hands, afraid that some inadvertent brush against a kitchen cabinet will be enough to trigger volcanic release. *She's* seducing *me*, right? God knows why – look at me. But she's directing this. I could halt it at any time if I wanted. Look – I'm your teacher. This is against the rules.

I carry the mugs back to the room and see that she's sitting in my swivel chair with an amused expression. She's reading a printout.

'You probably shouldn't . . . ' I try to move faster but the cups are full.

'"Fenella let her clothes drop to the floor",' she reads, '"revealing her fine, up-thrusting breasts, her taut abdomen, her lissom thighs and the shadow at the centre of her pelvic girdle . . . " What *is* this?'

'It's, er, a side project. It's nothing. That's an early, rejected draft.'

Her eyes hold mine mesmerically then move back to the page. 'The vocab is too anatomical. Not poetic enough. Breasts, abdomen, thighs, pelvic . . . '

I'm still holding the cups. 'That's why I discarded it. The *shadow* is OK. *Thighs* is OK.'

'You like thighs?' She swivels in the chair so she's facing me. She's wearing silky black leggings. Her eyes are embers.

'It's an evocative word in itself. Sounds like *sigh*. You get into trouble when you, er, look for synonyms or euphemisms for everything. It can become ridiculous.'

She looked at my midsection. '"His swollen weapon ... his twitching member ... " That kind of thing?'

I'm still holding the cups, which might as well be shackles. 'Yes.'

She shrugs off her denim jacket, arching her back in the process. Her torso is sheathed in a top of the same silky material. '"Ample orbs ... velvet mounds ... ",' she says.

'That kind of thing.'

She stands and approaches me with a sinuous, hip-swaying walk. More a languorous dance. She walks right up to me so I'm obliged to hold the mugs either side of her. She smiles and I stare into the abyss of her eyes as she moves closer still, tilting her head, opening her lips, kissing me with a softness and delicacy that threatens to precipitate insanity upon me. Her hands move slowly down the front of my body to cup the urgent swelling there.

I'm spilling the coffee.

'How would you describe that?' she says, her breath hot and sweet in my face.

'I'm ... teacher,' I whisper. 'Against ... rules.'

'Tom – we're going to fuck now.'

The expletive is twice as effective in her crisp, calm Anglo-Indian accent.

'I ... '

'We'll start like your doll here if that's what you like. Then I want everything, Tom. Everything you've thought about, I've thought about, too. I'm not leaving until I've had everything out of you. Let me be more specific: I'm not leaving until my mascara has run down my cheeks and my hair is wet. My lips will be swollen and my skin flushed. Do you understand? Total commitment.'

I nod.

She pulls the top over her head. No bra. She steps out of her leggings. A miniscule pair of lacy black pants. Her skin is flawless.

'Time to put the coffee down, Tom. We won't be drinking it.'

It's dark when she leaves, her lips swollen, her eye make-up on my sheets and on my body, her hair calligraphing my pillow, her tears and saliva still damp on my neck, her perfume on my tongue and permeating everything. I'm bitten, bruised, emptied . . . and yet full of her.

I must have more.

Impressionism

I AWAKE LATE from one of the deepest sleeps I've had since Lara left. I'm groggy and my limbs are heavy. The bed retains Mohini's marks and scents. Lying in it is a reminder and a promise. But I'm late for a staff meeting at MGU and a session with my most hated supervisee.

I pull on the same clothes as yesterday and slurp both cups of cold coffee in the living room. As I'm dribbling this down my front, I notice her tiny black pants on the arm of the sofa. Did she leave them here on purpose? A memento? (Did she leave the house knickerless, or bring some spares?) I stuff them in my jacket pocket and grab my mail off the doormat as I rush out of the house.

I'm last to arrive at the meeting. All the biscuits are gone and the desk tops are littered with wrappers. Jerry nods a welcome. Gwynn salutes.

'The late Tom Fynn,' says Janet.

'OK, let's begin,' says Jerry. 'Admin have told me that there are few MA supervisees who should be making final submissions this year. Are any of them ready?'

'Danny Glover,' says Janet. 'He's ready. I've told him to submit. And The Exorcist. Scooby Doo is still miles off; he knows when the deadline is.'

Jerry, who disapproves of the nicknames but who knows them all, marks his printout.

'I've got the Giaour and Dorian Grey,' says Gwynn. 'They've finished already.'

Jerry nods.

'Radio 4 will be submitting,' I say. 'She doesn't want to, but she's out of time. Do we all know about Percy?'

'I sent an email round,' says Jerry.

'Poor old Percy,' says Gwynn, shaking his head. 'Do you think he killed himself, Tom?'

'Probably. The book was his life. Can I submit his work for him?'

'It's a lovely thought, Tom, but he's not paid the final instalment on the course. You'd have to pay that if you wanted to submit. And, really, it's just a gesture. Who'll collect the MA?'

'I know.'

'But I'll be giving you a new supervisee now your hours are down.'

'Ashes to ashes, the show goes on,' says Gwynn.

'An American girl. Kalli. She's here on the USC transfer programme. It'll be for just a semester after Christmas. I'll put the file in your pigeonhole.'

'Kali — Indian goddess of destruction!' says Gwynn, with a wink I don't like the look of.

'Different spelling,' says Jerry. 'Two l's.'

'Double Hell,' says Gwynn.

'Yes, so there's also LUFC,' I say. 'I'm meeting him after this.'

'The creature from the black latrine,' says Janet, quoting *Blackadder II*.

'Is he ready?' says Jerry.

'He thinks he's ready. He thinks he's Christ Triumphant with a Nobel Prize.'

'I hope you're managing his expectations,' says Jerry.

'Right. "I'm sorry, Adolf, but you might have to rethink this whole Aryan supremacy thing ..." The guy's a psycho.' He's also someone who's already made two official complaints about me because I don't share his Messianic opinion of his work.

'Well,' says Jerry. 'All the better to get him through as soon as possible. If I were—'

His phone is ringing. He ducks out, holding up a finger. One minute.

Gwynn and Janet are both smiling at me. He nudges her. She nudges him.

'What?' I say.

Gwynn winks exaggeratedly. Janet sucks a finger with mock eroticism.

'There's no way you two can know ...'

'I was walking into Waterstones as you were walking out,' says Gwynn. 'Arm in arm.'

'"Intertwined" you told me,' says Janet.

'That was later, I expect,' says Gwynn. 'Look how pale he is.'

In fact, I'm blushing. 'I've never . . . '

'Don't sweat it,' says Janet. 'Just remember to keep a distance, all right? That's the main thing. And don't tell anyone. They'll know anyway, but you won't have told them. Deniability. And never for longer than a semester. These are the rules.'

'Thanks. But nothing happened . . . she'd hurt her ankle and I was supporting her.'

'With your crutch,' says Gwynn.

Janet nods approvingly. 'That's it. Deniability.'

'By the way,' I say. 'Did you get that note, Janet? I put it in your pigeonhole. It was in mine.'

'That was you? I thought it was a joke. It meant nothing to me. I put it in Gwynn's pigeonhole.'

'I always get away with what I do,' he says. 'Whatever it is I do.'

Jerry's back. 'Sorry about that. Had to take it. So we're done with the supervisees, yes? Next we have the . . . Vegas conference.'

'My turn!' says Janet.

'Sorry, J. It's Gwynn again.'

Janet's arms go up. 'For fuck's sake, Jerry. We're all writers.'

'Gwynn has the Eliot Prize. If you'd won at Sundance . . . '

'Yeah yeah. Blah blah MGU international reputation blah. Keats has published more recently than Gywnn has.'

'But pr'ythee do not stick/Thy latent talons in me,' says Gwynn.

'Let's not get into that,' says Jerry. 'It gets a bit Israel-Palestine, doesn't it?'

'Is the meeting over?' says Gwynn, shaking out a cigarette.

'Yes, OK,' says Jerry. 'I'll send round the minutes this afternoon.'

They depart, Janet pursuing Jerry. I'm left alone in the biscuitless room.

I look at my watch: five minutes to LUFC. I take the crumpled mail from my jacket pocket, bringing her tiny pants out with it. Memories of last night: she atop me, eyes closed, rocking; she below me, eyes burning; the spinal groove of her lower back, snaking slowly, traced by my fingers. Her breath and teeth at my ear. How am I going to concentrate on anything today?

There's a bill, some spam from the bank and a hand-addressed letter whose writing I don't recognise. I slit it roughly with a key and unfold a single A5 sheet of notepaper with a ragged perforated top and the same handwriting as the envelope.

Tom

You are a despicable person. You think you know everything, don't you? Think you're such an expert on writing even though the most successful of your 'books' is ranked 200,000th on Amazon and you're a 'teacher' at a university ranked 103 in the league tables for English. Somebody needs to bring you down a peg or two. Hope you and your colleagues liked Lexxi Cummins. Well worth your money, I'm sure. There's more to come . . . just wait.

Your Unfan

Wonderful. A rhetorical question, two stats, a cliché, an insult and a threat. No attempt at paragraphing to achieve greater emphasis. Clearly a nutter; just look at those scare quotes. The only glints of nascent style are the omitted *you* at the start of the third sentence and the omitted *I* before *hope*. Not sure about the ellipsis. A full stop would have more emphatic. And *Unfan*. Does that mean he (?) used to be a fan and now isn't, or that she (?) was never fan and just has no idea how to use prefixes?

I should probably show this to Jerry. And it might constitute proof for the bank that this moron did indeed hack my computer somehow. Must see about that, too ... So many things occurring ...

But now I have to meet LUFC, so named for the tattoo on his neck. He's a painter and decorator, as Hitler was, and believes himself to be the next Ian McEwan or Martin Amis (seeing no difference between the two). There's no reason, of course, why any manual labourer shouldn't be an effective writer, but this one is an irredeemable dickhead. I'm terrified of him.

I smell his cigarette-and-Lynx stench before I see him. He's sitting in the meeting room with his feet on a chair, ostentatiously reading Amis' *Money*. He's that terrifying educational chimera: an autodidact. And he's keen on telling you. It was in one of our early sessions I suggested he should call himself a polydactyl, which he took to be some higher from of autodidact until he found a dictionary and made his first official complaint. I still derive great pleasure from imagining how many people he told about his polydactyly before he picked up the big book of words.

'All right?' he says as I walk in. His eyes are pale blue and laser me like a sociopath's. He's wearing paint-spattered jeans and football shirt from a club I wouldn't know. The blued tattoo is fully revealed. 'Heard you on the student radio,' he says.

'Ah.'

'You must've been drunk, mate.'

Something in his tone. Was he the second caller: "John"?

'Well, what can you do? Some of these callers are just idiots, aren't they?'

His serial-killer stare is unblinking.

'I've had a look at your latest draft,' I say. Which took me three days (unpaid) to read. I could have been doing the masterpiece edit.

He leans back in his chair. 'And ... ?'

'And you've not really made any of the changes I identified last time.'

He smiles and shrugs, meaning: I know better than you what literature is. Just give me my MA.

'The thing is ... and I've said this before ... there's a very real danger of you not actually passing this course unless you hand in something ... credible.'

The tendons on his neck pop. He glares. I imagine myself in pieces in his fridge.

'What I mean to say,' I say, 'is that your entire premise is flawed. We've been through this already. A western set in modern-day Manchester, but with no explanation why everyone is wearing cowboy hats and riding horses? There are no cars — what happened to them? — but Rawhide McJohnson rides his horse to Superdrug for his moisturiser, stopping at traffic lights as he goes. Cat-House Moll works in admin at the Council ...'

'It's IR-O-NY,' he says, smirking.

'To what effect? What's the point? What's the allegory? It's amusing for a few pages, but then it's entirely gratuitous. You don't use it to make any comment on either society. The western thing might as well not exist.'

He's actually laughing. 'You don't get it, mate. You can't see it with your little academic mind.'

'Explain it to me. Explain the irony.'

'Nah. If you can't understand it ... I'll let the examiners figure it out.'

He hasn't yet understood that I am the examiner. I can't tell him because it's supposed to be anonymous. I wish I could grade it right now and hand it back to him. But he'd stab me.

'OK, OK,' I say. 'Let's put the premise to one side. Look at this bit on page seventy-three.'

> *Rawhide McJohnson tied Excalibur to the hitching post and walked into the juice bar, his spurs clinking. He looked at the menu like a man who's crossed a desert. Pineapple, Guava. Passion fruit. Banana. Orange. Carrot. Wheatgrass. Hen grit. Brass rivets. Lasso*

rope. Branding iron. Hiawatha, Geronimo, Sitting Bull. Campfire,
railroad. 'Gimme a Tropical Refresher with a shot of ginger,' he says
laconically.

'Yeah?' he says.

'That's supposed to be funny, right?' Certainly, I almost wet myself while reading it.

He glares.

'No? OK. Explain the list to me: the fruit and the western, er, cornucopia.'

He shakes his head, dumbfounded at my ignorance. 'It's impressionistic.'

'Impressionistic.'

'Yeah.'

I could be editing the masterpiece. I could be naked with Mohini. I feel for her pants in my jacket pocket: a promise to get me through this. More memories of last night: inhaling her raven hair — actually inhaling it six inches or more down my throat but too ecstatic to care. The hot clutching at her very depths. Her whispers in my ear: incantations in Bengali, Sanskrit or Kashmiri.

'Let me ask you ... Are we to understand that Rawhide McJohnson is gay?'

'Why?' He sits suddenly up his chair and I flinch.

'Well, for a cowboy, he visits a lot of juice bars and buys a lot of moisturiser. I know ... I know that doesn't mean ... but he's in the Saloon Bar glee club and he wears a lot of leather ... and he'll only ever share his saddle with Nubuck, the handsome young rodeo rider with the tight jeans ... and, well, he's very sartorially aware for a cowboy. I mean, he knows at least twelve ways to tie his neckerchief ... '

'He's not gay.'

'It's not an issue if he is. In fact, it'd be a very interesting—'

'He's. Not. Gay.'

'Great!'

There's really no reason to continue, but LUFC knows his rights and he knows that he's entitled to a set number of tutorial hours, even if we have to spend them on the delusional odyssey of a mind permanently damaged by white-spirit fumes. I must go through another dozen examples of his pure insanity, and he'll disregard all my advice. For he is a Great Artist. I may have to leave Manchester after I fail him. For sure, I'll sweat every time I go into a B&Q.

It's difficult, though. For all of them. All of us. The hardest thing as a developing writer is knowing whether you're really any good. You can listen to opinions, but how many people really know what they're talking about? The line between delusion and confidence is transparent, between arrogance and genius, invisible. To believe oneself a good writer is immediately to be wrong. The good writers are the ones who despair that everything they produce should be better. They're right.

I SMELL HER as soon as I open the front door: that lingering, ageless perfume. My urge is to go directly to bed, strip and lie in the sheets that still retain a memory of her body. I have no phone number or address for her. I won't see her until the next seminar unless I go back to Waterstones and walk around until she comes in.

I've done nothing on the masterpiece edit. The main problem is reading the thing — something I've not actually done in the year or so since it was finished. What if it's not as good as I remember? Will I have the confidence to go on? And even if it is, a close read onscreen will take me about two weeks before I can even think about implementing the edits. Two weeks I could spend rutting with Mohini.

And yet the masterpiece is my only remaining connection to any pretence of being a practising writer. Otherwise, it's just those three published books, becoming less relevant with every passing year. I don't want to become (sorry, Jerry) one of those writers who was published once. That's only one better than becoming the dreaded local writer: doyen of the regional writers' circles and tedious old authority by dint of that monograph on steam engines published in 1953.

Perhaps it's the nature of the edits that's stopping me. It's going to become a totally different book. Diet-masterpiece. Can I face a shorter, less bombastic version? Can I actually make the changes they want? Am I able to be the writer they think I am?

Lexxi Cummins is still bent over the sofa. Poor Lexxi. How pale and lifeless you are next to the Anglo-Indian goddess. Your auto-grip hands hold nothing. Your vibrating fundament is vacant (the ingenious perineum battery compartment still empty). We stood right beside you there at the sofa and you watched with envy how vivid, how responsive was the flesh of your rival.

I'm going to have to move the doll. Pretty sure there's a no-returns policy once she's come out of the box. Pun intended.

I turn on the computer and go to the inbox. The usual penis extension pills, the inept virus-laden spam ("Hi I saw your pic on Facebook!" I'm not on Facebook), and the various newsletters I've been too lazy to unsubscribe from. Here's an update on the forthcoming York Festival:

Special guest Avery Johns interviewed by Mark Lawson

The York Festival: site of my tragic fall and the end of my too-brief publishing run. I've not been back since that disaster. I've not been able to face it. *He* was there during my Luciferian Fall. Avery Johns. Would he recognise me now? Has he guessed that I'm the one intermittently trolling his site? And there was that handwritten letter in green ink I sent him just after Lara left – the one where I pretended to be in a lunatic asylum and yet also an articulate fan of his books. How long did I lose sleep after that one, thinking they'd find forensic evidence leading back to me?

Should I go again? Just to get over the stigma? Prove to myself I'm over Avery Johns' success, though I'm clearly not. Perhaps it would eradicate my fear of the masterpiece edit. I know I'm better than him.

Nothing on the work email from Mohini. I open a new message to her but my fingers hover impotently above the keys. What to write? 'Can't wait to see you again'? 'Being inside you is all I can think about'? 'Miss you'?

I realise I know nothing about her. We've never had a conversation apart from that brief exchange at the bookshop and the purely pedagogical transactions of the classroom. I have no idea what tone to adopt. I don't know what her attitude towards me is. Was it one-time thing? Will I expose myself by displaying inappropriate or disproportionate feelings? Writing doesn't work with Mohini. Only the senses. I cancel the message and pick up my phone.

'*Dottore!*' says Will.

'You got time?'

'Yeah. Carol's taken the kids to a Halloween thing. I was about to retire to bed with the iPad and a box of wet wipes.'

'A romantic evening in. I don't want to disturb your precious—'

'Forget it. I'm on hair trigger anyway these days. How about you? Did you manage to . . . what was her name?'

'Mohini.'

'Oooh!'

'What . . . ?'

'The way you said her name! Quietly, like a breath. You did, didn't you? Tell me you did.'

'She started it . . . '

'Tommo the dirty dog! You'd better tell me everything. How old is she?'

'I've really got no idea . . . '

'Well, how was it? Don't make me interrogate you.'

'She was here for about five hours. I . . . inhaled her hair. Will, I've never . . . not even with Lara.'

'You lucky bastard. Did she—?'

'Everything. Everything you can imagine. Well, maybe not *your* imagination . . .'

'Je-sus.'

'But she's left me feeling . . . I don't know. I'm ruined for everything else. I can't think of anything else. Not even the writing. That edit I emailed you about? I've done nothing on it and it's my big chance. My only chance. Every time I sit down to begin it, I start thinking of her instead.'

'The power of the pussy, Tommo. Greater than any muse.'

'Lovely. That's why you're a comms writer rather than a poet.'

'Ha! Get it while you can; that's what I say. The last time Carol touched my dong was accidentally while she was groping in my pocket for the garage key. Listen – did you manage to enter that *Guardian* comp?'

'Yes. Your name. Your address. Why? Got another one?'

'Yeah. I'll send you the details. Might be fun. You have to write a review of your favourite Avery Johns book.'

'Seriously?'

'Yeah, but a good review – not a character assassination. It'd be a real test of your skill.'

'I'm not sure I could do that.'

'Come on. If you can write the masterpiece, you can knock out a fake review in your sleep.'

'But I'd have to read his shit. OK, send it to me. I'll have a look. And I wanted to ask you about my computer. That sex doll I told you about – it was paid for out of my account. The bank said I might have been hacked.'

'Yeah? Have you got anti-virus?'

'I'm not sure.'

'That probably means no. This is important: you've probably got some virus that's reading your emails and following your internet use. And I'm not talking about cookies. It's probably reporting all of this back to whoever sent it. You need to stop using the internet on your existing laptop and get it to an expert to clean. You got an iPad?'

'No.'

'They're a bit safer than a Windows PC like your old piece of crap. I know you've got precious memories with it blah blah blah, but it's not safe anymore. Do you know who's hacked you? Who sent the doll?'

'No idea. Could be anyone I've pissed off.'

'Shit. You need to find out. Maybe an IT guy can trace it back, but I doubt it.'

'I've had notes and a letter. None of it's traceable.'

'You've got a stalker, Tommo. Thought about going to the police?'

'I don't know. The threats are very vague: "You won't get away with it" kind of stuff.'

'Have you done an especially bad review of anyone on Penthesilea?'

'They're all especially bad.'

'Any students dislike you particularly?'

'Most of them, I expect.'

'Is it a man or a woman, do you think?'

'It might be an older man. He might have called into a radio show I did.'

'Well there's a start. Can you look back at the Penthesilea reviews for an older man?'

'There are hundreds of them. A lot write under pseudonyms.'

'It'd be somewhere to start.'

'Yes.'

'And if you get any chance to enter into dialogue, go easy. It's no good ranting at them and calling them a moron or whatever. You need to find out what their concerns are and meet them on their own terms.'

'Know your audience. First rule of comms.'

'Fuck off. Are you worried?'

'Not yet. But I think he might know about Fenella. The doll looks like a message.'

'Does that really matter? So what if you write porn on the side?'

'MGU might not care, but it'd taint my name with the industry. I'd be known as a smut hack. I'm having enough trouble coming back from the real books I wrote. Good books. Can you imagine being known as the guy who wrote *Thad's questing ram parted fleshly folds and sank fathoms deep in enclasping voluptuousness?*'

'Nice. Is that from the new book?'

'I was riffing. Too many syllables in that last bit.'

'Well, look – let me know how you get on with that virus cleansing. And the rest. Enjoy yourself, Tommo. Life's short, then you have kids.'

'Yes. Don't let me keep you from your wet wipes.'

'Yeah. One last thing. Can I ask … ? What are you planning to do with Lexxi?'

'Goodnight, Will.'

So no more Internet at home. Great. How much is an iPad? I could check online. And would it hurt if I also bought a couple of tickets for the York Festival while I'm at it? It's this weekend. Maybe Mohini'll come with me.

Herod's child

MY FAME as a writer came, and ended, at the York Writing Festival. It lasted half a day.

My third book had come out to no fanfare and no reviews. Copies were rare in shops and the publicity machine was a lopsided child's tricycle ridden by an asthmatic octogenarian. My royalty statements showed that I owed the publisher more than they owed me. Even I could see the end was in sight. Other writers published at the same time had already yielded to the axe and retired into bitter blogdom, bargain bins and writer's-group celebrity. Only I and Avery "No Cliché Left Unwritten" Johns remained from that original party in London.

It was my suggestion that the PR sloths put me forward for the York Festival: a small, but relatively well attended soiree that always attracted a few big names. I filled out all the application materials myself, understanding the lethargic velleity of my publicity team. I also submitted an entire address concerning the value of good writing in the modern market, which I hoped would form the basis of a detailed interview with me. (Please note the use of *velleity* in the previous sentence: a word I first saw in Beckett and which I've been waiting twelve years to use).

Naturally, there was to be no interview. I appeared onstage in a panel with three writers and fielded questions from another. One of our group was that TV presenter who'd retired and produced a sub-literate family saga so bad that I'd laughed out loud when I read the first page. She was the draw. Nobody would have bought tickets to see the rest of us.

It went OK. Most of the questions were directed to the idiot presenter, whose answers revealed (to me) that her book had been heavily edited by a publisher desperate to recoup its preposterous advance. The interviewer had clearly read only the back cover and the first page of my third book, a fact reflected in the vacuity of her questions. I must have spoken two sentences.

Still. I was onstage in front of a few hundred people being addressed as a writer. I'd bought an expensive silk-blend jacket for the occasion and pretended that this was how a writer of my stature would dress (if he sold any books). The audience applauded sycophantically each time Daytime TV made a weak joke, but echoed only silence back at my deathless comments on writing. It was all downhill from there.

In the signing room afterwards, people queued in four lines for the four writers. Or rather, they queued in one line for the one famous writer as we other three sat behind a wall of unsigned books. A myopic old dear briefly approached my table but swerved away at the last moment with a muttered 'You're not her!' I signed all the books regardless, having been told by someone that they couldn't be returned to the publisher if they were marked in any way. All the while, my PR stood sour-faced behind me. She might as well have been holding a scythe.

It was after lunch (a sandwich; the publisher wouldn't pay for me to attend the Writers' Lunch) that I found out they'd given my address on good writing to Avery Johns. He'd apparently read it from a lectern to a rapt audience and then answered a series of (supplied) questions to show his mastery of English prose.

'How could you have done that?' I asked my lemon-shark PR. 'How?'

'We really wanted you to get a solo stage, but ...' She shrugged, as convincing as Van Damme in *Hamlet*.

'But you didn't even *ask* me! You just *gave* it to him.'

'Avery is ... his books are doing rather better than yours.'

'But he's a fucking moron! He thinks prose is the plural of *prostitutes*.'

'Let's go and mingle with the readers, shall we?'

'I haven't got any, remember? You haven't managed to get my books in the shops yet.'

The readers had no idea who I was, squinting at my name badge and revealing an instant lack of interest. This is fame: recognition. It would have been enough if my name had been Tom Tesco. Tom Eastenders. Tom Pot-Noodle. Anything to stir the fog of minds blind to obscurity. Those people weren't there for writing; they wanted writers. I got talking to a (staggering drunk) arts journalist from a local TV channel who told me she hadn't read a single book by any of the attending writers but that she was desperate to interview Avery Johns. Had I heard his amazing address on the value of good writing? No, I'd missed out on that. My black-widow PR pulled me gently away from the media.

That evening, the senior editor took me for a (soft) drink and told me that they wouldn't require any further books from me. For some inexplicable reason, he said, the public hadn't taken to these novels they'd never seen or heard of. I ranted, I raged, I counted off instances of ineptitude on my fingers (the wrong character name on the cover?) and he nodded wearily, having heard the speech a hundred times from a hundred writers, and having arrived at vague contempt for this breed of scribblers he'd once respected. If only machines could be programmed to write the books, there'd be none of this whining and recrimination.

Of course, there was the usual offer to look at "anything else you might produce", as long as it wasn't anything like the stuff that hadn't sold. In the event, every one of my emails or phone calls to the publisher thereafter was ignored. Perhaps I'd been blacklisted. I was dead to them.

The postscript was almost funny in its dark irony. For months, my name had been all over the net as an attendee at the York Festival. Piles of my books had been arrayed there. Local radio had mentioned it. Hundreds of people had bought tickets for the panel session and thousands had read about the TV presenter who'd sat right next to me on the stage. And yet my next royalty cheque showed that this brief blast of publicity had had not the slightest effect on my sales. The Amazon ratings had not fluctuated at all. The Google Alerts had turned up nothing but old ads for the festival.

Was I actually invisible?

I had to face the fact that my publishing run was over. My lifelong dream of being a working writer was over. But unlike the Olympic athlete who can at least use his profile to retire into brand endorsement, TV presenting and personal training, I was as unknown as I'd ever been. Worse, the name of TG Harkett was now poison. Who'd want a book by the guy who had cost his publisher money? The guy whose books wouldn't sell even after he'd been on stage with that famous TV presenter? My own publisher wasn't replying to my emails; why would anyone else?

I'd had my chance and I'd blown it. Or rather, I'd handed my baby messiah to Herod for safekeeping.

Now I faced the decision of the other ten thousand writers in exactly the same position. Did I give up and adopt the stoical attitude? I'd had my go; I'd been published. Pat on the head. Well done. Now go back to your empty life and make writing books a hobby – books to be read only by your no friends, your illiterate family or the bovine masses on Amazon who'll buy the book if it costs £0.01 and has a cover designed by a monkey using Microsoft Word. Print a few copies, perhaps, and spend eight hours a day on Facebook trying to become friends with each individual reader.

Or start again from scratch. New pseudonym, new genre, new style, new market ... anything to re-attract the marketing raptors. Become better, become different. Because you're a writer. Remembering the example of Bukowski, who struggled his whole alcoholic, minimum-wage life to keep on writing against a tide of utter indifference until, finally, he was recognised just before he died. He was a writer. Or Miller, whose life-defining novel *Tropic of Cancer* was banned as obscene for thirty years, leaving him poverty stricken, shiftless and unread. He was a writer. Or pale, obedient Kafka, tortured by noise and so pursued by fears of inadequacy that he demanded his entire output be burned on his death. He was a writer.

I chose the latter. I'm not sure how much longer I can do it.

Drop-out

SO I WALTZ down to Quik Market for some skins and a can of Red Bull and I'm thinking to myself 'Why did they miss the 'C' out of Quik Market?' And what is QM (as I call it) anyway? I mean, it's not Sainsbury's or Tesco or Co-Op or anything. Who owns QM? A Mr Quik? Was he one of the original Mr Men created by Roger Hargreaves — those beloved children's books (and now a full range of merchandise including my favourite, The Little Miss Daredevil backpack.) My attention was instantly taken by the huge variety of inventive pasta shapes on offer . . .

'Can I stop you there a moment?' I say to Dreadlock Twat.

He looks up from the creased and yellowed scrap he's reading from. Hand-written. Did he find it in a bin? It belongs in one.

'Is there a problem?' he says.

The problem is that your work is making my brain hurt. 'I think it might be good to pause briefly and get some immediate reactions.' I look to the others: Stalwart (disgusted), Mum (embarrassed) and Earnest Youth (incredulous). Mohini is not here. Not here.

'It seems very glib,' says Earnest Youth.

'Could you expand on that?' I say.

'Well, it's mostly just . . . noise. Empty chatter, but self-satisfied. There's little substance or direction. It seems a bit witless . . . unless it's supposed to be in character.'

I nod, reflecting that *glib* was used as a verb by Shakespeare to mean *castrate*.

'Is it supposed to be funny?' says Mum.

'Do you find it funny?' I say.

'No. It seems a bit silly, really. If it's in character, the character would have to be . . . I don't know . . . '

'An idiot?' says Stalwart. 'The character, I mean. Perhaps he has brain damage. I assume *skins* is a reference to drug paraphernalia.'

Dreadlock Twat is looking crestfallen.

'Is this a character piece?' I ask him.

'Er, yeah. I suppose it is.'

'How, though? Is he cerebrally impaired from excessive THC inhalation? Or is he bi-polar, perhaps?'

'I hadn't thought of that, but yeah. I think he might be. Bi-polar, I mean.'

'You don't know?' says Earnest Youth. 'I mean, you can't decide the narrative perspective *after* you've written it.'

'Why not?' says Dreadlock T. 'Sometimes the characters do their own thing.'

A mini-debate starts among them and I stare at the empty chair.

Is it me? Did I say or do something that night? Has she reported me to the university? To the police? Is she pregnant? There's every reason for her to be, though she said ... Do I need to go to the clinic myself? I just wanted to see her again. I needed it.

'—and the tenses are all over the place,' Stalwart is saying.

'OK, OK,' I say. 'I think the conclusion we need to draw is that the piece seems essentially purposeless. What was your intention in taking him to the shop? Character development? A plot point? Tone creation? Establishing narrative perspective and empathy?'

'I ... just wrote it on the bus on the way here. I wasn't really thinking.'

Earnest Youth leans back with a pointed sigh. Stalwart rolls his eyes. Mum bites her lip.

'Do you think that might be the reason it doesn't work?'

Dreadlock shrugs with a tobacco smile.

'This is a Master's degree,' I say. 'It's expected that we become an effective critical unit. Do you think it might be disrespectful to present your classmates with something you wrote on a fish-n-chip paper on the bus ten minutes before the session?'

'S'pose so . . . but, you know, I . . . I believe in spontaneous composition.'

'Can you play chess?'

'Er . . . What? No.'

'If I challenged you to a game of chess right now, do you think you could win using your spontaneous understanding of the rules of chess?'

'That's not—'

'Do you think Mark Twain jotted *Huckleberry Finn* on the back of a cereal box as he sat on the crapper?'

They're all looking at me now. I should probably stop.

'Do you think Thomas Mann spontaneously scribbled *The Magic Mountain* – Ian Fleming's favourite book, by the by – on a discarded sanitary towel as he was crossing the street? Writing is hard work. You learn the craft, you put in the years; you grasp and struggle towards a voice. You fail again and again. You dream of simply being able to achieve the minimum level of proficiency, after which you can only fantasise about developing a distinctive style. It might take you ten years if you're lucky . . . if you write every day. And *you* think you can circumvent a centuries-old process with your spontaneous bus-ride litterature? If so, do please take my place here at the front and I'll sit at your feet. Come on. Come up here.'

'Nah, man . . . I . . . I get what you're saying.'

His face is a variegated palette of crimson pallor: a raspberry ripple of mortification and humiliation. The others are staring at the desk tops.

'Excuse me,' I say. And I walk out.

JERRY FINDS ME at my desk about twenty minutes later.

'Tom. Have a word?'

'Go on then.'

'I hear the seminar finished early today. Want to talk about it?'

'I'll do extra next week.'

'I didn't mean that. Are you ... are you talking to anyone? Even your students are worried.'

'I'm fine. There've been a few things recently. Percy ... the masterpiece ... '

'Mohini?'

'What? Has she contacted—?'

'Not her. There's been an anonymous complaint from a member of the public.'

'The public? I ... '

'Look, I've checked the university's code of conduct and it says that "staff are strongly advised not to enter into an intimate relationship with a student for whom they have a responsibility in the areas of teaching/learning and assessment." It's not specifically forbidden. You know I wouldn't normally get involved − Janet *et cetera* − but there's been this complaint.'

'But not from her. Not Mohini.'

'No. Although she's dropped out of the course. No reason given. We haven't got any contact details on record other than the MGU email account we gave her. Very odd. I can't understand how that happened. I'm not sure the university will follow up an anonymous tip. But it looks bad. There may be an enquiry. Basic procedure. Can I ask if it's true?'

'Once. She came to my house.'

'OK. That's good. Not on the premises. Who else knew?'

'Nobody. I mean, Gwynn saw me with her in the street that day and he told Janet. Nobody else. I don't talk to anyone else. I don't think she would have ... Maybe the hacker.'

'The hacker?'

'That sex doll. Somebody hacked my laptop and paid for the doll from my account. If they've been reading my emails ... I also had a letter. A note really. I'm not going to "get away with it" apparently. No idea what.'

112

'You should have told me. Could it be a student?'

'Could be. But nobody knew about Mohini. They'd have to hack my email.'

'So you did write to someone?'

'Old university friend. There's no chance he told anyone.'

'Hmm. Any ideas why she's just disappeared like this?'

'You mean did I do something weird with her? Against her will?'

'No, no … I'm just trying to cover us, to cover you from any accusations of impropriety.'

'I wanted to see her again. I thought she'd be here today.'

'Why don't you go home, Tom. I'll ask Gwynn and Janet if they've told anyone. Get your laptop seen to. And do something nice over the weekend, all right?'

'Yes. Yes.'

He hesitates and raises his hand to pat my shoulder before deciding against it. He leaves.

Did I do something, say something, to make her leave? I remember that final kiss as she left my bedroom, naked, her body a play of shadowy curvatures. Long, slow, soft, that kiss. Her face so close that a quote came to mind and I whispered it into her mouth: *Therefore my mistress' eyes are raven black.* She smiled. Her eyes were wet. The last I saw of her.

I THOUGHT I glimpsed her on the way past Waterstones. A flash of raven hair and silken thigh disappearing round the corner. I ran to catch up, but there was nobody. I even loitered in Waterstones for an hour or so, standing in the same place in case she came in, but the assistant came over and asked me if I wanted to buy the book I'd been manhandling for the last month. He asked me to leave when I pointed out that it was shop-soiled and should be discounted.

Still a fading trace of her perfume when I open the door. I've not washed the sheets. Her pants hang off the corner of my screen (Joe Eszterhas wrote *Showgirls* with a pair of his wife's delicates as his talisman). I Google her image, but there's no Facebook, no LinkedIn, no Flickr, no blog. No group photos. Not even any girls with the same name who look like her.

Why would she do something like that? Seduce me, enrapture me and then leave me in a void of longing. Not love — let's be serious — but something beyond lust. Primal, like hunger. Like the urge to inhale after a long-held breath. I want to possess her so totally that I absorb her, and she me. It wasn't lovemaking; it was sex in its purest form. Fucking. Her word. I hear her saying it — that delicate Received Pronunciation *u* rather than my hacking northern vowel — and my pulse quickens.

I put a rectangle of cheese-topped cancer in the microwave and sit in my writing chair, not writing. Fenella is briefly unfilled, caught mid-paragraph in anticipation of some comprehensive outrage. The masterpiece edit (and therefore my resurrection) remains unstarted. I'm too incoherent to write.

And for the first time, I'm angry about this hacker. The doll was an expensive practical joke. The letter was an impotent tantrum. But if he has something to do with her disappearance . . . If he's the complainant . . . I'm assuming it's a man. Who is this person?

I go to the Penthesilea archive. Were any of these reviews especially bad? I can recall some that were excoriating.

> Death in Blackpool *is that rare thing: a crime novel in which you hope the criminal gets away with it and the detective dies. DI Thelonious Haberström (Black, Norwegian) is certainly trying to be different, but his dirty mac and his alcoholism, his hangdog nature and laconic dialogue reveal him as the grossest stereotype . . .*

> *The biggest problem with* Endless Passion *is its endlessness. Using a travel brochure as research, the author presents us with a love story so crassly obvious that it makes Mills & Boon look like Tolstoy. My favourite scene sees Mary throwing a coin into the Trevi*

fountain and raising Geraldo immediately to the surface (he's trying to break the world breath-holding-in-a-fountain record . . .)

Strike Force X begins as it means to go on: with casual racism, a pornographic weapons fixation and a pathological indifference to mass slaughter. Such things sell well worldwide, but not when the dialogue looks like this: "I'm gonna turn your ball-bag into a toupee and wear it to prom if you don't drop that M60 right now, boyo."

Any of these authors (and dozens more) might have felt legitimately aggrieved if they weren't able to see the genuine criticism behind my sarcasm. Few of them can. But any one of them could be the hacker. Do I just write a blanket apology on the blog and discontinue it? Would that stop them?

But why should I? I've had bad reviews myself and I've not tried to ruin anyone's life. I just wish them a nasty rectal infection and get on with it. That's what you do. The trick is to not release anything abysmal to the public in the first place. Make sure you know the book's weaknesses better than any critic can. That's what being a writer is.

The ready-meal is now lukewarm with a skin on the top. It looks like a blurry animal-rights photo of a vivisection lab. I eat it desultorily, thinking of the seminar debacle. I should apologise to them. But I'm proud of *bus-ride litterature.* That was inspired.

I decide that I'm going to attend the York Festival.

Brumming. Blumming. Blooming.

THERE ARE A LOT of festival-goers on the train, none of whom recognise me from my last attendance. I hear at least one person talking about Avery Johns' latest book and how excited they are to get their copy signed, but they move on to Ian McEwan before I have time to interject with a withering summation of Johns' talent vacuum. Just as well, perhaps.

The hotel where the talks are hosted is thronging. Memories flood back. The last time I walked in through these doors, it was on a wave of expectation. It looks like the same crowd: the bloggers, the journalists, the sponsors, the agents, the publishers, the readers. There'll be a few hustlers, too, handing out business cards or flyers or even manuscripts to anyone who can be trapped in a corner long enough to be harangued with a pitch. It was here that a renowned agent had a manuscript posted under the door of her toilet cubicle, captive audience as she was. Not sure that book ever came out, though its pages may have served a more immediate function.

There's a palpable buzz. On my first visit, I'd misidentified it as enthusiasm for the written word. Now I understand that this febrile atmosphere is the throb of commerce. The festival is a nexus for sales: selling brands, selling copies, selling tickets, selling merchandise — fame-polishing the reputations of certain writers whose editors were unable to do much with the prose. There are almost as many industry representatives as there are readers. Writers make up the tiny minority: oddly superfluous supporting characters until wheeled out to do their little dance for the customers.

I see one of them now, being ushered through the lobby by an editor and a PR. He's that American who's risen into the top-ten lists over the last few months. He looks nervous, out of place. He'd probably rather be at home, dusted with cigarette ash, sipping cold coffee and banging out his word count. A proper writer.

On the way to the toilet, I walk past a dining room set out with a buffet table and packed with industry people listening to a sponsorship spiel. I hear an amplified voice droning: '... and QuikLoans has always been a supporter of fine writing, which is why we've accepted the honour of sponsoring the Newcomer Award at this year's York Festival ... ' Cue applause.

I'm gagging on this crass insincerity when I smell her perfume. That ambergris, that sandalwood. That myrrh. Mohini's perfume. I look around the crowded corridor for a flash of dark hair but see nothing. The scent is actually warm, as if I've just passed through her bodily wake. A frantic circuit of the lobby reveals no glimpse of her black eyes, her voluptuousness. She must be here. She must have guessed I would be.

Sitting in the toilet cubicle, I determine to find her before I leave York. Even if I have to walk the corridors until the place closes. Though I admit it's tempting just to stay here in my private, speckled-grey enclosure. Anthony Burgess' quasi-autobiographical character Enderby wrote his poetry in the smallest room. Something to do with the peristaltic nature of creation.

Toilets flush. Taps rush. The fire door bangs. An occasional bubbling fart. Urinal cakes exude their overpowering dissimulation of antiseptic freshness. Someone has Blu-Tacked an A6 flyer for their self-published novel on the back of the door. *Golden Mile: The poignant story of one man's quest to something something something.*

I become aware of heavy breathing and the rustling of clothes in the next cubicle. Imminent dysentery or an impromptu bout of self abuse? There's a soft thud against the partition: a buttock or back. Whispers. The gasping becomes more rhythmical, more frenzied. A feminine gasp. The damp slapping of flesh against flesh. A masculine moan. A series of tiny cries from her and a breathless "Avery ... Yes!" He gargles a strangulated climax as she gamely moans in counterpoint. Obviously faking. Must be.

Great. Just great. A bestseller, a movie deal and now hot sex in the toilets at a literary festival. Maybe it's Johansson in there with him. He'll probably win a

117

prize later. I wait for the happy couple to leave before I emerge, headed purposefully for the bar.

I've got seven Mount Gay Extra Old rums inside me when I start talking to a teenager on the stool next to me. My mistake — she's an editor at my old publisher.

'A writer m'self,' I tell her.

'Really?' she says, her wince, turning into a pained smile. 'Anything I might know?'

'Doubt it. I'm TG Harkett.'

A furrowed brow. A little shrug. 'Sorry.'

'So you must do lot of readin'. What's your favourite book?

'Oh, it's so hard to choose just one . . .'

'If I put a gun t'your head.'

'Well, I'd probably say *The Curious Incident of the Dog*—'

'No, I meant your favourite book ever. In the history 'f literature.'

'Yes. *The Curious Incident* . . .'

'Not *Moby Dick*? *Don Quixote*? *Tristram Shandy*? *War 'n' Peace*? *Mrs Dalloway*? *Heart 'f Darkness*? *Catch 22*? *The Invisible Man*? *Lolita*? *Madame Bovary*?'

'I've heard *Catch 22* is very funny.'

'So what is't 'bout the *Curious Dog*? Why's it so good?'

'Its autistic narrative point of view is very interesting, very thought provoking.'

''Tis, but those other books I said also've very pought-throvoking points 'f view. Without 'em, *Incidental Dog* might never've been written.'

'I'm sure you're right.'

'How d'you become 'n editor anyway? What qualfications d'you need?'

'Well, I did a Masters in Creative Writing at Goldsmiths—'

'Tha's not right . . .'

'Sorry?'

'I *teach* 'n MA in Creative Writin'. How're *you* qualified t' judge *my* novel when you could be my *student*? You haven't *read* anything!'

'Well … It's more about a knowledge of the market and public tastes. I don't have to write the books myself — just assess them.'

'Based on wha'? Your readin'? Your MA in Creative Writin'? Most of the courses're *shit*!'

'Where do you teach, if you don't mind me asking?'

'MGU. Manchester.'

Another shrug of non-recognition. 'What's your name again?'

'TG Harkett. Three books on the shelves.'

'I'm afraid I've never … Who's your publisher?'

'You are. Printed wrong character name on cover …'

'It's been lovely talking to you, Mister Harkett, but I think I see my boss over there … Excuse me.'

She's soon across the room, joining the same senior editor who dropped me from the publisher, here in this very hotel. He follows her pointing finger, shakes his head, whispers something close to her ear. She shakes her head. No nod of recognition from him. No smile. I am invisible.

I scan the crowd for a swirl of midnight hair. I sniff for a trace of her and detect a delicate, saffron-fine thread of frankincense amid the beer and massed bodies. A familiar greying mane passes among them and I think for a moment that it's Jerry, but it can't be. Not here. A bell is ringing: signal for us to make our way to the room where Avery Johns will be interviewed.

I shuffle in with the rest, oddly disoriented on my feet. The pattern in the carpet seems to undulate in three dimensions.

The space is full, people crammed shoulder to shoulder on anonymous conference seating. As usual (planes, buses, trains), I'm sitting next to someone guaranteed to invade my space or thoughts. Here, it's a vast woman whose prodigious thigh-buttock mass rolls towards my chair on a wave of lavender-scented talcum. She's hurriedly finishing a family-size bag of crisps.

'You might want t' select some chopped carrots in future,' I mutter.

She hasn't heard. She's chatting to her friend and I realise that I have the privilege to be neighbours with the famous blogger/Twitterer "Judge Lady", who gave my second book two stars because she couldn't understand the criminal argot used by the burglars.

'You tweeting live?' asks the friend (apparently a human/cocker spaniel crossbreed).

'Yah. And I'll update the blog after.'

Judge Lady has her phone out and is tapping away on Twitter. The usual output I expect: *Sitting at the York Festival. Just eaten a trough of Prawn Cocktail. Yum! Avery Johns due on stage in 5. My IQ is 47 and descending fast.* [137 characters].

I touch her arm and point to a sign on the wall: no mobile phones.

'Oh, that's just for calls and videos,' she says. 'Not tweets.' And she keeps on tapping.

I touch her arm again. 'I'm 'fraid I muss insiss. I've a medical condition, see? Spermatorrhoea.'

'I'm sorry?'

'The radiation. Makes me 'jaculate.'

She leans over to her anthropocanine friend and they converse in urgent whispers before getting up and moving with portly indignation further forwards, stopping on the way to complain to a steward. Her place is taken almost immediately by a man so huge that he's brought in on a forklift. Or so I remember.

The lights go down and Mark Lawson comes on stage to much applause. Nice man. Always liked him on *Front Row*. He lists the manifold successes of Avery Johns, references his previous festival address on the value of good writing (applause), praises the current book, and mentions the forthcoming global Hollywood smash featuring Scarlett Johansson. No mention of the wooden dialogue, colouring-book characters or kindergarten descriptive prose. Lawson is a professional; he may only think such things.

And here is the man himself, surfing a wave of applause to the stage. The cravat. The tweedy jacket. Is that a pair of exquisite hand-polished, hand-made, cigar-hued brogues? I look down at my own mousaka/lasagne/placenta-splatted Clarks, wondering which descriptive phrase is better: the hyphens of his shoes or the slash-hyphen combination of mine. I win. Better rhythm.

> Lawson: *Avery – can you tell us something about the inspiration behind your new book?*
>
> Jones: *Well, Mark, it was actually a novel by Denis Diderot:* Jacques le Fataliste [with vigorous French pronunciation]. *This early work, published in the 1790s, is really quite experimental in the way that Sterne also was and it showed me that, yes, innovation has been a hallmark of the novel since the outset . . .*

'Pseud!' shouts somebody in the darkened auditorium, twisting the word into a faux-cough.

Ripples of embarrassment spread outwards from my epicentre, and towards it from the periphery as people turn to see who spoke. The two ripples cancel each other, disguising my location to all but my most immediate neighbours.

'Keep your mouth closed, buddy,' says the immense man next to me. American.

'A useful motto f'r *you*,' I riposte.

On stage, Lawson and Johns are only briefly distracted.

> Lawson: *Indeed. Yours is a very innovative approach. I'm thinking of your character Jacko, who speaks only backwards. Some have said this makes his dialogue difficult to understand.*

Johns: *To those people, I say, 'Are horses difficult to understand?' I think there's a basic idiom of empathy that transcends syntax . . .*

'Plagiarist!'

Me again. Another expressive cough. More people have figured out the source of the disruption. I see stewards moving subtly closer. There's a uniform of some kind.

'It seems we have a critic in the audience,' says Johns, leaning back in his chair, all avuncular smiles. A patter of laughter. 'Perhaps we should give him a voice. No, sir? Nothing more constructive to offer than heckles? I rather expected as much.'

'The perils of going live,' says Lawson, getting another (bigger) laugh. 'Perhaps I might move on to—?'

'Cliché-monger!'

The audience is now a choppy sea of heads, mutters, creaking chairs and twisting necks. I feel blood and rum thrumming in my legs. Brumming. Blumming. Blooming. I stand and a spotlight near the stage sweeps towards me, picking me out, dazzling me.

'Why're you payin' t' hear this shit?' I hear myself say. 'Man's a fraud. He stole my address! *Value 'f Good Writin'. I* wrote that. Ask 'im! Ask 'im where 'e got it!'

'Someone's had a little too much to drink,' chuckles Johns from the stage.

I can't see his face so I shout into the light. 'Where'd y' get that address, y'ponce?' *Ponce?* A subliminal *Withnail* prompt. Janet'd be proud.

Stewards are moving darkly towards me from both ends of the row.

'You're killin' writin'! Gimmicks. Marketin'. Where's the prose? Where's the style?'

A hand takes my arm. 'I think it's time you left, sir.'

'N'thanks. I'm enjoyin' myself. Got a ticket.' I fumble for the ticket.

'The police would like to talk to you, sir. Come on. Come with me.'

'Inconsistent narr'tive persective!' I shout as they pull me away. 'Imprecise vocab'lary! Wooden di'logue!'

The house lights have come up and all heads are now turned my way.

The beam of fame briefly upon me! 'Author TG Harkett!' I shout, and I struggle to remember the titles of my three published books ... but I can't. I just can't bring them to mind.

Two men in dark uniforms and hats pinion me at the end of the row and I feel my hands snatched behind my back into the cold metallic clasp of handcuffs. There are men surrounding me now.

A different voice addresses the audience from the stage: 'Ladies and gentlemen – I must ask everyone to vacate the room immediately and in an orderly fashion. Follow the directions of stewards once outside. Thank you.'

A fire alarm begins to ring throughout the hotel, its different zones out of sync so that it echoes and answers itself. I'm virtually carried out of the room and along the corridor.

Somebody says something like, 'Where's the device, son?'

'I wanna make 'n official complaint,' I say. 'That man stole my address ...'

'I'm placing you under arrest,' says another man.

I notice he's got a gun at his belt. Another armed one is coming towards me with a dog – one of those undistinguished-looking mongrels that sniffs suitcases at airports. This doesn't seem right ...

MY LEGS ARE STIFF when I step down from the police van. There's apparently not enough evidence to show that I made the bomb threat. Neither is there currently any indication who did. The police have said they'll look at my laptop, but in a way that makes me think it's not an urgent priority. Maybe the MGU geeks can look at it?

It's my hacker, obviously. He's escalating. A note, a doll, a bomb threat and my arrest. What's next? Should I be scanning the rooftops for a rifle silhouette? I asked the police about this but they told me, straight-faced, that a professional sniper never reveals his silhouette. I'd never know what hit me. Good to know.

The crowds have now dispersed. The disrupted sessions have been rescheduled for tonight. I'd like to go back into the hotel for a coffee or three, but I've been banned from entering and, indeed, from attending any future York Festivals. *Persona non grata.* I should make that my next *nom de plume.*

The winter sun is sinking red beneath a bank of plumbeous cloud. My breath steams. I stand near the barrier gate of the car park and accept that my only choice is to head back to the train station.

A car horn sounds and I step back to let a gleaming Jaguar pass. There's a glimpse of tweed sleeve, a flash of cravat. I bend to look into the car's rear and see Avery Johns entwined with a woman, his hand reaching for her buttock, her head descending into his lap. My eyes telescope. Black hair cascading ... café crème skin at the base of her back ... moth-wing eyelid veiling obsidian iris ... dark-painted lips opening to ...

Her.

I try to call her name but the car has gone with an infernal wink of brake lights.

Definitely her. Unmistakable. Her perfume in the hotel. Her ... her with him in the toilets? Retrospect matches the little cries to those felt hot against my ear.

Her. With him.

Is this as low as I fall?

Dildonics gold

THE STORY appeared online in a local York paper and soon achieved viral notoriety. Blogs, Facebook, Twitter, some shaky YouTube phone footage (the madman yelling 'Author TG Harkett!' as the bomb squad led him away). Judge Lady tops the pile with her exclusive scoop and libellous misquotation: "Failed author said he'd come on me if I didn't turn off my phone." Noted American reviewer Dexter Flagstaff follows up with his eye-witness, "Sizeist maniac Harkett called me gross." It's more publicity than the publisher ever managed to earn for my books.

It's not about me, of course. It's about Avery "Writing by Numbers" Johns. My own pathetic tragedy is news only because of him. I'm just a supporting character in his ascendance. I'm Osric. *A hit, a very palpable hit.* The university gets more print than I do. And nobody mentions a single one of my published titles.

The news also stirs communication from sources predictable and unexpected. Will is first with a call.

'How you doing, Tommo?'

'Fine. It was a hoax. The hacker again. The police know about him now.'

'You really say you were going to jizz on that woman?'

'Probably. I'd had a few too many Extra Old.'

'Is this going to . . . I mean, is your job OK?'

'Should be. Nothing happened to Gwynn when he tried to piss on the Queen.'

'But he has the Eliot Prize, right?'

'Yeah, and he was on industrial solvents back then. Out of his mind.'

'Well, you know . . . come and stay if you need a breather. We'll put the kids in a kennel or something.'

'Cheers.'

'Have you considered stopping the blog? Maybe put a blanket apology up and leave it for a while?'

'Maybe.'

'Any news about that old man's book you've stolen?'

'Nothing yet. It'll probably go nowhere.'

'I'm running out of optimism, Tommo. You got any booze in the house?'

I can't tell him about Mohini. I can't express my feelings about that. Jealousy. Humiliation. Betrayal. The words are just empty phonemes in the mouth, just shapes on the page. They evoke nothing of the visceral knot within. The hot acid. The deadening numbness. The palpable weight of shock. It makes no sense . . . no sense. How? Why him? Did she know? Did she *want* to twist the blade? I can't blame him, much as I love to. What man could say no to her?

I've been trying to do the masterpiece edit. To take my mind off the other stuff. But the scope of the task is crushing me. I look at the thing and I don't recognise it anymore. Reading it is like tossing a pebble into a crevasse and waiting for a splash that never comes. Its depths are bottomless — or non-existent and it's just a void. What I thought was the finest description known to literature now seems adjective-heavy and laboured. The finest parts are the simple phrases and the subtle shades of punctuation. Have I the will to dig out the verruca root of that main character and replace him with something better? Can I add foundations to these themes that were never designed to withstand a geological core sample?

I'm half-heartedly stripping out repetitive adjective-noun pairs when the mobile rings.

'Yes?'

'Tom?'

A single word: a powerful rush of associations. 'Lara?'

'I didn't know if you had the same number . . . Tom?'

'Yes . . . the same number.'

'I saw the stuff about the festival and I was just wondering . . . Are you OK?'

'Not having a breakdown, you mean?'

126

'Well, you know: bomb threats, ejaculating on bloggers, sizeist abuse … that video.'

'A lot of that's been exaggerated. The bomb thing was a hoax. Not me.'

'Yeah, I saw that. So … how're you doing generally?'

'Good. Good. The masterpiece might get published. I mean, they've asked for an edit.'

'That's great. Still channelling your frustrations into Fenella?'

'Ha! Yes.'

'Well … I just wanted to, you know … '

'Thanks. Thanks. I'm glad you did.'

'OK. I should probably go. Keep on writing. Don't let them stop you.'

'Yes. Thanks.'

'Bye, then … '

'Bye. Bye.'

I sit holding the dead phone to my ear. And how are *you* doing Lara? Seen Will recently? Are you with someone now? Are you happy? Did you ever do that Photography MA? Do you sometimes miss me? I'm sorry for what I did to you? I understand now why you left? It was good to hear your voice …

The phone rings as I'm still holding it to my ear.

'Lara … I wanted to say—'

'Tom? It's Jerry … said the cat to the mouse.'

'Jerry. Hi. I thought it was someone else.'

'Have you got a moment?'

'Yes, go on.'

'Can you go to Las Vegas this week? We can reschedule your class for the end of term.'

'What's happened to Gwynn? Doesn't Janet want it?'

'Gwynn's had a bit of a relapse. They found him naked in the library.'

'Ginsberg again? The *Howling*?'

'I'm afraid so. Janet wouldn't be able to pull something together at such short notice and we really need a CW lecturer there. Have you got anything you can use as an address? Modify something, maybe?'

'Perhaps.'

'I'd really appreciate it. The university would appreciate it, especially in light of these recent . . . you know. Might be good to redeem yourself. For everyone's sake. Sin City *et cetera*. What happens in Vegas . . . '

'Yes. OK, I'll do it'

'Fantastic, Tom. Get it all out of your system. I'll email you tickets and reservations. I owe you one.'

Vegas. America's playground. Roulette and hookers. I'm going to visit your homeland, Lexxi.

Lexxi is wearing only a flat cap and a pair of my black M&S pants. She looks good in everything. Keep looking at me like that, Ms Cummins, and I'm gonna have to put four AA batteries up your perineum.

Vegas.

I close the masterpiece. I open the latest Fenella doc.

Sports Day at the Academy. Fenella was ahead in the spit-roast relay, her thighs bespattered, her lashes bejewelled. 'Fine rhythm from Fenella!' cried the commentator. 'Like a shuttle on a loom!'

Her loins may have been awash, but her mind was a hurricane's eye of reflection. Why had Charles called her earlier that evening? Charles, who'd been her chaste companion in those innocent days before the jetting fluids and sweaty wrestling of Switzerland. His voice had been so uncertain. So much he'd clearly wanted to say but hadn't. Couldn't. Gentle Charles. Could she ever return to him now, after everything – after Thad and Dirk; after Chad, Sven, Helmut, the Vibratothon, the Mirror Chamber . . . the Dildonics?

Rough hands gripped her hips and she redoubled her efforts until there came a terrible roar: a bison brought down by lions, a bull skewered by the picador, a rhino goring the poacher who'd try to take his horn — Thad's cataclysmic climax.

'And it's gold! Gold for Fenella!' shrieked the commentator. 'An Academy record!'

But all she could think of was Charles and what he'd say if he could see her now.

Sweaty wrestling? This is going to need a redraft.

Apothetae and agoge

SIXTEEN HOURS to Vegas with an hour-or-so layover in Houston, TX. The jet-engine tinnitus has become acceptable white noise. I've looked (in vain) through the greasy, curl-cornered magazine for an article worth reading. I've put the blanket over my knees and plugged distractedly into a film featuring Sandra Bullock. The man to my right, naturally, reeks of stale cigarettes and drools as he sleeps.

I look through my notes for the address I'm to give at the Annual Las Vegas International Conference on CW Methodologies − not the most respected or best attended of such events, but it is in Vegas and they do tend to organise it close to the Strip. Its popularity is what academics tend to call a no-brainer, especially when there's a modest expense account.

I'd initially toyed with the idea of using my "Value of Good Writing" speech stolen by Avery Johns, but it was never intended for an academic audience and it's clear I'd be accused of plagiarising my own work. In fact, I've never approached the subject in anything like an academic manner. I have no feeling for the other papers detailed in the schedule, these "Derridean Utopias in Automatic Composition," these "AnthropoDigital Resonances in the Writer-Reader Dynamic." I don't believe any working writer gives a thought to such things, though the literary ones are often eager to mythologize their process retroactively, because, you know, God forbid writing might be simplified, made teachable and put in the hands of the humble housewife. Academic approaches are not remotely helpful to the tyro staring at the blank page. He just wants to know, simply, *how it's done*. So I'll be delivering a (not entirely academically rigorous) address entitled "Apothetae and Agoge: The Values of Laconian Pedagogics." It'll probably get me in trouble.

And I've been working on another idea since we left England. It's become clear to me ... No, that's dishonest − I've *always* secretly known but refused to acknowledge even to my own conscious mind that the main flaw in my published work − even in the masterpiece − is a fundamental mismatch between style and substance. My subjects have been the stuff of commercial fiction: the storyline, the episode, the catalytic character, the entertaining substructure. It's why I was published at all. But my style has been drawn overtly from the well of literature: the too-clever word, the self-conscious syntax, the theme or allegory, the freeform jazz of creative punctuation − all that stuff the commercial reader misses or dislikes on sight. A mismatch.

But what if I could rid myself of literary intelligence and style? What if I could express my knowledge of structure in the vapid neutrality of untutored prose, stripped of my lifetime of careful reading? In the absence of a voodoo-zombie Avery Johns, what if I had access to a handful of battery-farm writers I could bend to my will and direct in the production of a book designed cynically for the market as I understand it: a fickle, spoiled, not-too-bright child who just wants a new toy as long as it's durable, branded, brightly coloured and contains no toxic agents from the Third World.

Battery-farm writers. Yes: my MA group.

They each have to produce a 20,000-word piece by the end of course anyway. What if I structure a novel and distribute its parts evenly among them? They'll have a well defined plan to work with and we'll exhaustively workshop each section. Not only will they learn a huge amount in a short time, but they'll also have the concrete goal of producing an actual novel to deadline. A novel, I've decided, I'm going to put forward for actual publication.

Naturally, it'll be utter shit. Dreadlock Twat is virtually illiterate. Stalwart cares more about an errant subordinate clause than he does a shard of glass in his carotid artery (don't think I haven't pictured this). Mum is terrified of making "mistakes". Earnest Youth is my only hope. But I'll edit the thing until it chimes with crystal purity and let them in on the editorial process. They'll learn more than they would on any other course − more than they would if they were working on their own doomed projects. I'll make them writers if I have to beat them with their own severed limbs. I'll teach them to love the anguish and frustration.

And best of all, the finished novel will be a colossal joke on the industry: a committee effort produced by rank amateurs and edited by a shamed failure. Publish and be damned. It'll be at least as good as Avery "Narcoleptic Banality" Johns. I can't wait to get back and tell them about it.

But first Vegas.

The titles are scrolling up on the movie I've missed. The man beside me is drooling through a glistening saliva bubble. I recline the chair and drift off into a dream that sees, variously, a naked and screaming Lexxi Cummins pursued by a faceless hacker, Avery Johns sexually assaulted by a grizzly, Fenella entertaining a hockey team, and Mohini whispering the Mahabharata into my mouth. 'I didn't know if you had the same number,' she seems to say, though the words are indistinct.

THE STRIP. An Eiffel Tower, a Brooklyn Bridge, a Pyramid. Venice, Camelot. The Bellagio fountain. Caesar's Palace. Like the manure-reeking, inbred world of the travelling circus, it should only be seen via night's falsifying spotlight. In daylight, Vegas is tawdry and vulgar – the pleasure fantasies of man made idiotic under the rational sun.

I walk South Las Vegas Boulevard distracted by sleeplessness and the inevitable disappointment of fabled places. Giza: riddled with beggars and filth. New York: not that skyscrapery. Uluru: flies. Hollywood: seedy and small. It's the unrealised imagination that reigns. Only on the page do places achieve the immortality of perfection. Only on the page is true reality possible.

My hotel naturally has its own casino, a dim labyrinth of blinking lights, waitresses done up in cheap harlotry, dead-eyed gamblers and the pervasive smell of desperation: cigarette smoke, stale carpet, industrial deodorants and bad feet. Everyone carries a plastic vase full of alcohol. A place for the spiritually dead. I think of *Casino Royale*'s classic opening para: "… soul erosion … a compost of greed and fear". Can't imagine what Janet and Gwynn see in the place.

I hail a taxi near the Luxor and go directly to the conference venue, where my address is almost entirely unexpected. There hasn't been time to change the details of Gwynn's topic in the afternoon's running order. Just as well, perhaps.

In the event, the modest lecture hall is only about one-third full (the rest of them presumably AWOL in sex dungeons, MDMA fugue states or hospital trauma wards). Deep breath. Scan the faces. Hope what I'm about to say still makes sense. Hope nobody throws anything.

> *In ancient Sparta, sickly children were precipitated into a chasm of Mount Taygetos. Those males who survived entered the Agoge system aged seven, where they would be fed just enough to sustain their growth but not enough for them to feel complacent. It was a brutal and punitive school whose sole aim was to produce a practical, sustainable society. Overlooking the fact that pederasty may also have played a part, I wish to suggest that we might adopt the Spartan approach to teaching people how to write.*
>
> *This is not, I know, a popular idea. Educators talk of nurturing, supporting, engaging — giving people the tools for self-expression and applauding that expression regardless of how flawed and futile it may be. I submit, however, that writing is not finger-painting and our students are not — for the most part — neurologically impaired. We owe it to them to be unforgiving.*
>
> *Consider the professor of medicine supervising an operation. "Nice try," he says. "You cut the artery and caused a fatal haemorrhage in the patient, but I applaud your efforts. Have you expressed yourself satisfactorily? Are you sufficiently engaged?' No doctors are produced in this way.*

The patchy auditorium seems emptier now than when I began. An optical illusion, I'm sure. Faces look stern. I'm already regretting the gag about pederasty. And I saw one woman shake her head slowly when I quipped about neurological impairment. This is not my crowd.

So when John or Jane hands us an execrable nugget of dialogue, do we offer praise for their effort and invite them to submit some verbosely illiterate description further to their self-enabling? Or do we rip that dialogue a new hole, as Bruce Willis might conceivably say, and leave John/Jane in no doubt how it should be done? This is, I feel, our responsibility as teachers.

Better to drop a single A-bomb of criticism on the student than to inflict a million tiny cuts, each of which will heal before the next occurs. Writing is very often right or wrong, good or bad – especially at the beginning of the learning process. Grammar, punctuation, vocab, paragraphing, exposition, narrative perspective: all can be taught quite easily. Why would we hold back? Because we're afraid of hurting their feelings? Hurting them more than a lifetime of guaranteed rejection – unfairly earned rejection, because they're not even aware they can't write ... because we never had the balls to tell them so? Unequivocally? Shame on us. We know what rejection and humiliation is. At least, we do if we're genuine writers. Regular beatings thicken the skin ...

Nobody laughed at the Bruce Willis reference. Where's the gung-ho American spirit? Where's the whooping? I scan the thinning crowd for any signs of interest or support, but receive mostly dead-eyed disapproval, boredom and confusion. Many have missed my substitution for Gwynn and are riffling through the conference guide for verification. There's just one girl – an eager UNLV student? – watching with clear interest. She smiles as I meet her gaze and she nods, seeming to urge me on. Blonde. A mid-western farmer's daughter, perhaps. OK – for you, my audience of one.

> *Some might argue that publication is not always the student's goal, as if writing were a hobby, a Sudoku, or form of solitary masturbation (which, admittedly, it often is, albeit potentially parthenogenic when done with passion). I say never mind the motivation. The most inept painter understands that perspective is important, that colours are not interchangeable, that the picture only has meaning if it has some fundamental form. Even an abstract has its nuances of tone and contrast. The most inept painter – if he is largely sane – judges and gauges his (in)ability by his understanding of what proficiency looks like.*
>
> *The writer who doesn't care (or can't understand) that his writing doesn't work is not a writer. He is delusional. We are not in the business of enabling delusionists. Let us instead insist on the skills of basic proficiency because – and I must stress this single point if I achieve nothing else – this is our language. We are trauma surgeons with our hands in the hot viscera of a dying corpus. We are among the last defence.*

My UNLV girl is bright eyed and fixing with me an encouraging look. She's still smiling. Keep going, she seems to say. This is good stuff. Give us the essence. Drop the bomb. I put my notes away. I know this stuff by heart. It's the looping monologue of my consciousness.

> *When we close our eyes to the infelicitous adjective, the errant comma, the clumsy expositional dialogue, we allow the language to die a little faster. Nobody else cares. Not the bloggers and the Twitterers and the texters. Not the newspapers who've fired all their subeditors. Not*

135

the million-selling TV-presenter novelists who scratch their prose in mud with a stick, or beat a cloven hoof to be interpreted by a publisher's editor.

When we give our students short reading lists or let them get away with reading extracts rather than the whole work, we're betraying our future. I say photocopy the entire catalogue of the humanities library and give them that as their reading list. Read it all. Read it twice. They can never read enough. They should be reading like an obese child gorging himself into a Krispy Kreme coma. Eat it; drink it; breathe it — that's how we teach reading. Weep into your book. Come into it.

Come in a book? Krispy Kreme coma? I think I'm losing them. A woman in dungarees is striding purposefully for the exit. Only the farmer's daughter is still interested. She's actually nodding along, making notes on her pad before looking back up to me at the lectern.

We're ... we're holding the hot, sticky heart of language in our ungloved hands. With our cardiac massage do we ensure its vitality and survival. Enabling? Motivation? Nurturing? For me, that's not the application of soothing emollients or lullaby platitudes. It's breaking the ribs, ripping open the chest and squeezing that flabby heart until it learns what good writing feels like. Sure, some patients will die of shock. Others will be literary invalids. That's the apothetae; that's the chasm. Not all will make it. For the rest, it's into the agoge. Just enough praise to flourish, not enough to get sloppy. When the battle comes to them, they'll be ready.

I'm Tom Fynn, lecturer at Manchester Gallagher University in the UK. Thank you for listening. Will there be any questions?

An elderly woman raises her hand straight away. 'Yes,' she says. 'I was told thirty years ago that I couldn't write, but today I sit here as the author of three books [*sycophantic applause*]. I suppose I'm one of those you'd have thrown in a chasm?'

'May I ask what you've published and where?' I say.

'A historical trilogy on the YouPublishIt writers' portal.'

'I've not heard of that portal, but if I'm right in thinking you've failed to attract a proper publisher for your work over the last three decades, I'm tempted to suggest that, yes indeed, you can't write. I'd be a hypocrite to say otherwise, given the speech I've just made.'

The woman mutters something that looks like an insult and walks out of the hall, accompanied by sounds of general disapproval.

A man who can only be a humanities academic raises his hand. 'Writing takes time,' he says, 'but you seem to be suggesting that people should undergo some kind of instant proficiency triage. What about development?'

'Good question,' I say. 'My feeling is that writers can be taught a huge amount in a very short time. Thereafter, they need constant feedback on their work in progress. But, as you suggest, the process might take decades. We can't be there to hold their hands. We need to use our time with them to make them self-sufficient, self-driven – their own harshest critics. Then they're on their own.'

He nods, but smirks as if he's won the point.

Next is a woman with a pinched, vinegar expression and dry hair. 'You recommend reading the humanities library catalogue [*knowing laughter; she must be a local face*], but do you really expect students to read so far back when more relevant books are being published today?'

'More relevant how? Teachers of film don't encourage their students to see only what came out in the last decade. The history of film is a narrative that incorporates every successive film. Is literature different? In fact, I might even reverse your proposition and recommend that students read *only* Shakespeare, Rabelais, Homer, Sophocles and the King James Bible. All literature is there.'

She's shaking her head at my ignorance and saying something to her neighbour (her *neighbor*, as Noah Webster would have it), a man who looks like he's never had an orgasm.

Are we finished? No more questions for the profane and unpopular Englishman? People are packing bags and reaching for jackets in slow motion.

Then a pale arm rises beside a bolt of blonde hair. Farm Girl.

'Just a very quick question,' she says. A strong voice. Confident. Not a recognisably American accent. 'What do you think is the single most important factor in someone becoming proficient as a writer?'

That halts the audience's departure momentum. A lightning-rod question. An unanswerable question. A question they must all have asked themselves in some form, at some point.

I look at her. Is she mocking me? Is she trying to trip me up? Her face is open and willing.

The most important factor in achieving proficiency? Time? Practice? Feedback? Reading? Objectivity? Honesty? Discipline? All of those. But the *single* most important factor?

There's an uncanny quiet in the lecture hall. People have paused mid-departure.

'Wanting it more than anything else in life,' I say.

She nods and smiles with a strange finality. Like we've just shaken hands on something.

A conference organiser approaches to my side and tells the delegates that this session is now over and that drinks vouchers may be redeemed at the bar. There's a patter of applause − perfunctory rather than appreciative − then a mass movement towards the exits: to the bar, to the casinos, the stripper poles, the oil-wrestling pits, the adult-movie conference next door. I look among them for the Farm Girl but she's lost in the outflow.

I wait at the lectern until the last person has left the room, just in case she's waiting or decided to return. Instead, I'm left facing an invisible audience.

Satellites

MY VEGAS HOTEL room is a hermetic cell: sealed from the outside by windows that don't open, sealed from other rooms and the corridor by impregnable doors and walls. I can look out at the silent city, or through the peephole into a distorted Kubrickian corridor, but I might as well be the only living organism in this tower.

I've watched four episodes of *Law & Order: Special Victims Unit* on a channel that seems to show nothing else. I've seen almost as many minutes of adverts selling treatments for indigestion, leaking bowels and erectile dysfunction, all of which I am urged to ask my doctor about (as long as I don't mind side-effects a hundred times worse than the complaint itself). I've brought my laptop to do some writing, but the humming vacuum of my room and the viewing ecstasy of 500 TV channels has anaesthetised me.

I determine to go down to the casino bar and eavesdrop on potential conversations about my conference address. I've so far ascertained that many people believe it was Gwynn who gave the notorious "Rip Dialogue a New Hole" speech, so I feel some relief (apply Gwynno twice daily; side effects include guilt, liver failure and suicidal thoughts). There's also a good chance I'll be able to observe the prostitutes in action if I go downstairs: a must-do in the unofficial Vegas guide book.

And so it goes. I'm served my third watery whisky by another insincerely smiling waitress in a thighs-and-cleavage cocktail dress and I perch on a swivel stool at the edge of the casino floor. Old men in 1970s suits accompany girls who are not their granddaughters. Steely hookers stroll among the slots with faces twice as experienced as their bodies. A gorgeous blonde in a sheathing pencil skirt, a tight white blouse and black Louboutins arrives for a "date" with a guy she's clearly never met. He's drunk and nervous; she's the consummate pro, laughing at his jokes and entertaining his inane conversation. Whenever he turns away, she tugs down the skirt, which has a tendency to ride up on to her hips.

First time wearing it, probably. Did she buy it because she liked it, or because he would?

'And in four or five hours,' says a voice from the neighbouring/neighboring stool, 'after he's made her walk a few miles in those heels, he'll be using her like he's paid for it. Doesn't it make you sad?'

I turn. It's Farm Girl. She smiles and orders the same as me from a passing waitress.

'It does make me sad,' I say. 'I don't know what kind of a man would pay for that. The very act of paying debases her, even if she does nothing for the money. Look at her: pretty, intelligent enough to play the role he wants ... more of a human than he is.'

'Both are *too* human,' she says.

I turn and look again at Farm Girl. Something ageless about her; she might be twenty-five or a well preserved fifty-five. A straight nose, a distinguished forehead, strong lips. Sculptural. A classical profile. She's handsome rather than beautiful: a face you want to look at and admire but which stirs no base passions. Art rather than advertising. Her hair is preternaturally blonde and her skin marble pale. No farm girl, this one. Her perfume is only now enveloping me: a crisp scent of lemon and spearmint, green apple and eucalyptus. Clarity, if clarity had an aroma.

She holds out her hand and I take it for a firm shake that seems to sober me immediately. 'Kalli,' she says. 'And you're not Gwynn.'

'Yes. I'm Tom. It seems you enjoyed my address earlier.'

'I enjoyed your enthusiasm. It's something most of the rest of them lack. You might mock your students, but you care about teaching the subject. You care about writing.'

'I wouldn't say I mock them ... '

'Come on, Tom. You enjoy it. Be honest – the sadism appeals to you.' She's smiling. Lovely teeth. American teeth.

'OK. You've got me. Call it ego.'

'It's not ego. You're like the militant anti-smoking ex-smoker. When you ridicule and sneer at your students' errors, you're attacking the beginner writer in yourself, the errors you yourself had to transcend, one by one, through all those years of frustration. You've never been a patient man.'

I look at her. Here eyes are a very pale blue. Frank, unflinching. 'You're not a student, are you?'

'Actually, I am.'

'Hmm. Maybe you're right about the mocking. Maybe. But it's also fun. I have to admit that. My position legitimises it. It's a very English thing. John Cleese in *Fawlty Towers*. Do you study here, at UNLV?'

'No. At USC, Columbia. I'm here just for the conference, and to see you.'

'Really? Nobody knew I was going to be here. Last-minute replacement.'

'Jerry mentioned in an email that you'd be here if I wanted to meet you.'

'Jerry ...? Wait ... you said your name was Kalli, right? With two *l*'s? USC?'

She nods. 'Your visiting supervisee at MGU next semester.'

'Well. Nice to meet you, Kalli.'

'And you, Tom. Or should I call you Mister Harkett?'

'Oh God. Don't tell me you've read any of them.'

'I read the first one. It's always interesting to see what a writer does in his first book.'

'Yes. It usually falls into two categories: unrepeatable genius or malformed turd. I think I know which mine is.'

'Well, at least you can repeat it.'

'Yes. Go on then: give me your review. It'll tell me what kind of supervisee to expect.'

A smile. Amused, not coquettish. 'It's not as bad as you suggest. The writing is well formed and effective — you obviously spent years finding a voice before you attempted a novel. You must know, of course, that the style is out of proportion to the subject. You're a frustrated literary writer forced by the market to write more commercial stuff. Can I also say you have a problem with your first twenty per cent? The pace, I mean. It takes you a while to get the reader sucked in. But once you have them ... well, you know what to do with them.'

'That's ... that's pretty perceptive. You know your stuff.'

'Thanks. I know you'll be equally frank with my writing. I also Googled TG Harkett ...'

'Yes? ...'

'It seems he appeared at a festival very recently.'

'He did. He did. Mister Hyde, Mister Harkett — my dark half. You know that bomb scare was all a hoax? I wouldn't do that. I've got a would-be author with a grudge. A police matter. The thing about ejaculating on the woman's leg ... taken out of context ...'

I can't stop myself laughing at the ludicrousness of it. Kalli laughs, too.

'So will I make a good supervisee?' she says. 'Or will you be breaking open my ribcage and squeezing my heart? Will I need to wear a blouse with buttons?'

I examine her face for signs of flirtation. Nothing. Just a joke. 'No ... no. You're safe.'

'Mohini was at the festival, right?'

I stare. 'Did Jerry—?'

'Jerry said nothing. I know all about Mohini — what she's like. What she does. You have the look of a man who's known her. Your actions at the festival ... that looked like the Mohini effect.'

'I ... I'm not sure I'm comfortable ... How do you know her?'

'No need to be embarrassed, Tom. I know all about her. Best sex you've ever had, right? Turned your mind inside out. Left you almost crippled. Come on — no blushes. We're grown-ups. These are the facts. You'll never have better. Never. Trust me on that. It's how she works. Sure, you'll know other women and you'll be lovers. It'll be wild. But never again like Mohini.'

She's not mocking me, not taunting. Her face has an unchallengeable openness and truth.

'Have you spoken to Mohini?' I say.

'We don't speak. We're like satellites in opposite orbits around the same body. We've known some of the same men. She has a thing for writers. I suppose I do, too. If it makes you feel any better, she's careful who she chooses. She has her reasons.'

'She's with Avery Johns now.'

'I know. Pity him. You might not feel it, but you're lucky she dropped you so quickly. The longer she stays with a guy . . . well, never mind.'

'How do you know all this?'

'Gossip. History. It's not important. I just wanted to be honest from the start. You're going to be teaching me.'

'Well, thanks. I suppose.'

The prostitute and her john are still talking in front of us. His confidence is increasing as her charm does. He'll remember this night as his greatest triumph. No doubt she'll make him think he's the most fantastic lover. A symphony of faking.

'Do you think she has a boyfriend?' says Kalli.

'I don't see how she could. How could it be meaningful?'

'You don't believe two people can have good but meaningless sex?'

'Touché.'

'I don't think she's ruined yet. You can see it in her face. There's still hope for her. Did you find Mohini beautiful?'

I look at her again. 'You have a knack with those blind-siding questions, don't you?'

She smiles and lifts her glass in a toast. Raises her eyebrows: well?

'Beautiful? What's beauty? I found her mesmeric. I wanted to consume her. I think beauty encourages a gaze but not a rage. Beauty intrigues and invites exploration. Beauty is inviolable. It encourages a protective, rather than an insensate urge.'

'Good answer. Were you thinking of someone in particular?'

'No.'

Kalli smiles. 'Would you give me any advice on my writing before I see you next semester?'

'Not without seeing it first. Just keep writing. That's the thing.'

'Are you working on something yourself?'

'Me? No. Well, an edit of something. I'm not really into it.'

'So scrap it.'

'I've invested two years' work in it. There's a vague promise of a publishing committee.'

'But if you're not feeling it . . . '

'Sometimes you just have to write through the apathy. A good writer should be able to do that.'

'Sure. But also to know the difference between perseverance and flogging a dead horse. Forgive me the cliché.'

'Forgiven. You know . . . I never once had a conversation with Mohini. I don't know if she had family, how old she was, if she liked ice-cream, if she listened to music.'

Another Mona-Lisa smile from Kalli. 'I've got an early flight back tomorrow, Tom. I'm going to say goodnight. I'm really looking forward to meeting you again in Manchester.'

'Bring an umbrella.'

We shake hands again: firm, plain-dealing. She fixes me with those pale eyes and I feel briefly x-rayed. No men look at her as she walks across the casino floor, though she's slim, athletic, tall.

I go to the lifts entirely lucid and dart through the closing doors just in time. There's one other person in there: a young woman wearing one of those tight, plum-coloured velour tracksuits. The jacket zip is open to reveal a prodigious cleavage. Her make-up is heavy and she's wearing a thick, saccharine perfume that's too strong for this enclosed space. Her long, blonde hair is straightened.

Our eyes meet; she winks and licks the corner of her lips in a lascivious manner. Probably another prostitute on the way up to an assignation.

I bow out of the lift before she does. It's only as I'm walking along the corridor to my room that it strikes me. Entirely possible. The adult-movie conference . . .

That was Lexxi Cummins. In person.

Too late, I try to think of comments I could have made. Something about biologically accurate. Something about auto-grip hands. The perineal battery slot . . .

I think of the doll back in Manchester. The flat cap and the M&S pants. My Lexxi is better dressed. More class.

IN MY ROOM, I open the masterpiece doc and stare at it. I've sharpened up the prose as much as I can. I've tweaked themes. I've hacked away at the word count, constantly redefining what's necessary and what's for effect. Whole chapters have gone, and with them some of the second-tier characters: those inessential organs of fiction. You can live with one lung, one kidney, a third of your liver, one eye, even certain areas of the brain. Amazing, really, how little is needed to sustain life. Unless there's a sudden and unexpected infection – then it's a case of catastrophic organ failure and the whole organism croaks.

So I laboriously use the Find function to comb through the doc and eradicate any trace of characters I've killed: all the names they go under, every reference to them, every minor story membrane and narrative tissue. I'd call it surgery, but it's more like an autopsy. The book is only truly alive when it's being written.

There's little pleasure in editing a novel. Editing is epileptic reading: jumping from scene to scene, backwards and forwards in search of threads to be cut, threads to be stitched. Character arcs are pulled out of the organic whole to have their health examined. Cup the balls; cough, please! Actors already given a part are asked to re-audition. Do a little dance. Take off your top. Assume the position. Much-cherished passages of description experience the multi-blade-safety-razor effect: cut, cut shorter, cut altogether. Dab wound with a styptic pencil. Decide to grow a beard. So many metaphors to mix. The popular editing cliché refers to killing your darlings, but it's more than killing. It's going Fritzl on their ass.

An edit is never finished, just abandoned. No book is perfect. Like a corpse, it must be painted and dressed, have formaldehyde pumped up its fundament and its limbs arranged neatly for the open casket. Nobody must ever sniff the rot or imagine the Frankenstein patchwork within. Only the writer may see his book so naked and dead. It's how I'm beginning to see the masterpiece.

I think about Kalli's comments re scrapping it. Smart girl. But she's a new writer; she doesn't know the lure of the publishing committee or the burning yearning for the next book. I need this deal. If published, the masterpiece will erase the debacle of TG Harkett, obviate the need for any more Fenella and earn me the reputation my writing actually deserves. Whatever that is.

No more. I've done as much as I'm prepared to do. I've ticked all their boxes. I've doused the reeking cadaver with enough editorial perfume to hide the stench. Now I'm utterly sick of it. Let them read it again and see what they think. I save the doc and send it.

There are better things to do in Las Vegas. For instance, I've found a channel that plays nothing but *CSI* episodes all night long.

The dirt

'SO WHAT do you think?'

The MA students stare back at me: a spectrum of incredulity from stunned disbelief (Stalwart) to wariness (Earnest Youth).

'I understood that we'd be writing our own novel on this course,' says Stalwart.

'And indeed you will. But as you know, the first 20,000 words are ungraded. Just a warm-up. You can write your novel in the next stage using the skills you learn on this project. Now you have the chance to make that 20,000 words part of a published work. Good for the CV.'

'And you say that you'll tell us what to write?' says Mum.

'It won't be writing by numbers. You'll still need to make your own creative decisions. But I'll block out the broader structures of the full novel and distribute bits among you. You might get a series of character scenes and an arc, or you might be on description ... I've not formalised it yet. I'll make sure you all get an equal share of the work: dialogue, exposition, narrative perspective *et cetera.*'

'Won't it be, like, a zombie novel?' says Dreadlock. 'All bits sewn together?'

'I think you mean a Frankenstein's monster,' says Stalwart, lips pursed like a Grimsby fishwife.

'I'll edit it. Even better, you'll be part of the editing process and you'll learn that skill, too.'

'It sounds interesting,' says Earnest Youth,' but I've been working on my own idea.'

I compose an understanding face. I nod amenably. You'd think every one of them was poised to embark on a *1984*, a *Fear and Loathing*, a *Clockwork Orange* when in fact they're all fated to produce the same ill-conceived, chaotically structured and dull nugget of novel that'll never go anywhere: a *1942* (Spielberg), a *Dislike and Grumpiness*, a *Rotten Apple*. Not their fault – nobody does a good initial 20,000 words. They haven't yet got the structural skills. I'm going to have to appeal to the deepest core of their characters.

'Look. I'll be honest with you. Nobody on this course has yet produced a 20,000-word submission that was anywhere near publishable. Your basic skills should be up to standard by the end of this course, but your structural skills won't be. Not for years. You need to write a few novels just to learn how to do it. Whatever you were planning to write – whatever your big idea is for this long piece – it's not going to be of a publishable standard. Trust me.'

I look at Dreadlock. Are his eyes actually crossed? His tongue seems to be lolling from his mouth like a panting dog. God help me.

'But,' I say, 'if you go along with my suggestion. I can guarantee you'll be producing something of that standard. I'll be supplying the high-level structural stuff that'll take you years to master. Sooner, if we do this. It's a great opportunity. Something innovative that no other course is doing.'

'But it's not compulsory,' says Stalwart. 'That's why you're asking for our consent?'

I entertain the vision of a pterodactyl crashing through the window and seizing this hoary bore in its massive beak, dragging him from his seat with a horripilating *kraaaak!* and carrying his jerking body back out through the window, only to drop it twelve floors into a skip full of medical waste behind the hospital. No, it's not compulsory. It's not compulsory to welcome the defibrillator as your heart clenches fatally; it's not *compulsory* to grab the lifesaver as you slip beneath the freezing waves . . .

'No. It's not compulsory,' I say. 'You can write your own thing if you want. But the decision has to be unanimous.'

'I'm in,' says Earnest Youth. 'I came here to learn, not to prove anything.'

'Me, too,' says Mum, nodding. 'The discipline is what I need. My own ideas are a load of . . . Let's do it.'

Dreadlock returns from whatever stoner fantasyland he's been visiting. 'Yeah . . . like, why not? Bring it on!'

So it's just Stalwart now. He leans back in his chair, a deity of deliberation. He clearly hates me. 'The book would be published under our names,' he says. It's not really a question.

'Absolutely,' I lie. 'Full credit.'

He strokes his chin, but he's hooked. He's imagining the glory, the glamour and the groupies that'll attend his fame at the church writers' group. Women's Institute members dashing their marmalade to the ground in the rush to adore him. Oh, you're published? Really? You must be hung like a tyrannosaur . . .

'Very well,' he says. 'I'm for it.'

'Yay!' says Dreadlock, holding his hand up for a high five that goes predictably unreciprocated. I think we all enjoy his awkwardness.

'So when do we start?' says Mum.

'I'm going to work out a structure in the next few days and we'll aim to get it finished in the next semester.'

'You expect us to write 20,000 words in a semester?' says Dreadlock.

'That's a course requirement. I've written that many words in a week before. Trust me: it's easier when you have a plan to work to. The biggest problem in novels isn't the writing; it's knowing what to write.'

'I have a good feeling about this,' says Earnest youth.

'Great. That's the attitude. Now—'

'What about the Indian girl?' says Stalwart. 'Don't we need to ask her, too?'

They look at me. Do they know? Can they see it in my face?

'Mohini has dropped out of the course for . . . personal reasons.'

'I thought I saw a picture of her in the *Daily Mail*,' says Mum. 'She was with Avery—'

'Well, anyway, she's gone now so it's just the four of us. I'm going to be restructuring the course into more of a . . . well, more a Special Forces guerrilla training camp. Throw out the formal martial arts techniques and get straight to the eye-gouging, the eardrum bursting, the testicle-wrench. Trench warfare. The dirt. I need you battle-ready by next semester.'

Stalwart sits up straighter, this military talk evidently stirring his loins.

'Yah, I'm a pacifist, but, you know ...' says Dreadlock.

'Oh shut up,' says Mum, reddening when she realises she's said it out loud.

'What's first?' says Earnest Youth, turning to a new page in his spiral pad.

'Right. First of all, we're doing a crash course in punctuation. None of you have got commas yet and I'm not going to go blind trying to edit all of them. Dashes, colons, ellipses – you'll be using them like Newton doing calculus by the time this lesson is over. Let's start.'

I write on the board, elicit responses, offer withering ripostes, establish rules and exceptions. I point them towards reliable books on the subject, offer disquisitions on Celine's use of the ellipsis, Poe on the dash, McCarthy's full stops, Nabokov's parentheses and Dickens' long sentences. I stir their passion for the semi-colon and we peer together into the comma's profundity. They scribble, they scratch, they look from the board to the page. After today, they'll finally understand the musical notation that is punctuation used properly.

I SEE JANET coming towards me as I'm walking back to my desk.

'How was Vegas?' she says.

'Oh, you know: crass, vulgar. I met a porn star in a lift.'

'*Love in an Elevator*! I'm not angry, just so you know. Jerry was right: I wouldn't have been able to prepare something fast enough. Were you naughty? Any pills, thrills and bellyaches?'

'I watched a lot of TV ...'

'Tom. You really are a square. Although I did hear something about ... what was it ... ripping dialogue a new hole? A Krispy Kreme coma? Is that right?'

'You heard that?'

'Twitter.'

'Wonderful. How's Gwynn doing?'

'Sabbatical. Well, that's what we're calling it. I think there must have been some Persil in his coke or something. Sent him a bit ...' She twirls a finger at her temple.

'Right.'

Janet's expression changes and I turn to see a young girl coming towards us. Big eyes, mumsy dress, bit too much make-up. Doc Martens. Her smile is awkward: half knowing, half seeking affirmation.

'In my office, Sophie,' says Janet.

We watch the girl go inside and I raise an ironic eyebrow.

'Not a word,' says Janet. 'You're one of us now. On the Dark Side.'

'May the force be with you.'

She winks and closes her door behind her.

I fire up the computer, which takes so long to start that there must indeed be a stoker in the basement feeding coal to the server. The keyboard looks smearily opaque, like someone's spilled a cup of milk and wiped it with a rag. Or changed a baby on it. There're probably particles of bubonic plague between these keys.

My gaze lurches directly to the top of the inbox. The title of Percy's book.

Dear Mr Harkett

Thank you for sending us the manuscript of Golden Times. It is a beautiful book: poignant without being mawkish, detailed without being over-researched and narratively persuasive without yielding overly to the strictures of pace. We would like to publish the book, subject to a few very slight edits, and I'd like to invite you to our London offices to meet personally for further discussion ...

Shiiit.

First time. Home run. One submission and acceptance straight away. If only I'd written the book. Well ... haven't I? The work Percy submitted to me wasn't publishable. It was rambling and verbose and stiff with unexpressed emotion. There's two years of my editing in this manuscript. I made it publishable. If Jeff Koons can get someone to make him a chrome dildo the size of a bus and sell it as his own for $58m, then surely I can take credit for *Golden Times*.

Shiiit. A trip to London. Do I own up to my role as the unofficial executor of Percy's sole testament, or do I pretend to be him? I do know the book inside out. I could fake it. Who'd know? Nobody's seen the MS but me. No digital record of it anywhere. I typed it myself, m'lud. The typewriter? Broke, m'lud. Threw it into a canal ... threw it into a car-crusher. Came out the size of a Rubik's Cube.

It's wrong. Yes, it's wrong. But Percy's dead. Who gets hurt? I could dedicate it to him. His initials only, obviously. And ... well: TG Harkett back in business! Still alive and with something totally genre-defying. How do you do it, Mister Harkett? Your voice is so different in this book. Talent, my dear. Pure talent.

I could stay with Will in London. He wouldn't mind.

Other emails. One from G-Spot Books, probably nagging me about the latest Fenella deadline.

Tom/Jed

You'll be glad to hear sales of Fenella I & II are doing very well [Why? I don't get royalties]. *In fact, an option has been taken out by an adult TV channel on Book 1* [Wha?] *and Fenella's future may be looking brighter than any of us imagined. Our Europe editor will be in London for the next week and it would be really great if you had time to see her in person to discuss some exciting opportunities ...*

I read the message three times. This sudden glut of good news is making me paranoid. Is somebody sending these messages from inside the building as a joke?

And yet my bowels sink at the thought of more Fenella. She might be turning the tricks, but I'm the whore. Jed Tyler is a hack. The books are drivel. Lucrative drivel. Rent-paying drivel. If Fenella's loins become more famous, does that mean I do, too? As a low pornographer? As a literary joke? A rich pornographer. The joke's on you.

London looms.

There's an email from IT at MGU, who've been looking at my laptop while I was in Vegas. More good luck? They've found something remarkable hidden in my RAM or ROM? A golden ticket for Wonka's chocolate factory? Horse race results from the future? No. Just a few bits of cookie-style malware and some questionable "research" for Fenella on my hard drive. No sign of a Trojan Horse or a worm or whatever. My laptop hasn't obviously been hacked.

So what's going on? How was Lexxi paid for? How did he get my home address? Is he actually watching me? Following me? A stalker.

I try to remain rational. The police said he'll probably go away now. Most of these people are lonely weirdos, they said. A bomb threat is serious stuff compared to a sex doll. He's made his point. I've been very publicly humiliated and that's what he wanted. Eye for an eye. Fortunately, the bank has said they'll refund the money in light of this obvious nutter. But I get to keep Lexxi. Who's the winner now?

Rail tickets for London. I'd better book now if I want to pay less than for a new car.

At home, I'm selecting a rectangular death parcel when I pause to peer inside the upright white coffin of my fridge. I've got some Époisses cheese, a courgette on its way out, some double cream about to mutate. I've got penne, garlic and a sorry-looking basil plant on the kitchen window sill.

There's something automatic in the way I drop the crushed garlic into hot, peppered butter. The Damascus-steel knife (its edge so lovingly sharpened that I'd throw myself under it rather than have it chipped on the floor) whips through the courgette and the slices go into the butter with a sprinkle of sea salt. The penne's on. When everything comes to fruition at precisely the right moment, I sieve the pasta and it all goes into the same pan. I drop in the Époisses and the cream, give it all a mix and add the finely chopped basil as a garnish. It smells like a tramp's feet, but it's going to taste like heaven, like . . .

I still can't get her out of my mind. She's a dark splinter deep under my skin — one of those that are absorbed, not extruded.

I'm not thinking clearly as I sit down to eat. For some reason, I've brought two plates to the table. Two forks.

I look over at Lexxi. She has one of my cardigans draped round her shoulders. The flat cap. Her mouth gapes in dumb lubricity.

'Care to join me for tea, Lex?'

Big time

THINGS ARE LOOKING UP. I'm in London to meet two publishers and success is surely just around the corner, whether as Percy, Jed Tyler or the author of the edited masterpiece (pseudonym to be confirmed).

And yet . . .

Success is money. It's fame and recognition and the ziggurat of books at the front of store. It's proper reviews by people who (should) know what they're talking about. But I'm not sure that's the kind of success I want. Yes, I want people to read the books, to *get* them, to enjoy them. Be inspired by them, maybe – understanding at the same time that few readers will ever appreciate the books on the level they're written: the subtleties, the themes, the crafty colon, the cantilevered sentence. Was it Rothko who killed himself when he saw the kind of people buying his paintings?

Success for me is being able to do nothing but write: to exist purely for that onanistic pleasure. No teaching. No Fenella. Success for me means the next five or ten years accounted for in terms of books to produce, books to be published and read. A working writer. I don't believe in posterity. What's the point? Is Shakespeare sitting there in the bourne from which no traveller returns and stroking his beard in smug joy at his everlasting fame? Doubt it. He made his money, lived fast and died relatively young. He lived for the words. For him, it was all about the next line, the next scene, the next play. Writing was the drug.

Success means continuing to produce stuff that's right at the very edge of my reach: struggling always for the next millimetre of technical development. I'm not interested in being a production line, even if the books are multi-million sellers like the crime writer in Waterstones. That's rubber-stamp writing. No innovation allowed – the readers don't like it. Stick to the formula. Any flavour as long as it's vanilla. Think of Conan Doyle on the Sherlock treadmill, or Ian Fleming coughing out *The Man with the Golden Gun* – Fleming, who read Mann's *Der Zauberberg* in the original German and came to see Bond as the "cardboard booby". How many of those writers retain any literary integrity? Elmore Leonard, for sure. Raymond Chandler. Thomas Harris?

Nor do I want to write the gimmicky stuff that marketing departments love. The "Radio 4 Special": a whimsical, soul-searching tale of lost love, redemption, grief and family trauma in "lyrical" prose, designed to be orated by national-treasure actors in a slow, meaningful ... pause-ridden dramatic whisper. Or the "Exotico-Ethnic Special" whose first paragraph must contain italics: "Hajid took out his *umju* and carefully folded it into the delicate *ghanij*, muttering the mantra his father had taught him: '*Ghat al bzdura, skata malakies.*'"

Alas, success breeds success. If I get some recognition from Percy's book or a Fenella TV deal, I might then be able to push for more books. Better books. They listen to you when you're famous, when you're making money. Having a name opens doors. How else do you explain Paul McCartney's poetry collection? Even Tarzan's chimp chum Cheeta got a publishing deal.

So ...

G-Spot Books has its London office above a betting shop in Kings Cross. Or rather, it's a shared office with Beef Dreams (specialising in gay erotica), Black and Blue (S&M), Quim (lesbian) and Sugar Daddy (incest?). Notable titles are blown up as posters around the tiny reception: *Argon's Sword*, *Spank Academy*, *Cleopatra's Ass*, and the first of the Fenella Chronicles, featuring a simpering Fenella kneeling before a jodhpur-clad Thad, his schlong standing out like a beacon (credit: Jackie Collins).

The receptionist looks like an intern with attitude. Dyed pink hair, nose piercing, and a black t-shirt with *Whore* printed across her breasts in white. She wears a phone headset.

'Hi, I'm Jed Tyler. Here to see Carrie from G-Spot?'

'Does she know you're coming?'

Everything seems to have a double meaning here. 'Yes. Yes, oh yes.'

Pink Hair looks at me as if I'm a half-wit. 'Have a seat.'

There's only one. I wonder if I should wipe it before sitting, and decide to stand.

Pink Hair presses her headset and calls through to Carrie, who appears about three seconds later from an adjoining door. Her arm is in a blue sling and she has a black eye.

'Jed,' she says. 'Good to finally meet you.' She holds out her uninjured hand.

'Are you OK?'

'Fine. Fine. I was wondering why they kept repeating "Mind the Gap". Now I know.'

'Ouch.'

'Yeah. Come through. Can we get you something to drink?'

'I'm fine.'

Only the Beef Dreams editor is at his desk: a stick-like youth wearing a grey cardigan and a woolly pom-pom hat. He nods a brief greeting and goes back to marking up a graphic novel that seems to be a cross between Conan and a very popular sauna.

'So!' says Carrie. '*The Fenella Chronicles.* You know, they've got a growing readership among college-age girls back home. Must be the finishing-school vibe.'

'That's rather worrying, isn't it?'

'Not at all . . . wait, is this the English sarcasm?'

'No.'

'Well, they're doing well . . . and we're really looking forward to seeing the next one.'

Translation: the deadline's passed.

'Yes. I'm just about finished.'

'Great. That's great. Suri has asked me to remind you about the vocabulary? Something about obscurity? I don't know the details. She said you'd know.'

'Yes.'

'And she said to remind you about Thad being a little less … dumb this time? You have male readers, too, and they like to see themselves as thinkers rather than farm animals. She mentioned the scene where the horse is able to do arithmetic faster than Thad.'

'Right, OK. I get it.'

'So … How do you feel about the TV deal? Excited? I mean, I know it's not final yet, but they're talking about casting Lexxi Cummins as Fenella.'

'Lexxi?. That's … '

'You know Lexxi?'

'I have some experience with her. I met her in Vegas.'

'Wonderful! Of course, the TV channel doesn't want any screenwriting assistance from us, but the books' profile is going to increase. It's already increased. Suri has authorised me to tell you that we'd officially like to commission you for three more books at a new rate of £3000 per book. The TV company has made some suggestions where they might like to see Fenella going after graduation … but you retain full creative control. You're the writer. You're the creative genius!'

Creative genius. *Fenella straddled the prodigious staff … Thad's massive equine buttocks clenched as he …*

'You don't seem happy,' says Carrie. 'Is it the rate? I can talk to Suri if—'

'No. I'm just thinking. Three more Fenella books.'

'I know! It's great, isn't it? In a few years, you might be the next Chunk Hoffman, the next Brandy de Beurre. Big Time.' She indicates a couple of book-cover posters by these big-time authors: *Drill Bit* and *Petting Zoo* respectively. I'm not familiar with either.

'Have you read any of my books, Carrie?'

'Read them? I mean, I've looked at some scenes.'

'Which scenes did you like?'

158

'Let me think … It's been a while … Oh, the scene where Fenella has to sit on the different coloured dildos to decide which sorority house she's going to be in.'

'Did you find that erotic?'

'Well, you know … eroticism is a subjective thing, isn't it?'

'How about Thad and his colossal dong? Any attraction there?'

Pom-Pom Hat looks up from his sauna-fantasy fiction.

'Personally,' says Carrie, 'I prefer a man with a big brain. But … perhaps I'm not really G-Spot's target audience.'

'I'm just a little worried that, well, that the books are absolute shit.'

'Shit? Noooo. No no no. Your readership is very appreciative … I'm sure that Fenella is … is a … role model to many girls who aspire to … '

'A perfect fellatio technique?'

'Exactly!'

'Don't worry. I'll do them. I need the money. Tell Suri I'll do them. They're easier to produce than a bowel movement, albeit slightly more offensive. I'll do them.'

'Suri will be delighted. Look out for the contracts in your inbox soon. Sure you won't have a coffee?'

'I'm sure. And you be careful on the Tube.'

'Ha ha! Yes!'

'I'll see myself out.'

Pom-Pom Hat nods his goodbye and I go out into the reception, where Pink Hair is tapping at her mobile phone. I point to the Fenella poster on the wall behind her.

'I wrote that.'

She turns to look at it. 'The guy looks like a moron.'

I smile and go down the poky stairs to the street.

Three more Fenella books. There's only so many glistening pistons and swelling purses a man can take. I can kind of see why de Sade had the heroine of

Justine (Justine) struck by lightning at the end. Could I write all of them within a year and be out of that contract? Anthony Burgess wrote five and half novels in a year when he thought he was going to die. Philip K Dick wrote twelve, but he was on a lot of amphetamines (or similar) at the time.

I rush back into the station and on to the Tube for my second publishing meeting of the day. This one will be at a café a safe distance from their offices – one can never be too careful meeting a writer for the first time. A lot of them are unbalanced or just plain weird. Better to meet them in a public place where one can cry for help or get out of the meeting with some feigned gastro-enteritis. Indeed, I believe the main purpose of these initial meetings is to gauge exactly how insane the writer is before signing a contract with him. There's probably an established scale of literary sociopathy: from Salinger to Hunter S Thompson. My recent shenanigans in York can't have helped.

And, of course, there's the necessity to ascertain whether the writer claiming to have written the book does seem to have written it. Plagiarism can be embarrassing and expensive once the contract ink has dried.

The *rendezvous* site is a fashionable café somewhere in Hoxton: the kind of place where every male has a prodigious beard and every girl is "kooky". All have tattooed arms. It's the kind of place Percy would have dismissed as being "full of poofs". I need to remember things like that if I'm to stay in character as the writer of *Golden Years*.

I order a single-bean Nicaraguan mountain drip coffee with organic milk, which is served to me lukewarm in a chipped china cup by a twenty-year-old girl dressed as a 1950s Hollywood sailor. I could have got a Sunday roast in Manchester for the same price. My table and chair are cast-iron garden furniture and probably deeply ironic.

A young man waves at me from entrance and approaches. He's wearing thick-framed black glasses and a three-piece vintage suit with a mustard waistcoat.

'Hi! TG Harkett?' he says. 'I found some pictures of you on Google.'

160

At the York Festival? Being led away by the bomb squad? 'That's me. But call me Tom. Tom Fynn. Harkett is a pseudonym.'

'Oh, OK. Tom. I'm Ben. Are you drinking anything good?'

'The Nicaraguan. Lukewarm, over-roasted and exorbitantly expensive.'

'Sorry. I don't usually come here myself. It's just near the office.'

He orders and comes back to the table with a similar china cup: single-source Peruvian Peabean.

'So,' he says. '*Golden Years*: a remarkable find. I must admit I'm surprised you're so young, given the subject matter.'

'It's all research. I really try to get into the period and the characters.'

'And it shows. The detail is superb: really persuasive without being laboured. You might be eighty years old.'

'Thanks.'

'You know . . . I had a look at a couple of your other published books and they were very different. Stylistically, I mean, and in terms of subject. Very different. How did you manage that?'

Well, Ben. Let me explain something to you. It's a revolutionary concept, but bear with me. I'm a writer. That means I'm able to write. It doesn't really matter what – sci-fi, romance, historical contemporary, comedic or serious. I could do all of them. You're not surprised if a journalist writes about wind farms one week and TV the next. That's their job, right? But if I write a crime novel, say, it's assumed that's all I can do: I'm a crime writer for all eternity. Or rather, that's the assumption of your marketing people. Readers couldn't possibly conceive of an author writing different kinds of books. That's a career ender, isn't it? What, you've written three travel books and now you've produced a novel? Impossible! Can't be done. Nobody will believe it. How could we market that?

'Imagination,' I say.

'Well, it's remarkable. If we needed you to produce a short story for promotion, could you do that for us? Something in the same style?'

'Of course.'

'Tell me something about the genesis of the book. If you don't mind me saying, it's an odd choice of subject matter for a man of your age.'

'Well, I suppose it started back when I used to listen to my grandfather's stories about the war and the post-war years. Granny died while he was fighting in Africa and I suppose his way of keeping her alive was through anecdotes. He left a journal when he died ... In fact, it was more a series of notes. Perhaps he was planning to write a book. Who knows? I liked that idea of retelling one's story just to keep it alive — as if the past and the present are never really separate. So I used the inspiration of those notes and got into the research, which suggested its own stories. It was that simple.'

'Remarkable. Does his notebook still exist?'

'Cremated with him.'

Ben nods solemnly.

I stroke my chin. Ask a writer to start lying and you reap the whirlwind, sonny.

'You're a lecturer at MGU, is that right?'

'Yes. I teach the MA Novel course.'

'You must be a very good teacher.'

'Some might challenge that assertion.'

'Really? Well, look. One of the reasons I asked you down to London ... I'd like to talk to you about the name. TG Harkett is known as, well, as ...'

'A failure? A lunatic? An Avery Johns stalker? A bomb hoaxer?'

'No no. I haven't seen ... It's just that the name has certain associations and we feel that *Golden Years* might ... not benefit from these associations. Would you object to releasing it under another name? I mean, the truth would probably come out in the end — these things usually do — but it would help us to steer initial perceptions.'

'I have no problem with that, Ben. Suggest a name if you like. It doesn't matter.'

And it really doesn't. If the book is a success, nobody will care if Idi Amin wrote it. I'll just say I'm the author of *Golden Years* and editors will lie back like Fenella at the Dildonics. Poetry collection, Tom? Great! Gardening guide? Lovely! A-level Physics textbook? Excellent!

'Well, we can come to that later. I know I mentioned that there isn't a great deal of budget for an advance. The current market and everything ... I'm afraid we can only stretch to £500.'

Five-hundred quid for thirty years of Percy's work and two years of mine. I know for a fact that Ben's employer has recently given a six-figure advance to that 1970s sportswoman who won *I'm a Celebrity*. She's apparently going to have an autobiography written for her. Think it'll ever break even?

'That'll be fine,' I hear myself say. I can buy half a new boiler with it.

'And the edit will be very light,' says Ben. 'But I'd expect that with a writer of your experience. Just a few political correctness issues, you know.'

'Yes. I left those in because they reflect the world view of an eighty-year-old man. The poofs and the cripples *et cetera*. I could have filled it with darkies and wogs, but I appreciated that such terms are, you know ... '

Ben is blushing as if I'd slapped my genitals on the garden furniture and invited him to palpate them. This is the TG Harkett who threatened to come on a blogger: the volatile nutter. I'm veering towards Thompson when I should be on the Salinger side.

'But I entirely agree with you,' I say. 'Maximise the readership — that's my overriding concern.'

'Good. Good. I'm glad we agree on that, Tom.'

'How's the Peruvian single-peasant magic bean?'

'It tastes like strong Nescafe. Only lukewarm.'

'Not lukewarm, Ben. It's *cool*.'

'Yes indeed. Well, Tom — it was good to see you. Apologies for such a short meeting, but I have to be getting back to the office. We'll be sending you a contract and I'm looking forward to collaborating on a swift edit.'

We shake hands and I walk with him out to the street. He lopes off, looking behind him a few times to make sure I'm not going to track him back to the office and enact some Harkettian outrage. I wonder if he'll really send a contract.

I look at my watch. The pre-rush-hour crowds are massing. Time to get back on the Tube and head for Euston, where I'm meeting Will for a quick chat before we both head home.

Arriving late, I find him at a station bar packed with people trying to euthanise memories of their work day or anaesthetise themselves for the long commute back into domestic asphyxiation.

'*Dottore!*' he says, already three Stellas in.

He embraces me, London style.

'What's with all this hugging now?' I say. 'I don't even hug my own family.'

'Homophobe.'

'Already drunk?' I say.

'Well on the way, mate! Listen, I owe you a drink – your competition entry won us a trip away for Christmas. First prize: luxury bloody hotel in the Cotswolds. We're leaving the kids somewhere ... in a lay-by if necessary.'

'Congratulations.'

'I've bought a catering-size box of condoms.'

'Catering? Where do you eat?'

'You know what I mean. Are you OK, Tommo? You look thin. You look like shit. You sleep in those clothes?'

He's wearing a white shirt and a lilac tie. His jacket is slung over the back of the bar seat. He smells of wife-purchased aftershave and middle-aged masculinity.

'Lara called me.'

'Yeah? Shit. When? What'd she say?'

'It was after the festival. I think she thought I was going insane.'

'But she called, right? She must care. Do you think ... ?'

164

'I don't know. Maybe she's different, but I'm still the same. Worse, probably.'

'Don't start all that. Things are on the up, aren't they?'

'Do you still see her around?'

'Yeah. I mean around London. A gallery, the Tube. I think she works somewhere near the office. I've not seen her recently. Tell me about your meetings today. Good news?'

'Three more Fenella books at £3000 a pop and a possible £500 for my plagiarised novel.'

'Only £500 for Percy?'

'Massive dongs sell more copies than sensitive geriatrics.'

'I guess so. You don't seem very happy about it.'

'I'm waiting for the masterpiece. That'll make everything right. I can hold my head up when that gets through to the publishing committee.'

'Yeah. Right. But have you . . . have you thought about what you might do if it doesn't. I mean, what's next? How long can you . . . ?'

'I don't want to think about that.'

'Good strategy.' He looks at his chunky watch with its multiple crowns and dials and he offers me a sad *moue*. Time to go. 'Listen, Tommo. We'll be gone all over Christmas. Come down. House-sit for us. Feed the cat. Or don't feed it – you'd be doing me a favour. Spend Christmas in London. See some shows, offend some tourists. I'll get some food and drink in for you. Rum. Mince pies. I can't think of you alone up there with your fingerless writing gloves and your sex doll.'

'I'll think about it. Cheers.'

We both rush off to our respective trains and I find myself on the late-running Manchester Piccadilly wedged next to Britain's female Munch-eating champion. Her chin is glistening with pickled-onion flavouring and her lips slap grotesquely as I unfold my laptop to attempt some solace in the patchily delivered Wi-Fi.

There's a photo of Avery Johns on the *Daily Mail* site. He's pictured emerging from the rear of a London club with an Indian girl of surpassing beauty and sex appeal who's rumoured to be his lover. She's smiling, her black gaze burning into the camera. There's a sliver of that perfect skin exposed at her right hip. The ample cleavage. That's enough newspaper browsing.

It's been a week or so since I've done a Harkett search. Not since the York debacle. Evidence of that is still lingering on blogs, but there's something new ... something very disturbing.

The link takes me to Amazon, to the exact URL I have stored in my favourites: the TG Harkett page. Only now it seems there's a new book by Harkett: *Toad of Stone*.

Toad of Stone? The cover has been designed to look very similar to my other books. The font looks the same. But it's clearly the work of an amateur. Nothing in the copy suggests that the author is a *different* TG Harkett. Why didn't I get a Google Alert about this? There're already a handful of reviews.

I enjoyed a couple of the author's previous books, but this one is a very serious disappointment. The plot is idiotic and the writing is just terrible. I can hardly believe he wrote it ... (one star).

Harkett's descent into madness (as evidenced at the recent York Literary Festival) finds further evidence here. The book is a mess: chaotic, illiterate, cliché-ridden and full of frankly gross detail ... (two stars).

RIP TG Harkett. I can't imagine why anyone would have put this rubbish on Amazon, let alone Harkett. Hasn't he heard of proof readers. It reads like he wrote the whole thing in one go while on intravenous Red Bull ... (one star).

I feel like I'm hyperventilating but in fact I've not been breathing at all as I read through the reviews. With a quivering hand, I choose the *Look inside* option and click through the blurb and chapter listings to the first page.

> *Rain lashed the windows and thunder rumbled like a giant explosion as the lightning crackled down like a giant silver fork. I pulled the knife out of the prostate body of my grandmother and held the bloody blade up to the light with a blood-curdling cry: "Come to me, thy agents of Shaitan!" I exclaimed, my voice a howl like a werewolf.*

I feel bile rising to burn my throat. A bubble of acid-tinged Nicaraguan coffee pops at my tonsils. And all the while, the pickled onion-reeking heifer next to me chomps and gobbles, crunches and smacks, rustles and grunts her way through the industrial-sized nosebag of Monster Munch. The table is dusted with yellow crystals from her feeding.

I feel an outburst coming. It's not going to be very politically correct.

Static

I WAS EJECTED from the train at Watford Junction for causing a disturbance, but they allowed me to catch the next one after I'd calmed down a bit. The Monster Munch woman was tranquilised by someone from a local zoo and persuaded not to press charges following my one-minute-and-thirteen-second rant (somebody recorded it on their phone). Fortunately, my face does not appear on the YouTube video, which has so far achieved 1,456 hits for its aria of profane invective.

Naturally, I contacted Amazon straight away. It seems that there's no law against two writers having the same name. The TG Harkett page is not *my* page, apparently. It's the page of anyone deciding to write under that name, though one would expect any sane writer to check if they had the same name as another. As for the question of this imposter clearly copying the appearance of my books, Amazon tells me that's a matter for the copyright holder of the original designs.

I sent an email to the publisher, who of course didn't reply because I'm dead to them. What do they care anyway? The original books have a radioactive half-life that'll be darkening their balance sheets for the next fifty years. Will thinks that the designer himself might own the copyright, but I have no idea who that might be. In short, there's nothing I can do about the fake TG Harkett.

Or rather, there are a couple of things I can do, insane as they are. I've been on the site and written a lacerating review of *Toad of Stone* under the name TG Harkett, denying any link between my own published books and this excreta. I've also hinted in the review that a more structured and less restrained condemnation of the book might be found on a review blog called Penthesilea. It's there, on my blog, that I've had the surreal experience of eviscerating this novel by someone with my own pseudonym: raining down a righteous cataclysm of Sodom-and-Gomorrah vituperation that makes my previous reviews look evasive in comparison. Barely a cliché or a moronic plot twist has gone unbrutalised. I've utterly Jack-the-Rippered *Toad of Stone*, although some bloggers are already saying I've attacked *myself* on Penthesilea – that I'm schizophrenic and don't recognise my own declining work.

Partly because of this, I've also decided that this ouroboric review will be my last on the blog: simultaneously a nadir and a zenith. No more nasty hatchet jobs. Not a single writer ever seemed to learn from them, and Kalli's comments in Vegas made me see that the negativity was essentially self-destructive. I've written a note on the blog saying something along these lines. Perhaps now my stalker will desist.

What more can I do? I'm dealing with an evil genius. Everything he does seems to be untraceable or quasi-legal. Does he know this, or is he just lucky? Even as I attempt to dig myself out from the heaps of manure he drops on me, I somehow bury myself deeper. I mean, what kind of absolute nutter am I faced with? Hacking my bank details is serious. A bomb threat is very serious. But now he's actually written an entire novel (albeit a short one at 60,000 words) just to spite me. Who writes a novel just to spite someone? How long has he been working on it? Did he write it in his own piss-poor style and just post it as me, or has he written it on purpose to tick all the boxes I specifically warn against in my blog? If the latter, he might even have some talent because *Toad* is celestially awful. It might actually, literally, be the best worst book ever written.

Theoretically, I've now got enough of a sample of his prose to try and make some comparison with the few snippets I've seen elsewhere. Alas, those other snippets are so minor that they offer very little similarity other than their shared propensity to cliché. He's very clever.

The fact is: I'm no nearer to figuring out who it might be. A student? A disgruntled reviewee? Somebody in publishing? They know where I live. They know about Fenella. They know about my long-standing hatred for Avery Johns. They must have read a few Penthesilea reviews to so accurately create a novel containing all of the most common flaws. Is it Will? Is it Lara? I could easily start getting paranoid.

It's the last MA seminar before Christmas and the students are itching to get started on the novel I've yet to plan. Even Dreadlock seems to have new purpose and focus.

'What are we doing today, Drill Sergeant?' says Mum, nervous with attempted familiarity.

'Silent killing!' says Dreadlock. 'Slipping it to the reader unseen.'

Stalwart allows himself not to scowl this time. His pen hovers expectantly.

Earnest Youth just waits, a fresh page of his pad open.

'In fact, you might be right with your stealth approach,' I say to Dreadlock (surprising him with the acknowledgement). 'Today, we're thinking about narrative perspective: who tells the story? How does the reader enter the story and pass through it, live inside it? To see it another way: what lens do we choose to picture the scene? Do we take a wide-angle lens to encompass the whole scene? Or do we go for a close-up? Do we choose soft focus to suggest a mood? Or sharp focus and harsh lighting to create starkness? If you remember one thing about narrative perspective, remember William Goldman's words (oft quoted by our own Janet Freeman): the screenwriter writes for the camera; the novelist *is* the camera.'

And we're off: them scribbling, me grandstanding and gesturing and throwing out Socratic allegories like a pedagogic Catherine-wheel. First person brings the reader closer to the action, but complicates matters when dealing with other character points of view; second person evokes an over-friendly, slightly unhinged perspective; third person is the classic omniscient focus but with the added pitfall of encouraging too much telling if the writer is inexperienced.

'The thing is,' I say, 'you're seldom choosing just one of these. You're negotiating among them. You might write a polyphonic novel with multiple perspectives and various voices. You might have a first-person narrator who is able to imagine the perspectives of other characters because the story is told in retrospect, or overtly made up through an unreliable narrator (see Kinbote in

Nabokov's *Pale Fire* or Stevens in Ishiguru's *Remains of the Day*). You might opt for third-person with the added benefit of free-indirect voice . . . '

'Invented by Joyce,' says Stalwart.

'Invented inadvertently – by necessity we might say – in Austen, used by Kafka and perfected by Flaubert and Joyce. Nabokov claims he was using it before he ever read Joyce, but then he would, wouldn't he? This can be your secret weapon, obviating a lot of narrative scaffolding to get right into the heart of the characters and action. Right into the very thoughts of the *dramatis personae*.'

'An example?' says Earnest Youth.

'OK, so instead of saying, "John opened the door and he saw nothing", we say "John opened the door. Nothing." It's clear that's what John is seeing – we're seeing it through his eyes. Indeed, there's a scale of narrative distance that we can narrow as the novelist camera. When we use the character's name, we're speaking as the story-teller (the character doesn't think of himself in the third person); when we use *he* or *she*, we get closer with more ambiguous perspective; when we use free indirect, we eliminate the idea of the narrator or the figure of the character and go straight to his mind. Your job is to move between these perspectives invisibly as required.'

They're nodding, but I'm pretty sure they don't get it. Certainly, their workshop pieces show they don't get it. I launch into a Homeric catalogue of examples, thinking:

Stalwart moved his fountain pen irritably across the page. If only Tom wouldn't talk so quickly. A knowledgeable lecturer, perhaps, but a cocky and self-absorbed one without the obvious advantages of age. Self-knowledge. Patience. Piety. Look at the way he dresses, with his creased clothes and food down his front. He hasn't even noticed he's stained! Nevertheless, quite a well read fellow. Wrong about Joyce just now, but it doesn't do to argue with the teacher. A brief word afterwards . . .

He flicks a dread from his face as he writes. Bloody things. More trouble than they're worth sometimes. Can't write all this stuff so quickly. Too much to remember with all the other things I've got to remember ... getting de weed for de party on Friday and making that difficult phone call to daddy about spending all my allowance before the end of the semester. Better smoke one before *that* particular chat! What did Tom just say about Ellroy ... ?

Got to get bananas and garlic from the Co-op on the way home, thinks Mum. And toilet paper. God knows why nobody else in the house can't go to the supermarket. I'm writing this stuff, but God help me if I can do it myself. He makes it look so easy, like Roger Federer serving an ace. He doesn't tell us it'll take us ten years of practice to make it so easy. Why doesn't he tell us that? At least then I'll have an excuse. Socrates? What's he have to do with novels? I'm never going to get this ...

Yes, yes, and yes again. Good examples. I thought I knew free indirect but this is useful stuff. He knows what he's talking about ... when he's talking sense. Must admit he's a bit less showboating now that hottie's left the group. Good for us. Or good for me anyway — these other jokers aren't going anywhere. It's just going to be me and Tom carrying this collective novel. Should I volunteer for more words? Don't want to seem like a suck-up, but that dreadlocked tit'll be lucky to write his own name ...

Tom dashed off another book title on the whiteboard — child-like handwriting, never corrected by generations of teachers — and started giving an example of first-person free-indirect address as part of a third-person narrative. And all the time, he thought: is it LUFC? He hates me. Maybe Radio 4. But they couldn't know about Fenella. Might it be Stalwart? He's the passive-aggressive type. The sort of church-goer who'll listen to a sermon about charity and then sneer at a beggar loitering outside the Sunday School. He's the kind who'd stab me in the back, but only after he's got the high mark he thinks he's going to get. Could it be a long-term blackmail strategy?

And so they jot, scribble and note, becoming slightly better writers with each new example I give. Will I be able to bring them up to anywhere near a workable standard? Nobody can accuse me of not trying.

After the seminar, I follow up an old message on my monitor from Jerry saying that he wanted to see me about something. Turns out he's not at work today. He's taken a day off. Very unusual for Jerry – I thought he lived in his office at MGU.

'Doing anyone nice for Christmas?' says Janet in the ship's-galley staff kitchen.

'I'm house-sitting for a friend in London. Visit some bookshops. Get mugged. You know . . . '

'Nice. I've decided to treat myself to a few days in Vegas. 'Cause I'm worth it.'

'Have you heard from Gwynn?'

'Yeah, he's back after Christmas. MGU has advised him to see a counsellor. It seems a lot of people are saying he gave your address in Vegas. They're calling him the "New Hole".'

'Apt. The programme there hadn't been changed to my name. Too late.'

'Lucky for you, perhaps.'

'Indeed.'

'Well, have good one. I've got to go and explain to young Sophie that her silly infatuation needs to end now.'

'Heartbreaker.'

She winks and waves over her shoulder as she goes.

At home, I'm trying to get to the end of Fenella (so to speak). A home-made Bolognese steams by the side of the laptop. Lexxi sits behind me at the dining table, her auto-grip hands grasping cutlery in anticipation of the next dinner invitation. She wears Lara's scarf around her shoulders because I've not yet put the heating on.

I'm just about to describe another Thaddean orgasm (*taurine* or *ursine?*) when a Skype call comes through. I never use Skype. It was set up for Lara and I've not got round to taking it off the computer. It's a caller I don't recognise: *Mousai69*. I click it away and get back to Thad, but the caller tries again. Again I reject it. I'm about to turn the Skype off when a message flashes up:

Tom. It's Kalli. Want to talk?

I call her and hear her voice, tinny and distant. The video appears and I see her against a blue sky wearing sunglasses and silvery dress. Sitting on a balcony, perhaps. The sun makes her skin and blonde hair appear even more ethereal.

Kalli:	Are you there, Tom?
Me:	Yes. How did you manage to call me? Did I tell you my Skype ID?
Kalli:	In Vegas? I'm sure we discussed a possible call.
Me:	Yes? I can't remem—
Kalli:	I can't see you. Is it dark there?
Me:	I haven't turned the camera on. My house is a bit ... disgusting. Where are *you*? Looks like you're in heaven.
Kalli:	At home. Outside. Turn your camera on, Tom. Don't be shy.
Tom:	Really? OK ... Can you see me now?
Kalli:	I'm not sure ... Are you a balding man living in dim squalor with a sex doll?
Tom:	I warned you. The doll isn't mine. It's ... well, it's a story for another time.
Kalli:	How's it going? What happened with the masterpiece?
Me:	I emailed it to them from Vegas. Just waiting.

Kalli:	Waiting how long?
Me:	However long it takes.
Kalli:	What are you doing now? Have you got time to talk? I just saw you online and thought ...
Me:	Yes, it's fine. I'm not doing anything ... I've been thinking about novel structure. I'm doing something ... interesting with my MA class.
Kalli:	So go on: tell me something about structure. It might help me with my work.
Me:	There's so much they need to know. I suppose the basic idea is like a satellite zooming in from space. The novel is initially an empty, shapeless space. Then you define its borders by setting yourself a notional word count.
Kalli:	How do you know how many words?
Me:	The market pretty much decides. Sixty-thousand is the minimum; anything beyond ninety-thousand is "long" and needs to be justified. But it's practice. You shouldn't be writing a novel at all if you haven't yet got a sense of how many words you need to build a scene, build a chapter, build a pattern or whatever. Practice gives you that.
Kalli:	I suppose ...
Me:	But the point is: once you know how many words, you can define a mid-point. Now you have a beginning, middle and end with which to structure a story. You might further divide that into a three-act structure, or a five-act structure. The first twenty per cent is for introducing storylines and characters, the last twenty for climax and denouement. So then you divide your fifths into chapters and populate them with storylines, characters. Then the chapters are subdivided into scenes, dialogue, openers, closers—

Kalli:	Zeno's paradox.
Me:	Eh?
Kalli:	A Greek philosopher. His idea was that a runner could never conceivably finish a race if you subdivided the distance into infinitely smaller increments. A paradox, though ...
Me:	That's about it. And across your thirty chapters, or whatever, you have independent character arcs, story skeins, thematic developments, the acts ... all the puzzle pieces.
Kalli:	Like a jigsaw. You begin with the outside and work in.
Me:	Or a labyrinth. Same principle. The novelists sees all the passages, but steers the reader down the right one.
Kalli:	You make it sound simple.
Me:	Isn't it? The biggest challenge for my students is accepting that writing a novel is as much a structural as a creative endeavour. A novel is a map for the reader's journey.
Kalli:	You don't believe in the muse?
Me:	I believe in practice, planning and hard work.
Kalli:	How about luck?
Me:	Not sure I've ever seen any of that. The good stuff, anyway. Avery Johns knows what it's like.
Kalli:	Don't you make your own luck?
Me:	Have you got the recipe?
Kalli:	Ha! Sorry − it's an old family secret. Did you start anything new? A new book while you wait for the masterpiece, I mean.
Me:	Nothing new. Nothing. I probably shouldn't be saying this to you, but I sometimes think ... well, that there's no point in going on. At least a painter can hang his unsold pictures on the wall. What do you do with unread novels?
Kalli:	Isn't an unread novel like an unexpressed thought? It still exists, just not out loud.

176

Me:	That's a nice idea but books are created to be read. Only in the reading do they come alive. A novel is like … like a bolt of lightning — it needs to ground if there's going to be any light and heat. Otherwise, it's just … static.
Kalli:	I think you're a good teacher, Tom.
Me:	You know what they say: those who can't do, teach.
Kalli:	Vonnegut taught. Nabokov taught. Burgess, too.
Me:	You're difficult to argue with.
Kalli:	I'm looking forward to seeing you at MGU after Christmas.
Me:	Me, too.
Kalli:	Look … I know this might sound a bit presumptuous … I know I'm just a supervisee … but would you consider sending me a bit of your masterpiece? I'd be really interested to read what you consider to be your best work.
Me:	I'm flattered that'd you'd even be interested. Of course I'll send you a bit. In fact, I'll just send the whole thing. I'm not precious.
Kalli:	The Apothetae. The Agoge.
Me:	Exactly.
Kalli:	I can't wait to see it. Well … I guess it must be late where you are. I'll let you go. Good luck.
Me:	Thanks. See you in—

Her screen goes blank, leaving me with the fuzzy image of my own face, sickly in the electronic light. Lexxi haunts the background, a busty spectre. I click my image into blackness.

Something about Kalli — the way she seems to come out of nowhere and vanish just as quickly. Like when you're writing and the exact word you want — the one word that fits — flits tauntingly at the limen of deep memory. You see the shape, the vowel and consonant combination, but it won't come at your bidding. Only in its own time.

177

Something about her appearance, like she's been lit by a director of photography on a sound stage. A Golden Age starlet, all pallor and shadows — not of this world. Beauty as a concept only. It's odd, but I feel as if I can smell her presence here in my foetid living room. Lemon, spearmint. Eucalyptus. There's none of the fire I felt with Mohini — none of the onrushing lust, the visceral twist, the penile quiver. I believe I could lie with Kalli naked and feel no stirring except that of my mind.

I shut down the laptop and swivel the chair to face the kitchen. This is where she sat, her silk-sheathed legs opening. That's where I stood, pinioned by coffee and libido. Now only Lexxi gawps at me, her loose-lipped silicone vapidity going dark as the screen blips off.

Showing and telling

FENELLA CUPPED Thad's hairless baubles in her cool hand. Her nails were painted "Christmas Red" and she wore a tinselly blindfold. Thad was dressed as Santa: red coat, white beard, black boots, vast swollen erection twitching before his angular oiled abs. He had playfully tied a ribbon around its prodigious girth and leered now as he invited her to open her present. Fenella grasped it (forcing a porcine squeak) and squeezed. 'Is it a baseball bat?' she asked. Thad whinnied as she descended upon his Tannenbaum. 'Oh Tannenbaum! . . . '

I know. I'm even disgusted at myself. I've already deleted a previous version set in a stable. There was a donkey. It wasn't pretty. Plus, I think the G-Spot publishing group probably has an imprint for that kind of thing anyway. Doolittle Dreams? Ee-i-ee-i-Oooh?

I stand on stiff legs and rotate my shoulders. I'm at Will's place in London and it's Christmas Eve. He has a tree festooned with baubles and tinsel and flashing fairy lights. An inept origami angel (fashioned by one of their kids?) sits askew on top. Toys are cleared away in a box. There are coffee-table books of photography (Salgado), painting (Turner) and fashion (Chanel). The room is warm and smells of the mince pies I've warmed up in the oven. I have a glass of rum to hand. On the radio, Kirsty McColl is abusing Shane McGowan. This is nice. This is how Christmas should be. It used to be this way, back before . . .

My phone rings.

'Will? Shouldn't you be halfway through your catering pack by now?'

'Yeah. Had a bit of a tiff, Tommo. She'll come round. Listen – just a quick one. I got you a present . . . or rather you got yourself a present. Remember that competition you entered a few weeks ago?'

'No.'

'The Avery Johns review. Well, you won it. The prize is in the top drawer of the dresser. Enjoy it. Got to go now … she's doing something with scissors. Bye!'

I go to the dresser. He's put it in a golden envelope like I'm at an awards ceremony, the flap hanging open. I pull out the A4 sheet and unfold it. *Congratulations … very thoughtful piece … vouchers to the value of £500 … personal audience with Avery Johns …*

Will has scrawled a note at the end: 'Johns chose the winning entry personally and wants to meet the competition winner — that's you! Stick it to the man! I've already set the date (below), but you can change it if you want.'

I can't believe it. Will planned this. He's long known about my feelings for Avery. What does he expect — that I'm actually going to take his name attend this intimate dinner with Avery Johns? I surely won't get past his PR and security. And what would I say to the man? Crap books, mate. Aren't you ashamed? I was lying in every sentence of that review. Every line was a smear of sarcasm. How's Mohini? Are you two rutting like racoons?

I read the letter again. Avery Johns chose *my* piece from over 1600 entries. What does that mean? Is his opinion worth anything at all? Has he damned me with his faint praise? Or does it prove conclusively that he recognises I'm a better writer than he is? And a voice calls to me from the Greenean ice-sliver in my brain. A wheedling, insinuating Judas voice that tells me my work has been officially approved by Avery Johns. Avery Johns is famous. That's the same as being reviewed. That's the same as an endorsement. I could … I could use this to sell the masterpiece. I could use an endorsement from a man whose ability I hold in utter contempt. Perhaps when I meet him …

Is this the black rot in every writer's heart?

The doorbell rings. Carollers, probably. I ignore it.

Another ring. A tentative knock. No discernable wassailing. Charity people? I ignore it. Then a voice that seems to come through the letterbox.

'Will? Will, it's me: Lara. Are you there, Will?'

I walk to the front door, where a familiar figure is silhouetted against the urban sodium glow. I open the door.

'Oh!' she says.

She's just as I remember. Same serious eyes, same subtly pretty face, same social-camouflage clothes. But she's also different, and that difference is everything she's seen and thought and felt in the years since we split. Her difference is the absence of me, the addition of something else. Some*one* else?

'Will asked me to come round . . . ' she says. 'I didn't know you'd . . . '

'Will's away for Christmas. I'm house-sitting.'

'Ah. I see. That's very naughty of him. We just met briefly at the Turner exhibition and he said . . . '

'That's Will. I've got mince pies . . . Do you want to come in?'

'I was really just passing. You know, just being polite. Christmas,'

'OK. If you have to be somewhere else . . . no problem. Nice to see you. Merry Christmas.'

'You, too.' She turns to go but pauses. 'How long are you staying?'

'Back up north after Boxing Day, probably. You can, er, call round another time if now isn't convenient.'

She nods. 'Have a good one, Tom.'

I watch her walk down the street, standing at the door in case she looks back and I can wave. She doesn't look back. In a book, that would mean something.

I go back to the computer like a dog going back to its own vomit (credit: Proverbs 26:11). There's a new email. It's from the publisher looking at the masterpiece. Here we go:

Many thanks for the quick turnaround on these edits, Tom. You've done a great job, but I'm afraid I still have a few qualms about the main character. What's his motivation? Why does he do what he does? He remains a bit flat. And I think we need to lose at least another 10% of the overall length. I've attached a document with a few more little things that I feel . . .

Fifteen more pages of editing notes. As if my previous edit counted for nothing. Do they even want the book I originally submitted, or can they see another book inside it – the sculpture inside the sculpture? Seems to me they don't know what they want. Just keep chipping back until we've got a deformed stick man and a mound of gravel. Then they'll say, 'Nah, never mind. That's not what we were looking for.'

More edits. How long can I prettify this corpse? Must I become a necrophiliac (I could write for G-Spot's most arcane imprint: *Le Petit Mort*)? Or do I just bury it as Kalli suggested?

Merry Christmas, Tom.

CHRISTMAS DAY. I'm woken early by car alarms and by an ambulance (?) racing down the street. Vestigial dream-tissue tears on my sharpening consciousness: Lara turning into Mohini turning into Kalli, faces and bodies merging. I'm asking Kalli, 'Why doesn't your breath steam when it's cold?' The kind of dream you can't remember ten minutes later but which returns a year on as *déjà vu* or insomniac revelation.

It's a crisp, clear day: cars frosted and naked branches still against the blue. I decide to walk into central London without purpose or direction. I've got an *A-Z* just in case, but I follow the main artery on a whim. The streets are virtually deserted – just the occasional car, the odd cyclist, people in hijabs or saris or turbans or djellabas for whom the season must be surreal. The more central I get, the fewer people there are. Fleet Street is post-apocalyptic, the Strand wiped clean by some pandemic, Trafalgar Square flickering with Hitchcockian hordes of confused pigeons.

I'm heavy-legged and footsore by the time I'm passing somewhere near Covent Garden. There's an Indian man noisily positioning a sandwich board outside his second-hand bookshop: "Free Cuppa As you Browse" (offer limited to one cup per customer before 12 noon). I can't say no to that.

I've always loved second-hand bookshops. They're where my reading began and they've been kinder to me than the others. It's rare I see one of mine among the foxed and faded ranks of the used – not enough were printed to achieve that level of ubiquity. One must be an *Oliver Twist*, a *Catch-22*, a *Clockwork Orange* or a *Da Vinci Code* before one becomes a fixture in every shop.

But such place are museums of writing rather than shops. This is where careers *end*. Scan the titles and count the unknown authors and titles: first books, second books ... and then the yawning void of oblivion. How many of these writers are now dead? How many celebrating with their families today, remembering vaguely the time they once had a book published? How many sitting bitterly alone at the keyboard, typing a Jacob's Ladder back to the light?

What I love is the randomness. It was in places like this I first met Cendrars and Celine and Gombrowicz – writers I'd never heard of when I bought them. Writers I probably wouldn't have found in my local Waterstones. If I never read another book published henceforth, I'd still need a dozen lifetimes to unearth the good stuff hidden here under the cloak of failure and obscurity.

I'm looking at a clothbound hardback with its fake gilt title worn away when I simultaneously smell lemon and hear the words:

'That's a good one. The only book he ever published. Out of print now.'

'Kalli? What ... ?'

'Came in to Heathrow this morning. This was the only open bookshop I could find.'

She doesn't look like she's been flying all night. She looks pristine in a tailored wool coat and a stylish scarf that covers her hair and oval-frames a pale face: 1960s Hollywood.

'Well ... merry Christmas!' I say.

'You, too. You looking for anything in particular?'

'Almost never. Just drifting. I recently bought a vintage hardback of *Moby Dick* just for the woodcuts in it. I already had two copies in paperback.'

'I know that edition. Beautiful illustrations.'

'You know ... this is the second time within a few months I've met a student in a bookshop. Mohini was the last one.'

'I think I can guess how that must have ended. Knowing her.'

'Yes.'

'You know it's not how *this* meeting is going to end, right?'

'Of course. I don't even feel like that about ... It's a totally different ... '

She smiles. Her icy eyes scan me. 'Come with me. I want to show you something.'

'Where are we going?'

'Drama. Or poetry.'

At the drama shelves, she reaches for a complete Shakespeare and turn immediately to the back, flicking just a couple of pages until she finds what she wants. 'Read that,' she says.

The expense of spirit in a waste of shame
Is lust in action: and till action, lust
Is perjured, murderous, bloody, full of blame,
Savage, extreme, rude, cruel, not to trust;
Enjoyed no sooner but despised straight;
Past reason hunted; and no sooner had,
Past reason hated, as a swallowed bait,
On purpose laid to make the taker mad.
Mad in pursuit and in possession so;
Had, having, and in quest to have extreme;
A bliss in proof, and proved, a very woe;
Before, a joy proposed; behind a dream.
All this the world well knows; yet none knows well

To shun the heaven that leads men to this hell.

'Sonnet 129,' I say, 'One of the Dark Lady set? I've not read that for ages.'

'Remind you of anyone? Of a recent experience, perhaps?'

'It might have been written about her. He might have known her.'

'It was. He did.'

'Sure. Her type. Her effect.'

Kalli smiles and replaces the book.

'You know,' I say, 'I think I actually quoted a Dark Lady sonnet to her. The last words I said to her.'

'She would have appreciated that. It was her finest hour.'

'You said in Vegas she has a thing for writers.'

'She does.'

'So why is she with Avery Johns?'

'Not always the best writers.'

'That makes me feel better.'

'She goes where there's attraction. She has a sense. How do you understand the sonnet? What is Shakespeare saying?'

'Lust sucks you in. You think of nothing else before, during and after. But it ruins you with disgust and regret. It depletes you.'

'Right. Now apply that idea to writing.'

'You're talking about success?'

'No, but it's interesting you should go there. You've said you don't believe in the muse — how about an anti-muse?'

'Who enervates rather than inspires?'

'Right. Who fosters apathy rather than interest, immediate gratification over diligence and patience. As Shakespeare said, lust is easy. It intoxicates but it doesn't sustain. It's a promise never fully delivered.'

'This is good. You're saying Mohini is perhaps demonic. A kind of anti-muse?'

'*The* anti-muse. Think about it. When is writing about easy victories – about the thunderous orgasm? It's a pleasure that's always deferred, isn't it? We spend years honing the craft, experiencing frustration at lack of progress, knowing that we can always be better. No writer worth the name ever *arrives*. OK, perhaps one or two, but the gods first make mad those they intend to destroy. Homer told me that. Think of Joyce in *Finnegan*, Melville's *Pierre*. Much of Poe. The ecstasy of perfect ripeness soon turns to rot.'

'My students think they'll reach perfection within the span of the course.'

'Of course they do. It's lust they want, not love with all its pains and promises.'

'Are you sure you're just a student?'

'Ha! Aren't *you* still a student?'

'I am. That's why I'm here in this bookshop.'

'Right. But Mohini didn't want you in a bookshop. She wanted you inside her. She wanted you living for the next thunderous orgasm. Twitching for the next encounter so that you lost all sense of yourself as a writer. Oh, Tom, you're blushing!'

'You Americans are very frank.'

'But aren't I right? Wasn't Shakespeare right? What's happened to you since you met her?'

'I can't blame her . . . '

'You should. I said she has a sense, that she feels a certain attraction. She sensed your weaknesses and sought to exploit them. She was coming for you before you even knew her name.'

'Sounds like you two have quite a stormy relationship. You say you've never met?'

'Never. Just the same men sometimes. I won't say I hate her; she's just my opposite.'

'I wouldn't want to get between you both.'

Kalli smiles. 'All I'm saying is: writing is control. Control of the material, controlling time, self-control. Restraint. Patience. She represents none of that. She's the opposite.'

'OK. Enough about her.'

'I agree. Did you get any feedback on the book you were editing in Vegas?'

'Last night. More edits. It's like the first load didn't make any difference. It's turning into a piece of *decoupage*, you know? You snip here and there with the scissors, unfold the sheet of paper, the pieces blizzard away and you're left with a lacework of gaps. Only, the scraps on the floor are the bits I liked. I never set out to make a doily.'

'So don't do it. Self-publish.'

'You don't understand . . . The publishing committee.'

Kalli shrugs. 'I thought you held the whole industry in disdain, and yet you're slavish in your recognition of it as the only meaningful standard.'

'You don't . . . The industry is like . . . is like a parent. It doesn't matter how old you get, you still recognise your dad's authority. It's his approval you seek. Sure, you can show your work to a friend or a lover, but it's daddy's opinion that matters. Even if daddy is an abusive, ignorant shit. A thrashing from daddy has more love in it than praise from a friend. Self-publishing is like the self-help industry: empty platitudes and the universal pat on the head.'

'Have you considered counselling?'

'Has anyone ever told you about tact?'

'Yeah, that old woman in Vegas. Remember? You told her she'd wasted thirty years pretending to be a writer.'

'*Touché*. Again. Did you read any of the masterpiece version I sent you?'

'I did.'

'And?'

'It's long. Very long. The writing itself is remarkable: what you do with perspective, rhythm, punctuation, the character interplay and the themes.'

'But . . .'

'But I think there's a difference between writing and a book. You've produced some virtuoso writing, but I'm not sure it coheres.'

'Hmm.'

'You're thinking that I didn't get it, that only you — the omnipotent author — knows the truth about this book. You're thinking how to answer without patronising me.'

'No . . .' Yes. Exactly that.

'Listen. Don't respond at all. I think I saw a café open on the corner. Do you want to go?'

'I'm reminded of the last time a girl in a bookshop made me a similar offer.'

'Just coffee,' says Kalli. 'Let's go.'

She loops her arm around mine and it feels natural. Her body is hard, spare, athletic. Her perfume invigorates.

We're walking to the corner arm in arm when Lara appears from round the other side of the café. She continues walking towards us. She looks, looks away. She looks back with recognition and surprise, slowing her pace as we meet. Kalli grips me inexplicably closer.

'Tom . . . Hi,' says Lara, her gaze flickering between me and Kalli.

'Lara. Er, merry Christmas . . . again. Are you on your way somewhere?'

Her eyes take in my proximity to Kalli: the intertwined arms, the easy rapport. She's waiting for an explanation by way of an introduction.

'This is Kalli,' I say. 'She's one of my MA supervisees. American.'

'Hiya!' says Kalli with uncharacteristic animation and a cheddar grin.

Lara looks at me with something like reproof. Like disappointment.

'No . . . it's nothing like that . . .' I say.

Kalli leans against me, taking her arm from mine and putting it around my waist.

'Right,' says Lara, who (I know) is not dressed or made-up to be meeting a stylish, striking woman in the street. Tracksuit trousers. Hoodie. Probably out on a quick errand — running to or from an idling car nearby.

'It really isn't . . . We just met in that bookshop and—'

'We're going for a coffee,' says Kalli, resting her head against my shoulder.

'Nice to meet you, Kalli,' says Lara, meaning not a word of it. 'I've got to run. Bye.'

I watch her walk briskly back the way we came. No departing glance for me.

I turn to Kalli, who has now disengaged herself from my waist with her usual sardonic smile. 'What was all that about?' I say. 'The down-home cheesecake smile, the head-resting?'

'Showing, not telling. You're familiar with the concept, I'm sure.'

'You know what she's thinking now?'

'I know exactly what she's thinking. Conflict. Motivation. Don't you teach that in your classes?'

'That's in books. This is real life.'

'Oh, Tom. You know there's no difference. Trust me. Everything is going to be fine. Come on, I'll buy you a muffin with my crisp new currency.'

I look at her, with her *Picture Post* sunglasses and her Jackie O headscarf. Her teeth are perfect. She lowers her head and looks at me over the top of her shades: a frank and unflinching stare.

'OK,' I say. 'But make it a millionaire's shortbread.'

WE SAT THERE until they threw us out around half past three, at which time the near-solstitial dusk was bloodying capital spires. Kalli went off to her hotel and I took a taxi back to Will's, paying an unexpected seasonal surcharge to a driver I strongly suspect does not recognise Christmas as a legitimate holiday.

Now I'm crammed with a family-sized Christmas pudding I heated to fissionable temperatures in the microwave and then doused with double cream. There's a shot glass of good rum beside the keyboard and I'm idly surfing the net looking at writers. That's what we discussed for most of the time in the café. Writers we admire, writers we'd recommend, writers we'd like to be. She's promised to email me her work in progress so I can start reading it prior to our first tutorial. No sign of it yet.

And I'm thinking about her summary of the masterpiece: writing, but not a book. It's a devastatingly simple and perceptive critique that's been echoing around the vault of my increasingly drained ego. Like any man, I'm not going to acknowledge the truth of an argument in the flash of battle; such acceptance comes later (if at all) and is absorbed quietly. But the more it rattles inside my head, the more I see its essential truth. How does a writer come to produce the stuff that suits his style? A voice is not automatically a song.

It's not about structure. It's about matching personality and text. I've been singing pop songs with an opera voice, or vice versa. I can't possibly start looking at the masterpiece in this frame of mind, so I allow myself to swallow the lure of the TV.

I'm settling in for a box-set when the doorbell rings. Something makes me get up to answer it.

Lara.

She's wearing a red dress. Dark stockings. Heels. More make-up than she used to wear. Clearly on the way to a festive party. She has a package under her arm.

'Lara.'

'Can't stop. I'm just on my way to ... Look, I got you a present. It's nothing special. Just, you know ... '

I take it from her. Clearly a book. Heavy.

We stand looking at each other.

She leans in and kisses my cheek and I smell her perfume on the heat of her skin. That favourite, discontinued scent that still hides in folds and pockets at home. 'Merry Christmas,' she says, close to my ear. And then she's gone, looking back with a little wave as she turns out of the gate. I hear a car rev and see exhaust fumes billow over the hedge.

I take the book inside and open it on the sofa: a Chambers dictionary, seventh edition: the same one I used at university. You'd look in vain for *dot.com* or *cyberbullying* or *quidditch* in this dictionary. And why would you? Context and regular usage makes those words clear; we need dictionaries for words like *ensorcellate*, *settembrinian*, *esurient* and *subfusc*. The etymologies seem fuller than in my current edition.

A note falls out.

I don't know anyone else who'd appreciate this. Lara.

Kalli was right. Showing, not telling.

Monkey business

JANET STICKS her head round my door at MGU. 'Visitor for you at reception, Tom. A girlfriend?'

I trot down the corridor but the only person waiting is an elderly woman leaning on a wooden walking stick. She looks me over with a scanning glance.

'Yer must be Tom,' she says.

'Yees?'

''E won't've mentioned me, I 'spect.'

'*He?* I'm sorry ... I don't know ... '

'Percy. I've been 'is bit o' stuff these last ten years. I've come for manuscript.'

'Would you like to talk in a meeting room? I ... '

'I don't mind wettin' 'ere. Just bring me it and I'll be on me way.'

'The thing is ... It's not here. There's a meeting room just through those doors.'

'Aye, go on, then.' Resignation in her voice as if she expected such a thing.

She follows me with a wobbling sailor's gait — one leg shorter, perhaps — and puffs like an old bulldog until we're seated in the Vader suite.

''E tole me there were only one typewritten copy,' she says, 'and that yer'd 'ave it.'

'It's, ah, been put forward for marking. That means it's somewhere between four or five internal and external markers.'

'But yer muster med copies. What if someone loses only copy?'

'I suppose admin might have ... '

She crosses her arms in classic I'm-not-leaving-until fashion.

'The manuscript is Percy's property,' I say. 'Why—?'

''E's dead, i'n't 'e? There mebbe some munny in that script. Mebbe not Arry Potter money, but ... Well, 'e's left me bugger-all. I'm invisible woman. Scarlet woman.'

Her face is creased and gravity-ravaged. It looks like a monkey scrotum. Some orthodontic catastrophe has left her mouth pinched and shrunken: autumn's puckered windfall uncovered in a winter thaw.

'He never mentioned you,' I say.

'Course he di'n't. Too busy polishing the saint — 'er — while I were polishing 'is knob.'

I'm afraid I wince or grimace.

'Aye, 'ave a laff. Yer young. I mebbe seventy-nine, but I still got me ways. I got a queue of 'em at Friday-night darts since Percy passed.'

'So . . . did he show you what he was writing?'

'No. When 'e said it were about 'er, I told 'im I weren't interested. I'm still not. I just want what's comin' to me.'

'I can certainly try to find a copy, but do you understand that Percy's book is very unlikely to make any money? I mean, I've had three books published myself and I still have to work here. The odds of him getting a deal, especially as a dead unknown, are very slim.'

'I espected yer'd say that. Like the antiques shop man told me mother's Meissen teapot weren't worth more than a fiver. Five 'undred quid I got for it in end. Five 'undred. That's a few days in Blackpool.'

What a literary legacy.

'Well, as I say,' I say, 'I haven't got a copy of it to hand. If you give me some contact details I can—'

'I'll be back in a week.'

'Right.'

I see her to the lifts and then drop into my office chair. Percy — you old rake. A thirty-year opus on uxoriousness and you were 'avin yer knob polished all along. Now what am I going to do? Tell her the copies have vanished and give her a five-hundred quid payoff? I doubt she's read any of it; she probably wouldn't notice if it was published. Besides, she's pretty old — she might die within the week. All that darts-team action . . .

Anyway, the publisher still hasn't sent a contract or the edits. Perhaps they're still nervous about the TG Harkett associations.

I see Gwynn walk past the doorway and call his name, whereupon he walks backwards in mock slow-motion and leans against the jamb. He looks thinner. His skin is greyer, but his eyes have the same impish animation.

'How was Vegas?' he says.

'You gave a great speech, citing Bruce Willis and Krispy Kreme.'

'I accept all praise for it. The criticism I direct to you.'

'How're you doing?'

'I've started writing again.'

'Really? Poetry?'

'We'll see. It's just for me at the moment. Call it therapy. But I'm excited.'

I nod, remembering Gore Vidal's dictum: *Every time a friends succeeds, I die a little.*

'That's great,' I say.

'By the way, I didn't know you were born a polydactyl.'

'What? I wasn't.'

'Oh? You might want to take a look at Wikipedia, then.'

I turn to the screen and go straight to the site. I'm already familiar with the pages on me and my published books (presumably written by a fan), but there was never anything about birth defects.

I scan the lines. *TG Harkett ... born 1973 ... author of ... pseudonym of Manchester Gallagher University lecturer Tom Fynn ... also writing as Jed Tyler ... Fenella Chronicles ...*

Heat suffuses my face. I feel myself wobble on the chair. My real name and Tyler's loathsome *nom de plume* have never been revealed in print anywhere. With onrushing dread, I scroll down to *Early life*:

> *Born as a polydactyl (six fingers on each hand), Harkett was initially rejected as Satanic by his fanatically Christian parents and*

spent his first four years in an orphanage, where nuns sprinkled him
with holy water before and after every meal. Sold into a circus aged
five, he was taught to play piano duets with a monkey named Sir
Monocle . . .

Lies. All lies. I scroll through this tissue of insanity to *Critical reception*, where the page's author has collected together every poor review I've ever received, including the one mentioned by that caller on Student Radio. A note at the end of the entry observes that I am now the official Writer in Residence at Chadderton Sewage Treatment Works, where I am working on a collection of short stories that explore the poetics of excreta.

I click *Edit* and delete all of the untrue information, stripping out the negative criticism at the same time. How long has this stuff been live? Why didn't I get a Google Alert? Who's doing this? LUFC? He was the one who made the complaint about my polydactyly jest. But is he capable of the measured prose of this libellous farrago? He hasn't the skill or the imagination. And how could he possibly know about Fenella?

My alter egos are threatening to eclipse their creator. Harkett and Tyler are Poe-esque doppelgangers gradually arrogating more quiddity and immanence than the literal truth of Fynn (a Selfian sentence if ever I've written one). The more I fight against them, the more dominant they become, the less real I am. It'd be a good idea for a novel if it wasn't my life.

I walk distractedly to the seminar, worrying how many people might have read the Wikipedia entry. Why would they? Unless they were Tyler fans searching for Fenella titbits (pun intended) or straggling Harkett fans checking to see if I'm dead yet and whether their signed edition is worth a fiver more. Or a publisher already nervous about taking on a notoriously unstable writer and double-checking all details before agreeing to a contract . . .

The class has that post-festive apathy. Mum looks enervated by a traumatic family Christmas; Stalwart is florid faced from too much whisky, religion and mince pies; Earnest Youth has counted off another year of wage slavery and non-publication; Dreadlock has trimmed his matted pineapple of hair and sits straighter in his chair, no doubt threatened with excommunication from the ready-meal millions unless he cuts down on de weed, mon.

I've got just the thing for them: detailed plot notes for the portion of novel they're going to write, character portraits and arcs, thematic structures, tone and pace diagrams — even chapter breakdowns detailing the scenes they're to write (for example: *Fiona goes into the quirky record shop and gets talking to/flirting with Brian, who accidentally reveals his sister's affair with Jonas. Fiona buys a Smiths album to flesh out her character*). All they need to do is knock out the words and I'll finesse them into something readable.

'Any questions?' I say.

'I'm writing Brian, but I'm not writing Fiona,' says Earnest Youth. 'How do I get round dialogue?'

'Simple. Initially, you write both parts according to the necessity of the scene, then Fiona's author will read over your dialogue and amend Fiona's words to match Fiona's character. And vice-versa. After some time, we'll all understand the characters. It's how the writing's done on American TV sit-coms. The script teams all have a good sense of how the characters think and speak.'

Earnest Youth nods and glances to Mum, who'll be writing Fiona. They seem relatively happy.

'And what about the overall style?' says Stalwart, glancing at Dreadlock. 'I don't want to feel that my rather formal, precise writing is going to clash with, ah, other voices.'

'You'll see that I've written the first chapter myself and I've given examples of how each character speaks or thinks. Use these things as your guide and we'll iron out any inconsistencies in the workshops as we go.'

'And if we think of something new?' says Mum, 'Something not in the plot?'

'Go with it. We can absorb whatever works.'

They're sorting through all the copies I've given them and I wonder briefly if this is a very bad idea. Too late now. I'm committed.

'I'm glad you mentioned dialogue,' I say, 'because we're going to do a bit of a crash course today. Specifically, we're going to look at some of the different ways it can be handled and how those ways affect our perception. We're used to speech marks and *he says/she says*, but there are other ways.'

Stalwart: Like a script.

Tom: Exactly.

Mum: But why would you use that in a novel?

Tom: Any suggestions . . . ?

Earnest Y: It speeds up the action. Less punctuation and speaker tags.

Tom: Right.

Dreadlock: And I suppose, like, it's good when you have a few people talking.

Tom: Definitely.

Earnest Y: But it doesn't work so well if you want to show physical stuff.

Tom: True [*nodding*]. You'd need to use square brackets.

Is it possible to just avoid a script layout and still omit the punctuation? says Stalwart.

Cormac McCarthy does that I say.

Doesn't it get confusing who's speaking?

It can. Sure.

So I suppose it's best limited to pair dialogue.

I'd say so. It's a very distinctive method. Spare and evocative.

— I've seen some writers use long dashes, says Earnest Youth.

— Indeed. Irvine Welsh, for example. It obviates the need for a lot of punctuation.

— And I suppose it's good for pace, says Stalwart.

— Yes, but with the drawback of making narrative interjections trickier and more overtly signposted, I say, thinking that the class is responding particularly well today.

— Better for pair dialogue? says Mum.

'Probably,' I say. 'But I think it's important to stress that dialogue becomes much easier when characters have distinctive voices. Then you don't need to signpost as often who's speaking. It's just clear from their voice and their interaction.'

'I, like, totally agree with that. It's Kerouac's thing.'

'No. I really don't believe people are so predictable in speech.'

'I think we are. Everyone has some quirk. It's good to give a character a voice.'

'I don't know. I suppose so. Is it difficult to do?'

'Not at all. You just need to establish certain traits and patterns early on. As the writer, you're God breathing life into the Genesiac clay.'

'Might I request we avoid outright blasphemy in the classroom?'

I smile. I look at Stalwart. A voice in my mind whispers: *'Could it be him? Is he the Wikipedia character assassin?'*

'The rest is just punctuation,' I say. 'Show interruption with—'

'A long dash,' says Earnest Youth.

'And pauses with . . . ?'

'Ellipses,' nods Stalwart.

'Right. And remember that the most effective dialogue is evoked by what's not said: what the reader infers from the spaces in between. Do you see what I mean?'

'I . . . I suppose so,' says Mum.

The Wikipedia entry had some of his verbose formality.'

'And we can add a certain ironic narrative distance by switching to reported speech at key points. We might use this to draw attention to a character and, in so doing, implicate them or imply something about them. If you want to blacken someone's character or libel them anonymously, for example. Do you see what I mean?'

Stalwart answers that he does indeed understand. His eyes avoid mine.

'And finally, be wary of the redundant or laboured tag. It's usually enough to use *say/said*. Let the dialogue tell us *how* it's spoken. OK?'

'Of course,' says Stalwart.

'*Count his fingers!*' says the voice.

'Yeah. No probs,' says Dreadlock.

'Uh-huh,' Earnest Youth.

'I ... suppose so,' says Mum.

'And finally, I suppose we might mention a technique made famous by Flaubert in *Madame Bovary* where an extraneous source of dialogue seeps between the characters. It might be an overheard conversation or an internal voice. Have any of you read the book?'

'I have,' says Stalwart. 'It's rather overrated.'

'Is this a hacker I see before me? Or a hacker of the mind, a false creation, proceeding from the heat-oppressèd brain?'

199

Bounces like Castle

NEXT MORNING, I see that my Wikipedia entry had been restored to its original ridiculous form. It seems that I, as the person being described, have no power over the factual truth of the entry. Being TG Harkett is not enough; I must have citations to prove that he was not born a polydactyl and did not play piano in a circus with a monkey.

And this is where the infernal genius of the hacker lies. I have followed the footnotes provided in the entry and discovered – with commingled terror and respect – that he has fabricated a tissue of evidence to justify his work. An obscure reviewing blog has an interview with me that I never gave. A circus blog describes someone's reminiscence of seeing the young Harkett deliver a barnstorming rendition of "Knees Up, Mother Brown" with Sir Monocle at the keyboard beside me. A spurious Sister Assumpta contributes to an obscure ecclesiastical site with anecdotal evidence of the six-fingered Satan freak and the holy-water showers. Why didn't I get a Google Alert?

It seems there's nothing I can do other than faking my own evidence to counteract the false stuff. I can't even prove I am Harkett because he doesn't exist beyond the pseudonym. The only link between him and me is the Wikipedia article that reveals it. True, there's no footnote for the Jed Tyler link and I might be able to get G-Spot to counter the claim . . . but would that look even more suspicious? Apparently, Wikipedia won't reveal the identity of the poster unless I can provide a strong case for libel and an official subpoena. As if I've got the time and the money for that.

Will insists that he's not told anyone about Fenella except Carol, and that Carol wouldn't voluntarily raise the subject of obscene books even at gunpoint. I'm afraid I shouted at him on the phone – still embarrassed about this Avery Johns meeting he's engineered, and (unaccountably) still agitated by the emotional engineering of Lara's Christmas Eve visit. 'So don't see Avery!' he said. 'I thought I was doing you a favour,' he said.

Someone at G-Spot, then? Perhaps Suri, who's been battling with my irrepressible literary leanings for three books? That bobble-hatted editor of Beef Dreams I met in London? But why? There's no reason for such a labour-intensive campaign of retribution from those people. This is the behaviour of a madman. An obsessive lunatic. Very probably a writer, writing being a kind of obsessive lunacy in itself.

A reasonable person might say I'm overreacting about all of this: the Wikipedia thing, the fake book, the bomb hoax (*overreacting* about a bomb hoax?), but this reasonable person might like to look over the email I received from the masterpiece editor late last night.

Tom

There's no easy way to say this. Someone at a recent editorial board raised the subject of your pornographic alter ego Jed Tyler and a series called the Fenella Chronicles. I had not been aware of this writing activity and I was disheartened to see the kind of books they are. Following this revelation, and the seeming inability for us to reach consensus on the edits of your novel, I feel it may be best to part ways on this one. I fear we would not be able to market and earn critical respect for a serious novel if its author was also known to be a pornographer . . .

Naturally, I dashed off an intemperate response, which has so far been (and will continue, forever, to be) ignored:

Benedict

In your original response, you wrote that my book is "accomplished, inventive, humorous and experimental". You called me a terrific

writer. Evidently, those things are no longer true now you discover I have written in another style. Don't worry. I understand — the book itself is the empty tin can. It's the packaging that matters, no matter whether the can is full of caviar or cat shit. Perhaps I should have revealed to you that I suffer from agoraphobia, or synaesthesia or anosmia — some kind of inoffensive but interesting condition that makes me easier to market. Perhaps I should have told you I was raised by wolves, or in a fundamentalist commune, or that I lived until my late teens inside a pickle jar at a Mumbai circus. Anything except pornography (which Miller wrote, and Flaubert). Did the idea of a pseudonym never cross your mind? Congratulations on your utter spinelessless. I trust the hardback party-planning book you published by that reality-show winner has sold well over Christmas? I'll look out for it in the remainder bins at my local homeless shelter
. . .

Not too pleased with the homeless-shelter jibe. It doesn't really make sense. But I've read in *Private Eye* that the party-planning book has gone down like a ton of elephant manure at a royal reception. A six-figure advance they gave for that foetid turd.

Anyway, that's another publisher I'll never be able to approach again. No publishing committee for me. Back to the futile cycle of submission and rejection. This book, my masterpiece, that strode into the amphitheatre so confidently and armed to the teeth has returned to me once more, maimed and limping. Can I send it back to fight? Which version do I send? I'm not sure if it's got any fight left in it. The *magnum opus* has been defeated in the popular bestiary by a shapely nymphomaniac called Fenella (whose contract for three further books lies, still unsigned, on my desk).

I think the masterpiece is dead. I think I have to accept that. It's not the years I spent on it that sting me now; it's the passion and hope that have passed their use-by date. The book was the best I could do. It wasn't good enough.

I look at Lexxi. Or rather, I look at the tuft of blonde hair and the crescent of silicone hip emerging from the cupboard under the stairs. She looks like she's trying to escape. Might she sneak up behind me as I'm writing and put her auto-grip hands over my eyes: guess who? Or is she — the woman scorned — more likely to grasp my neck in a homicidal auto-grip as my fingers flutter fadingly at the keyboard. That's the kind of death I anticipate. The obituary writes itself:

> *MGU lecturer Thomas Fynn leaves a testament of three out-of-print books. His reputation as a plagiarist and base pornographer is mirrored in the nature of his demise: asphyxiated in an unexplained encounter with a high-end sex doll — a death described by friend Will Trewitt as "somewhat characteristic". His one-time university sweetheart Lara James described the failed writer as 'underendowed, but enthusiastic'.*

I ARRIVE on campus in a better mood. Today is my first proper tutorial with Kalli, whose frankness and humour act as smelling salts to my stuporous sensibilities these days. There's still no physical attraction — not even an erotic dream (to which virtually every female mammal I ever meet is subjected at some point). She's just so … intuitive. It's like having a conversation with the truest part of myself: that part I normally keep locked in ego's cellar and whose occasional yelps for freedom are stifled by ever-accumulating cynicism.

I've also been reading a sample of her work and I've been quite humbled by its perfection. Not flashy, not overtly clever — no stylistic pyrotechnnology. It's as simple and effective as one of those masters who's been writing so long and so much that their craft has become entirely invisible. Elmore Leonard. Kurt

Vonnegut. You search in vain for the clockwork of their writing. Great style has no fingerprint, no blood type or DNA. It just is.

Let's hope my meeting with her can rejuvenate my positivity. I'm meeting LUFC straight after.

She's waiting for me in Vader's asthmatic cell, her invigorating perfume signalling her presence all the way from reception. She's wearing a white dress that should wash out her pale complexion but doesn't.

'Hi,' she says. 'Six fingers must have made you a damn hot pianist.'

'Ah. You've seen that, have you? I'm afraid Sir Monocle was the real talent. Like a little, very hairy Richard Clayderman.'

'So you're taking it as a joke?'

'What choice do I have?'

She shrugs and spreads her hands on the table.

I sit. 'I've read your work,' I say, 'and I don't think there's anything I can teach you.'

'Really? Perhaps you haven't read it closely enough. Nothing's perfect.'

'True, but there's a point after which criticism is hardly relevant or just comes down to taste. I might be able to find something wrong with Elmore Leonard if I really searched, but why would I? There are pages of Burgess or Nabokov I might want to skip, but the quality of the rest is so stellar that I can't begrudge them any inconsistency. You mentioned Poe last time we spoke. He's a perfect example, isn't he? He'll write something sublime like "Masque of the Red Death" then write that crap about the guy with bad eyesight.'

'"The Spectacles".'

'Right. I think that's a hallmark of genius: inconsistency. Bursts of brilliance.'

'Is my work brilliant? Am I a genius?'

'No. It's just very good. It's good enough that you probably see its flaws better than I can. A literary voice is like a bell. You hear the ringing note as you write and you know instinctively when it's out of tune.'

She smiles. 'Some of the description is tonally out of proportion to the action around it. That's vanity.'

'I'd expect as much from any writer talented enough to make that kind of distinction. Style is vanity. It's also arrogance born of confidence. Was it Gore Vidal who said that style is knowing who you are, knowing what you want to say, and not giving a damn?'

'I think it was. You know, Tom – you talk so passionately about writing, but you're not doing much of it. Apart from that edit, I mean. And the porn, if I can believe Wikipedia.'

'No, the edit is gone. They backed out because of the Fenella thing.'

'So you're writing nothing serious at all?'

'That's about it. Yes.'

'Don't you miss it? Don't you feel the need? Isn't it time to – forgive me – stop wasting your time with the cheap porn and aim for something new? Something higher? Don't you have ideas? Things you'd like to write?'

My smile is stiff. 'Aren't I supposed to be leading this tutorial? It's about *your* work.'

'Is it this hacker stuff that's getting you down? The bomb hoax, the Wikipedia page, the *Toad of Stone* imposter – yes, I've seen that, too. And your review of it.'

'It's been on my mind a little bit. A writer's reputation is—'

'Is based on their writing. You know that. Think of them: Rabelais the blasphemer; Celine the anti-semite; Burgess the brawling philanderer; Nabokov the arrogant snob; Flaubert the whore-hopper; Faulkner, Chandler, Poe and Fitzgerald the drunks; Shakespeare the syphilitic adulterer. Miller selfishly abandoning June to the asylum. The abusers, the hypocrites, the murderers, the perverts and the egotists – these are the people who made art. You wouldn't want to be friends with them, but their writing is transcendent.'

'I'm no Faulkner or Chandler.'

'Not yet, perhaps. But if you write something with the fullest degree of your ability, will it matter about Fenella? Will it matter about those three early books? If Celine can be cited as a great writer after what *he* said, you have nothing to worry about. You just need to write. Prove yourself. Then it doesn't matter what idiots say.'

'You remind me of a speech I gave recently in Vegas.'

'Yeah, right. Am I gripping your bloody heart too tightly? You already know that a writer's greatest responsibility is to be true to his voice: to know his work better than anyone else and set higher standards. If you don't, you're not a writer. Sure, you might fail. But as Bradbury said, you only really fail when you stop writing.'

Her voice remains calm all the time. There's no passion in her tone; these things are so clear to her. She might be talking about a shopping list or the weather. In fact, she's acting ventriloquist to that voice I've got locked in the cellar beneath my ego – the voice I'm afraid to acknowledge. Her pale eyes hold mine without challenge or opposition. She smiles as she speaks. Her cool hand sometimes touches my arm with transatlantic familiarity, but there's no sensual frisson.

'There's a quote from Orwell,' I say.

'I think I know the one you mean. He refers to a demon? Yeah. Socrates also spoke about one, but his was a daemon. There are demons and daemons. Orwell's was the latter, I think. But you don't believe in things like that do you, Mister Agoge? Mister Apothetae. For you it's about "hard work".'

'I see where you're going with this . . . '

She nods. Her teeth are so perfect. 'You know what you have to do.'

'Just start again. Something new.'

She shrugs and spreads he hands. 'Want another quote? Try this: "What more is required than a kind of stupid, insensitive doggedness, as a lover, as a writer, together with a readiness to fail and fail again."'

'Beckett?'

'Coetzee.'

'Remind me: who's the tutor in this room?'

'Ha! You realise you haven't mentioned the Dark Lady yet?'

'No, but now you have. I might see her. I'm meeting Avery Johns for lunch – it's a long story: proxy competition winner – and she might be around. I think they're still together.'

'This is a development.'

'Isn't it.'

'Will you be taking a bomb?'

'Funny.'

'How do you feel about seeing her again?'

'You know . . . I actually feel very much like Sonnet 129. I really do.'

Kalli's glacial eyes laser me with something like approbation, affirmation.

'But I'm not sure I'll even go to meet him. Why would I?'

'Because you're a writer and you're curious? Because there might be a story in it? Because it's a free meal?'

'You know my weaknesses.'

'And your strengths.'

'Have we met in another life, Kalli?'

'You don't believe in that stuff. It's OK. You don't need to. So are you going to tutor me at all? Or do I get thrown down a chasm?'

'Right. Right. You said your description was tonally off. Let's start with that . . .'

I'M STILL SMILING as she leaves, even though LUFC is filling the hallway with a smell of cigarettes and insecticide deodorant. He's wearing an England football shirt. As she passes him, he leers at her with his best barroom pick-up face and says, 'All right?'

She seems not to notice his existence, passing through the double fire doors with a backward glance that promises to sustain me through the next hour.

'Shall we go in?' I say to LUFC.

I've wasted another few unpaid hours of my life reading his turgid bowel movement of a book and, yet again, he's taken none of my advice. Rawhide McJohnson the closeted cowboy is still risking melanoma with the amount of moisturiser he's buying; Nubuck the tight-jeaned saddle-sharer is getting perilously closer to a Brokeback moment; Saloon Lil's part-time job at the fish-bait shop is in jeopardy because ... I don't know, because Sheriff Patel drank a bucket of mescaline and scalped himself with a Bowie record. It's all bollocks.

'She's fit,' he says, slouching back in his chair.

'She's a proper writer.'

'Sayin' I'm not?' he says, with a pigeon jerk of the head.

And it's suddenly as if I'm hearing Kalli's voice. Everything I was going to say — the evasions, the euphemisms, the dancing round McJohnson's love of panto — falls from me and I realise I need to take a new direction.

'I've read your book again and ... I owe you an apology.'

'Eh?'

'I didn't get it before: the western/Manchester thing. But now I see that it's a profound allegory on late capitalism and the crisis of identity in post-modern culture. You're positing a new frontier in the sphere of dress and historical regression. That's it, isn't it?'

'Er, yeah ... you could put it that way. Yeah.'

'I see now that McJohnson *isn't* gay. He's playing with gender stereotypes — the Marlboro man as transvestite. Nubuck is a comment on the innate femininity of masculinity.'

'McJohnson isn't gay.'

'That's what I'm saying. But I think I've seen some opportunities for you to make this brilliant allegory even greater. Just a few edits that would really bring it out.'

'Yeah?' He casually clicks his pen and moves it towards his pad.

'For example, what about if McJohnson slept in a wardrobe?'

'He's not gay.'

'I know that. He's ... he's a rigid beef jerky of a man. But sleeping in a closet would emphasise his essential isolation from other men. It's kind of metaphor: like a coffin. Death is sleep.'

He writes *coffin* on his pad.

'And your Apache character, Bounces Like Castle — the guy who works at the fun fair. Maybe we could include a scene where he opens a casino. It would be a provocative comment on the American reservations.'

He nods, trying not to look interested, and writes *Casino* on his pad.

'Cat House Moll,' I say. 'Her job at the council is boring and she hates it, living for the weekend when she can do the can-can at Rusty's Saloon. She's a tragic character really. I wonder if she might go on a prolonged peyote trip? You could narrate it like Molly Bloom's monologue in *Ulysses*. You've read Joyce, haven't you?'

'Loads of times.'

'Great. I think ... I think we might be looking at a future masterpiece here.'

He nods, triumphant on his throne of delusion.

I feel no guilt. I've tried for two years to make this guy a better writer and he's ignored every word. Kalli is right. Writers take responsibility for their own work. They are their own most reliable critics. True, they need guidance and close supervision in how to achieve objectivity, but this guy is unteachable. He doesn't want to learn; he wants a medal. He thinks if he goes to a publisher with a Creative Writing MA it'll be like a passport — A Get out of Talent Free card.

'In fact,' I say. 'I think you should start sending it to publishers as soon as you've made these changes. Don't wait 'til after submission.'

He writes *masterpiece* on his pad and underlines it. 'Can I quote you on the cover?' he says.

'Of course. If this book is published, you can say I said that. Now — let's talk about the moisturiser. I can see a man like McJohnson buying a fuller range of skincare products ... '

I'm probably going to lose my job. I might even lose my life when LUFC gets the marks back for this faecal nugget. How low can I go? Twenty per cent? He'd get that much just for being able to sit up straight. I imagine the laughter that'll resound from publishers' offices all over Britain when this lands on their desks, and I plough gamely on with my sabotage.

Pork pies

I'M SITTING at my desk laughing to myself when Jerry's head pops round the door.

'Are you OK, Tom?'

'Yes. Fine. Just thinking about something.' Rawhide McJohnson saddling a bidet.

'Have you got fifteen minutes? Gwynn and Janet are here and I thought it might be a good opportunity for a quick chat.'

'Fine.'

We use the Vader suite, which carries a composite scent of Kalli and LUFC.

'My God, what's that smell?' says Janet. 'Like a salad in a teenager's y-fronts.'

'Like Olympus in the back of a Ford Transit,' says Gwynn.

'That's the smell of writing,' I say, 'from A-list to Z-list.'

'Did I see Kalli here earlier?' says Jerry.

'Yep. First tutorial.'

'Good student? Getting on OK?'

Gwynn and Janet snicker and offer exaggerated winks.

'Perfect,' I say.' I wish they were all like her.'

'I wish they all could be Carolina girls!' croons Gwynn.

Jerry shoots him a doubtful glance. Is out poet fully recovered? Gwynn mimes closing a zip across his lips and intertlaces his fingers in a show of seriousness.

'Just a few things while we're all here,' says Jerry. 'First, we've had a complaint about the MA course. It refers to a particular lecturer, but it's something we've all heard before.'

'Our marking is a matter of taste rather than judgement?' says Janet.

'Our idea of poetry should be widened to encompass birthday-card doggerel?' offers Gwynn.

'Our teaching doesn't tally with the opinions of their hairdresser?' I say.

'Our standards are too high,' says Jerry, barely masking a smile.

'*What?*

'Bollocks!'

'Shoot me now.'

'What does "too high" mean,' I say.

'Too high for them to achieve,' says Janet.

'This person claims that we're judging them based on professional rather than academic standards,' says Jerry.

'Well, of course,' says Janet. 'Think about how many screenplays are produced academically each year. I think Oxford Brookes were up for an Oscar in 2013.'

I nod. 'Publishers all over the country are looking at novels and asking themselves if the work meets their rigorous academic standards. Let's be honest about this. Most of the students are obsessed with marks. They want a high mark even if they learn nothing about writing during the course. As if the mark means anything. Would *The Da Vinci Code* get a first? Probably. Would *Ulysses?* Probably. Because the criterion is publishability. The professional standard is the only standard that matters.'

'We need to remember,' says Jerry, 'that the students are paying for the course and the qualification.'

'Exactly,' says Janet. 'But not necessarily the learning. They can take or leave the learning.'

'If I were doing the course,' I say, 'my only measure of satisfaction would be if I came out of it a better writer than I went in, regardless of marks.'

Jerry's expression is pained. 'The Quality team won't see it like that. We may need to look at the marking in light of the other similar complaints.'

'Raise all the marks!' says Gwynn with an antic disposition.

'Yeah, give 'em all firsts,' says Janet. 'That's what they're paying for, right?'

'And what happens after they get rejected by every publisher in Britain because their work is shit?' I say. 'Then they write and complain that we didn't prepare them for the rigors of professional writing.'

Jerry raises his hands in surrender. 'A complaint has been made and it has to be addressed. Just be ready with your defence when the Quality team comes calling. Can I also check that you've been in contact with all of your BA supervisees?'

Shrugs all around.

'Does that mean no?' says Jerry.

'According to the list, I've got seven,' says Janet. Only three have contacted me.'

'Same,' I say.

'Four,' says Gwynn. 'It's their responsibility, isn't it? We don't know their email addresses.'

'Yes. They should be contacting you,' says Jerry.

'They will,' I say. 'The week before submission, with a jumble of pure crap they expect us to sort out.'

'It's a life lesson,' says Janet. 'Let them learn that they get shit marks when they leave everything to the last minute. See how that approach prepares them for a career.'

'They'll become university managers and administrators,' says Gwynn, 'and get the last laugh when they become your boss.'

'Too true,' says Janet.

Jerry shakes his head. 'Do you realise how much they're paying for their degrees?'

'All the more reason to crawl out of bed and actually attend,' says Janet. 'That's surely the minimum academic requirement.'

'OK, OK,' says Jerry. 'I've mentioned it. Just one final thing. A small announcement, really. I've got a novel coming out. My first in ... well, in too many years. Macmillan are bringing it out next year.'

'Congratulations!' says Janet.

'To the victor the laurels,' says Gwynn with a salute.

I nod acknowledgement, my throat so constricted with envy that I can't even verbalise a platitude, thinking: even Jerry ... even Jerry whose career was deader than the public phone box can get a publishing deal while I flog a dead penis in the Fenella books.

He's enough of a writer to guess how I feel and dutifully avoids my gaze.

'Any other business?' he says. 'Janet? Tom? Gwynn?'

'I'm meeting Avery Johns for lunch at the weekend,' I say, just to say something.

'Call the bomb squad!' says Gwynn.

'Ooh! Can I get an autograph?' says Janet. 'Or does he have them ghost-written?'

'Is this a good idea?' says Jerry.

'It was a competition I entered for a friend. Now he says he doesn't want to go. Maybe I could, you know use the opportunity to ... clear the air.'

'Clear the venue,' says Gwynn.

Jerry looks at him sternly then back at me. 'You're still having problems with this stalker/hacker aren't you? Something about having six fingers? The porn thing?'

'I am. But ... I think I've found a way to get over it. It's just like a bad review. I've got to rise above it.'

'Good for you,' says Jerry.

'Six fingers?' says Janet.

'All the better for onanism,' says Gwynn.

I have to remind myself sometimes that he was once one of Britain's best poets.

We're all leaving the room when Jerry touches my arm.

'A moment, Tom?'

'It was my student, wasn't it? The complainant. Radio 4?'

''Fraid so. Obviously, you shouldn't raise this with her.'

'Naturally. Better for the tutorials to proceed in an atmosphere of unspoken accusation and mutual resentment.'

'Give her what she wants, Tom. She might understand five or ten years down the line — if ever. And just one more thing: your MA Novel group is telling other students that they're writing a collective novel. Is that right?'

'It's an experiment. I got their consent. I figure they'll learn more from this than their own stuff.'

'But they have to write their own novels. That's the course requirement.'

'I know. And they will. But right now none of them has any idea what they might write so this is a useful exercise.'

'I'm just trying to prevent further complaints.'

'Canute amid the crashing surf.'

'Quite. Just take it easy, Tom.'

He rests a hand on my shoulder as we leave the room and all I can think of is his new book and the fact that the corpse of my masterpiece lies dismembered and rotting on my hard drive.

THE AFTERNOON finds me standing in the cold on a Manchester street near where Lara's parents live. An email from Will — overly nonchalant and ostensibly about something else — has mentioned that Lara is up north to see her mum and dad and I know that she always used to visit a particular butcher's shop famous for its pork pies. (A fugitive thought: has Kalli ever eaten a pork pie?) The shop is just across the road from where I'm freezing and pretending to wait for a bus.

Why?

Maybe it was that perfumed kiss on the doorstep at Will's. Or the dictionary she gave me, containing all the words she didn't say. Maybe it was the red dress and the stockings and the make-up that stirred memories of our early years when she was wild and I hadn't yet poisoned myself with disappointment. We had fun then. Never like Mohini, but close. Close. And I loved Lara. My first love. The only one.

Memories have started to come back to me since Christmas. That break we had in Paris. Lying naked together in bed, my head resting on her stomach, she reading — the street sounds rising through our curling net curtains. The custard tart I bought that was runny in the middle and which I lobbed into the Seine like a salmonella grenade. She laughed so much that her tampon popped out and we had to find a public toilet which, she said, looked like a trench latrine at the Somme. We re-enacted that famous Doisneau kiss outside cafes in Montmartre, where I sought the footsteps of Miller and Sartre but found only piss and litter. A waiter in an Italian restaurant leered openly at her breasts.

I've been writing some of this stuff. I couldn't have written it even two or three years ago, but it's easier now. Stories come retrospectively out of the chaos of immediate impressions. I've realised that there's a book in this: a fictionalised autobiography of my journey — our journey. It might not be commercial enough to be publishable, but it'll heal and soothe until I'm ready for something else.

A figure in a hoodie and trainers. The face is hidden but the walk is hers. She goes into the shop.

I dart across the road and follow her in to the smell of refrigerated meat.

'Tom?'

'Oh! Hi. Here for the pork pies?'

'Will told you I'd be in Manchester.'

'No ... Yes.'

The butcher hands her a paper-wrapped parcel and looks to me.

'Small pork pie, please. Look — have you got time for a coffee?'

'Why?'

'Two quid, mate.'

'I've only got a twenty. Is that OK? Because of London and the dictionary and ...'

'What about blondie?'

'I told you, she's a student. She was … just messing about. She was trying to make you jealous, didn't you see that?'

'Your change, mate.'

'Thanks. When you came round to Will's in your red dress—'

'Let's go for a coffee,' says Lara, who never liked a public confrontation.

We walk to the corner where there's an independent café with virtually no customers. Nothing is said on the way, both of us furiously rehearsing lines that aren't conspicuously loaded with meaning.

When we're seated at the window with a flat white (me) and a latté, she says: 'So …'

'Thanks for the dictionary. It was a nice thought. My eleventh edition is jealous.'

'No problem,' she says, looking out at the street.

'Were you on the way to a party that night? You looked … like you were going to a party.'

'Yeah.'

'You *were* jealous, weren't you?'

She turns to me and I wonder if I'm about to be lashed with hot milk.

'I was surprised to see you in London,' she says. 'That girl irritated me with her behaviour.'

'Lara … I'm glad we're talking again. I'm glad you called me after the festival disaster. I'm glad Will engineered these meetings. I'm not saying everything's going to be OK and we'll live happily ever after but … you were my best friend before we were together and I miss having you as my best friend. I'd like to be in contact again. Just to talk now and then. I don't care if you've got someone else. Is that something you'd like, too? Could you tolerate it? Could you forgive me?'

She's looking at the smeary Formica, her face half turned away. She says nothing.

'I'm beginning to realise that … that the writing oppressed me when it should have released me. I'm not saying I'm cured. I'm a recovering scriboholic. There's no such thing as "just one metaphor" for me. I can't pass an adjective without having a noun. My colons don't know whether to dash or stop.'

Is she smiling or crying?

'And, well, you did look very hot in that red dress.'

Her head drops, still not looking at me. 'That's the Tom I recognise.'

'But, you know, there's no need to rush straight into bed. I accept that I don't deserve any trust, and that you might … you know, have someone else. A chat sometimes – that'd be nice. Maybe a meal further down the line. A back rub …'

Her eyes are wet when she finally turns. 'You've never really grown up, have you?'

'That's the wonder of me.'

'Let me think about it, OK? It's been a long time. I don't know if I'm ready, or willing, to go back. Even as friends.'

'Of course. Just so you know: I'm working on something now. A novel about me – about us. I'm writing it as an experiment. I can show it to you, if you like. I won't try to get it published if you object.'

She nods and stands, taking her pork pie. She seems to deliberate a moment before saying:

'I'll be in touch. You can send me some of your new experiment.'

No departing kiss this time. She's almost out the door when she turns.

'I'm not with anyone else,' she says. And she's gone.

I promise my pork pie that I'm going to write this book just for her. A readership of one. I'm going to make her see that I understand now what I lost. And I realise, only now, that I'm going to use every atom of ability I have to get her back.

Literary jihad

THE REVIEW of an Avery Johns' book I wrote for the competition was one of the hardest things I ever had to write. That was partly my reason for doing it: the challenge. Of course, I had to endure one of his books, which, at the time, seemed like one of those craps that so soils your posterior that you have keep wiping and wiping without any sense of the taint diminishing. I must have spent longer reading it than I spent on *Foucault's Pendulum* or *The Glass Bead Game* or *Vanity Fair*. I had to look up new words to express my disdain for it.

The breakthrough came when I understood that all I needed to do was write the diametric opposite of how I felt: an exercise in clinical irony. *Avery Johns is a truly visionary writer ... his description transcends reality to create something purer ... to read his dialogue is to be an audience in the most literal sense ... his themes and motifs lay bare the very strata not only of culture and society but also of history and literature ...* Coincidentally, it also helped to imagine I was writing a review of my own work.

And he liked it. He loved it. He wants to meet the reviewer for lunch in Sheffield, where he's in the middle of a national book tour. I've changed my mind so many times since Christmas whether or not I should go. What would I say to him? Would I embarrass myself? Would I be tackled to the ground within feet of him? Would I back down and snivel before his superior fame and confidence? I recalled the anecdote of a disillusioned Labour Party door-stepper who had the chance to meet Blair at an annual conference and who'd rehearsed a heartfelt tirade to deliver to his face. But when the grinning warmonger held out his hand and congratulated her on all of her hard work, all she could do was gush her simpering thanks. That's the allure of power and success.

I might not even get to him. They know what I look like. My only hope is that his PR team is so obsessive that they'd rather see conciliation than confrontation. Better copy. Good for the man's reputation. Avery Johns sits down with his would-be assassin, forgives him. Next week: Avery Johns releases doves in Palestine as Hamas and Netanyahu enjoy a picnic at the writer's expense. Hummus. Falafel. Gefilte fish. Olives.

So now I'm sitting in the reception of a chain hotel in central Sheffield, the city where Larkin changed trains and ate an awful pie, and where I'm drinking a coffee from a vending machine. It tastes like sooty dirt. There's no sign of Avery Johns, who's probably seated in a Waterstones somewhere, wearing his cravat and brogues and signing autographs for a line fawning imbeciles who, presumably, will reverently stroke that signature. His hand rested here! These marks were made by him! Like it was the Magna Carta or Christ's own notes for the Sermon on the Mount.

I should go. I'm not in the right frame of mind for this.

I'm getting up and making for the exit when I see the man himself entering with a gaggle of publisher's reps and hangers-on. The cravat, the tweed, the brogues. The vulture-like PR is first to see me and instinctively moves in front of the writer as if to shield him.

'You!' says the PR.

'Will Trewitt,' I say, holding my hands up. 'I'm the competition winner.'

'What's going on?' says Avery Johns, looking between his handlers and me.

'The competition winner you're supposed to lunch with, Avery. It's this guy: TG Harkett — the one from the York Festival. The one we had to ban from your website.'

'Oh.'

'Look,' I say. 'I entered the competition for a friend and he didn't want to come. I suppose that invalidates the rules, so shall we all just go our separate ways? No harm done?'

The PRs Machiavellian spin gland is secreting overtime, testing potential Tweets and press-release titles. Might there be a story here?

'Did you write the review?' says Avery Johns.

'I did.'

'And you mean me no physical harm?'

'That's right.' Mostly.

Avery Johns turns to his PR with a shrug. Could we do this anyway?

'Would you consent to a body search prior to any meeting?' says the PR.

'You think I might have a Semtex waistcoat or a sniper rifle under this jacket? OK . . . Yes. If you must.'

The hotel security guard is persuaded to give me an inexpert frisk, during which he concentrates his search in the buttocks-and-high-inside-leg regions, offering me a wan smile as he does so. Then I'm invited to accompany Avery Johns through the dining room to a private area where a table has been arranged just for him. As we walk, I can smell Mohini's scent emanating from his clothes (his body?): that ambergris, that frankincense, that myrrh – a scent that brings back memories of her as powerfully as if she were in my arms. Her skin. Her hair. Her lips.

The PR is about to take a seat with us when Avery Johns says:

'Actually, Josh, would you leave us alone for the meal.'

'Are you sure, Avery?' looking sidelong at me, the maniac.

'I'm sure. I'll shout if I need help.'

'Unless I slice your voice box,' I offer with a smile that nobody shares.

'I'll be fine,' says Avery Johns.

The PR retires to the doorway, where he loiters nervously.

A waitress brings two bottles of wine: a white and a red.

'So,' says Avery Johns. 'That was a truly wonderful review. I suppose you didn't mean a word of it.'

'I meant to win the competition . . . but no: I'm not a fan.'

'Hmm. I remember you, you know. From that awful launch party in London. The plastic glasses and the hideous nibbles. When was that? Four, five years ago?'

'Something like that.'

'We were all so green back then. When I think of the deal they were offering me. They soon changed their tune when I changed my agent. You haven't got an agent, have you?'

'No.'

'Don't believe in them? I admit, even I resent the fifteen per cent. It's me writing the bloody things, after all. Would you like me to put you in touch with mine? I mean, I can't promise she'll take you on, but . . . '

'I'm not sure I've got anything for her to sell.'

'Not writing anymore?'

'Not writing the kind of stuff they want to publish.'

'Is that your problem with me? You see me as a sell-out?'

'My problem is your writing. It's cynical and sloppy. You clearly care nothing about the prose or the craft. The clichés are just shocking.'

'I'm sure you're right. Do you know who I wanted to be? Who my hero was? Have a guess.'

'Jack Higgins? Harold Robbins? Arthur Hailey?

He smiles stiffly. 'Ford Maddox Ford. Yes, you may smirk. I soon realised I would never be that good. But here's the thing: my readers don't care. They wouldn't even notice a fine prose style. They just want a story and perhaps a theme to work with. Books now are things to discuss in groups and online. They're things to plan a radio show around. Books are a kind of social media. Sometimes I think the marketing plan is created whether there's a book or not. They just look for one to fit.'

'People still love reading alone.'

'True, but they don't want style. Style is a hurdle between them and the stories. Readers no longer see reading as exercise, as some sort of route to betterment. If I want to be published, I have to acknowledge that.'

'I can't agree. If that were true, would Henry James still be in print? Joyce? Beckett? Shakespeare, Chaucer, Rabelais, Amis, Self, Woolf, Wolfe, Roth, Updike, Dos Passos—'

'Nobody reads those books. They're "reading list" books. Students buy them and never finish them.'

'Do you really believe that? Daniel Defoe has more readers today than I've ever had. Have you been inspired by nothing?'

'*The Curious Incident* was a very good contemporary novel. *Captain Corelli*, another.'

'Yes, they're good books. But they're not Sterne, Swift or De Quincey. They're not Cervantes or Diderot ... but you're a fan of Sterne and Diderot, aren't you? *Jacques le Fataliste*?'

'Ah, much of that interview at York was pre-prepared. There's so little time for me to ... '

I'm nodding. 'Do you remember your first York Festival? The celebrated address you gave on the value of good writing?'

'Celebrated indeed. In fact, I'm in discussions with Cambridge University Press to turn that into a small monograph that—'

'I wrote it.'

'I beg your pardon?'

'I wrote that address and sent it to our publisher. They told me that it was unsuitable and then I heard you reading it virtually word for word at the festival. They gave it to you because you were selling more books. Remember? Who gave it to you? Did it come through PR?'

Avery Johns is looking to the doorway where the PR seems to be talking on his mobile. 'I ... they told me they'd prepared it for me. I honestly had no idea ...'

'It's OK. I believe you. It's exactly the kind of thing they'd do. But I'd reconsider your deal with CUP if you want to avoid a plagiarism case. I have emails proving I wrote that address.'

'Hmm. I can see that you'd be bitter. Red or white?'

'White.'

He pours and the starters arrive, described to us as miniature rabbit pies with *jus* and a green salad. I think of Larkin and smile. Avery Johns' tweedy sleeve wafts a wave of that dark perfume across the table and again she's with me. I wonder if he knows.

'Mohini,' I say.

His fork pauses between mouth and plate. 'Excuse me?'

'Mohini. She used to be my student in Manchester.'

'Really? She hasn't mentioned anything.'

'We were also lovers for a short while before she vanished. The next time I saw her, she was fellating you in a car.'

He returns the unmasticated rabbit pie to the plate. 'I'm not sure I want to discuss—'

'What happened? How did you meet her? I'm not a vengeful lover; I'm just confused.'

He's thinking, gauging how much to say without the PR there to guide his thoughts. But he's enough of a writer to love a story more than caution. He leans forward.

'It was quite remarkable,' he says. 'I'd been in the building not ten minutes when she came up to me ... Well, you know what she looks like. And that unusual perfume. She took hold of my arm and whispered in my ear that we had to go into the gents immediately to ... to copulate. I was stunned, of course. But ... I just couldn't refuse and, my God ...!'

'I was in the next cubicle.'

'Ah. Hmm. She kind of disappeared during my talk with Lawson but returned again when I was leaving and just got into the car with me. Barely a word of conversation. And she's been with me since then.' He grabs the glass and downs half of it in a gulp. 'I'm afraid ... I suppose I can tell you this because you'll know ... I'm afraid I'm addicted. She just doesn't stop and I seem to have reservoirs of energy I never thought ... You'll laugh, but I sometimes think she's literally going to fuck me to death and ... that's somehow what I want. It's a suicidal passion.'

He stares at me plaintively, willing me to understand. And I do. I've felt it myself.

'I can't write,' he says. 'I'm past my deadline and the publisher is starting to nag. I've told them it's the pressure of the tour, but it's her ... it's her. I'm thinking about her even now: what she's going to do next. She's probably waiting for me in the room right now wearing nothing but a silk choker, or stockings or thigh-high leather boots and ... God, I'm getting aroused just thinking about it. I can't think about anything else. I'm neglecting people. I'm losing sight of things. Do you understand? Have you felt this? Tell me I'm not going mad.'

'You're going mad. She is a madness.'

He finishes the rest of his wine and pours another glass. 'You say she vanished from you?'

'Exactly that. Left the course without a word. We were together for just one night.'

'And?'

'And I'm still feeling the shockwaves.'

'She barely talks. She appears and disappears. Sometimes I wonder if I've dreamed her. Did you get that?'

'Yes.'

The waitress circles the table, sees that the rabbit pies are untouched and wanders back to the kitchen.

'Do you want her back?' he says. 'I'll give you my room key. I'll wait here.'

The word *no* begins to travel from the right hemisphere of my brain but gets short-circuited by static from the amygdala, which whispers synaptic sweet nothings. The smell of her perfume. The texture of her skin. That image of her wearing nothing but a silk choker. Upstairs. Now.

He's actually holding the card key over the table.

I see my hand moving towards it, when ...

'Oh, what's this?' he says, moving his seat back.

I turn and see the PR striding towards us flanked by policemen wearing guns.

Again?

One of the men drags me to a standing position and locks my arms behind my back. Avery Johns is removed to a safe distance by the PR.

'What's this about?' I say.

The second policeman takes a creased sheet of paper from his breast pocket and reads:

> *I, Thomas Fynn of Manchester Gallagher University, will strike a blow for the literary jihad today when I obliterate the infidel Avery Johns in Sheffield. Allahu Akbar!*

'Seriously?' I say. 'Do I look like a Muslim fundamentalist to you?'

'We're trained not to discriminate, sir,' says the taller of the policemen.

'Isn't there some sort of Police Internet or something? CopBook? Aren't you aware that the same thing happened before Christmas in York? It's a hoaxer. The same one. Clearly an absolute nutter.'

'We have to take these threats seriously, sir.'

'But I've already been searched and all they found was a scrotum. How was I going to obliterate Avery? With my fork? And why would I send you a message if I wanted to get away with it? Aren't these things normally sent after the fact?'

The policemen seem to be coming round to my point of view. One of them turns to Avery Johns and asks him if I've manifested any signs of threat.

'None at all – only cynicism and bitterness, but he's a writer, so . . . '

'Look,' I say. 'Look. Only four people knew about this meeting. My friend Will, in whose name I entered this competition, and three colleagues at work. I can't imagine it's any of them, but you might start with them. Perhaps they mentioned it to someone. I'm sure I've written no emails about it.'

I haven't mentioned Kalli. There's no way it could have been her. No way.

'We're going to have to take you to the station,' says the tall policeman. 'You're not under arrest, but I understand you'll be keen to help us with our enquiries.'

'Naturally,' I sigh.

Avery Johns comes forward and holds up a business card: *Avery Johns, Writer*. He slips it into my jacket pocket with a meaningful expression. He has the look of condemned man who must now eat his last meal and retire upstairs for some lethal injections, some electric bolts. I should envy him, but I can't.

No charges are pressed or brought. At least, not yet — and not against me.

Montage

WINTER PLODS pluvially towards a crypto-spring and my MA seminars proceed with both the regularity and the typical result of peristalsis. The students' collective novel is shit.

I should have known this, of course. But optimism and a fundamentalist faith in my teaching skills led me to believe I might counteract ignorance, apathy and chronic lack of ability. There have been flashes of hope. Earnest Youth has been the best, turning in regular pieces with strong evidence of improvement in each one. He's learning and adapting. Stalwart, too, has impressed me with a consistent work ethic and even a willingness to modify his creaking prose style to the median age of the class. In his mind, he's clearly taken on the mantle of the elder statesman – more probably, the *éminence grise*. Mum has gamely plugged away at the task like a woman coaxing response from a flaccid dong, but her heart isn't in it and her work is at best perfunctory. As for Dreadlock ... well, his writing, when he remembers to do it, bears all the hallmarks of a classic idiot. I may have to turn his contributions into a character with some kind of impairment.

Certainly, my hopes of being able to cobble this mess into something coherent looks like a task beyond my ability. There's no doubt each of them has learned a very useful toolkit of skills, not least the discipline to churn out the word counts and successfully edit their own work after feedback. I'm happy with that. My decision to work on a collective novel was a good one, for them. But the overall product looks utterly unpublishable unless written by/for a soap star. Marking it is going to be an issue. What was I thinking? I wasn't thinking; I was caught in a haze of toxic introspection. I see that now.

The clarity has come from my new project, code-named "The Lara Book". It's the first proper thing I've written since the masterpiece and I feel resurrected.

Something I forget between books is that the act of writing is quasi-conscious. You can think and talk about writing as much as you like. You can read and plot and make character diagrams. But it's only when you sit at the keyboard, face the blank screen and start to write in earnest that those mysterious parts of the brain wake up and sing. How else do you explain the serendipitous idea that comes out of nowhere to twist a scene, or the precise adjective you didn't even know you knew, or the felicitous phrase you'd never planned but which just ... comes as you arrive at it (see the first sentence of this chapter, which began with *Winter* and wrote itself thereafter)? This, this is the ecstasy of writing which I forget and which, between books, is present only as a nagging sense of absence. It's the sensation you're always secretly afraid will have vanished next time you call on it. Like prayer for the tentatively faithful.

The Lara Book is giving me that in potent doses. For the first time in my writing life, I'm writing with feeling — a dangerous thing for the habitual fiction writer, who must be the consummate faker, who knows that pleasing the reader is everything. Give them what they want and leave them panting for more. That's the kind of writing I've been used to. Now I'm negotiating reefs and undercurrents I've never before addressed, trying to find ways to simplify them for myself and for a reader. Emotion in writing is difficult. You can't just hang it out like washing to dry. Emotion is approached obliquely: suggested, alluded to. *I love you* is the emptiest phrase in the language when uttered without context. I've been re-reading Pat Barker's *Regeneration,* in which the horrors of the Great War are relived in Scotland rather than on the Somme.

I've also been sending pieces of it to Lara. She didn't respond at first, except to say that she'd received the stuff. Did she read it? I haven't pushed her. It's been enough to have a target reader: the one person I wanted to move. I asked myself early on if I was attempting to manipulate her with my writing and the answer, always, is: yes, of course. That's what writing is. The writer's job is to steer a reader through a story, evoke highs and lows, suggest and convey. Manipulation. Like Sartre said, reading is engineered creation.

But that doesn't mean I've sought to lie or mislead her. I've just been using the tools I know to make her see. Her initial comments were laconic; she knows enough about me to guess what depths may be hidden in the prose. She corrected some details, which has been welcome and necessary given the unreliable narrator of the writer's memory. Then came the praise – tentative and restrained at first, then increasingly personal. I knew I was writing well when she told me I'd made her cry. She remained silent for a while after that, perhaps wary of what the prose might do. What it did was increase the assault with ever greater subtlety, honesty and even simplicity, which has never been an element of my style.

We haven't met since that café near her parents', but I'm hopeful. I'm waiting for an invitation.

I have Kalli to thank for any breakthrough I've made. Subsequent tutorials have followed the pattern of the first: me struggling to find anything wrong with her work and she probing the weak spots of my psyche. An hour with her is like a month of therapy. She's a blonde manifestation of that little-discussed phenomenon of writing: that the good criticism you receive from a dozen sources during your formative period eventually coalesces into the single source of your own independent objectivity. Our best writing is the product of everyone who ever steered us the right way. I'm going to miss her when she goes back to America, though I can't imagine we'll be out of touch.

I wish I could say all tutorials were such a pleasure. Radio 4 has been back to the Vader suite for an hour's evasion, hypocrisy and mutual disregard. I couldn't use the same methods I used with LUFC because her IQ is in triple rather than double figures. Instead, I admitted to her that I'd rethought her excessive description after re-reading Eliot (George, not TS) and that, perhaps, there was indeed scope for a five-page exploration of tea being brewed, or a three-pager detailing Henley's quizzical eyebrow-raise in the seconds before she's bludgeoned and violated peri-mortem by Sir Thralgeon (a scene that would truly have benefitted from five pages of description). That should be enough to tip her book into the will-never-be-published category it was already flirting with.

As for Percy's septuagenarian bit-on-the-side, she's been back each week in her quest for the royalty millions. I've managed to avoid her during the book's very slight edit, and, being old, she's been happy to accept a series of sick notes from me via pube-wig-woman at reception: "caught a nasty chill," "gammy leg", "colostomy bag *etc*". But this darts-club Delilah won't be put off much longer. She knows the law, she says, and Percy, God rest his uxorious soul, would have wanted her to enjoy Blackpool.

I'm not even sure I want to go ahead with that deception anymore. Kalli made me see as much. Five hundred quid isn't going to change my life. Knowing that I shaped and edited the book is sufficient. I've got my own to write. So I've arranged for her to come and see me this week. I'll probably just hand over the cash to Delilah and let her know the book's already being published. She wouldn't have achieved that herself. The publisher will probably be happier with a dead Percy as their author rather than a live Harkett.

The Fenella book is finished, too. Fenella came (ooh!) top of the academy with a practical demonstration so outrageous it caused a black-out across the canton and left one of the instructors with limited vision in one eye. Thad, alas, was crushed and torn beneath a stallion that escaped from the stables and mounted him. It seems likely that Suri will request significant edits, which'll be a good opportunity for me to turn down their multi-book deal. The loss of the money is going to hurt a lot, but I just can't write that shit anymore. Lara doesn't approve. She's says I'm above it.

The biggest shock has been the revelation about my hacker/stalker. The jihadist flavour of the threat evidently meant that the police were obliged to take the investigation more seriously, and so they talked to the four people who knew about my lunch with Avery. I'm sure you've guessed already. It was Gwynn.

It all seems to make sense now. The sheer lunacy of that final threat was the work of an unhinged, possibly drug-assisted, mind. The entire awful novel that was *Toad of Stone*. The Wikipedia entry with its fantastic corroborative tissue. Lexxi Cummins, so perfectly judged to insult the culture of academia. My bank details? The knowledge about Fenella? My home address? Just a matter of snooping through my pigeonhole and sitting at my free-for-all MGU computer, which I apparently leave logged-on quite frequently. Turns out I'm constantly signed in to some shopping sites like Amazon, whence Lexxi may have come. All my own fault, they tell me. Was he also the old guy who called into the radio show? Or was that just another hater? Does it even matter anymore?

As for *why*, he apparently called it the "Iago Defence": no particular reason. Just to entertain himself. Just for a laugh. He was apparently well off the wagon when it started and he just built up a antic momentum, writing *Toad of Stone* over a single sleepless weekend on cocaine and some veterinarian pharmaceuticals intended for livestock. He held no personal contempt for me, he said. Quite liked me. Just couldn't stop himself. Laughed so hard writing *Toad* that he shat himself. Poets, eh?

I do feel slightly guilty that they've taken him away for rehab and counselling. I said I wouldn't press charges over the money stolen for Lexxi, but there'll probably be consequences for wasting police time in York and Sheffield. Jerry's hinted it's not a first offence. Something about repeated fire alarms at MGU before my time, back when Gwynn was into MDMA and Rohypnol. He was due for another crash, according to Janet. Just a pity he had to hit me.

Extra virgin

'WHEN CAN WE EXPECT to see the finished novel?' says Stalwart.

'That'll be a few weeks,' I say. 'I need to chop it down to about 80,000 and impose some stylistic consistency on it, but then I'll make sure you all see a copy.'

'Will we have an editorial sign-off?' he says.

'None. But that's good practice. If you ever get published, you'll have to accept whatever edits they give you, no matter how ludicrous or counter-intuitive they may seem.'

'So how will you be marking it?' says Earnest Youth.

'I have your individual contributions collected in their original form, along with the plot structures we drew up. I'll be marking your work according to the tasks you were set, just like in any sphere of professional writing.'

'Oh God!' says Mum.

'Don't worry about it,' I say. 'You know this grade counts for nothing. You'll each start your own novels next semester. Then you can worry.'

'And how, like, do we get paid?' says Dreadlock. 'I mean the royalties or the advance or whatever.'

'You can forget an advance. Only stand-up comedians get an advance these days. And even if the book did get published — which might take up to three years of fruitless submissions and a further year of production process — it'd be six months after that before you'd see any royalties. Fifty per cent of published UK writers make less than £5,000 a year from their writing, so your earnings by five, take tax off, and I think you'll see you don't need to see a financial advisor any time soon.'

'Why divide by five?' says Stalwart.

'Because I wrote the story and did the edit,' I say. 'You're technically my ghost-writers.'

Stalwart crosses his arms, purses his lips.

'I think you've all done very well,' I say, mentally omitting Dreadlock (whose portion will account for most of what I cut). 'You've learned the essential skills and you've used them in a large writing project. Do you feel you've got what you wanted from the course?'

'I do,' says Earnest Youth. 'I like the way you've drilled us. I didn't want book-club seminars where we just talk in generalities about whatever failed to win the Booker last year; I wanted a boot camp that taught me to write. I think I got that. And . . . I'd like to say thanks.'

Am I blushing?

'I found it hard,' says Mum. 'I've realised I haven't really got the time . . . not even to read all the books you've suggested. It's been a real struggle to produce the words each week.'

'But you did it.'

'I know . . . I know. But the kids have been complaining the washing isn't done and . . . '

'A washing machine is easier to operate than a games console,' says Earnest Youth. 'Teach them.'

'I know . . . It's just that I see now just how much work is involved. I used to enjoy writing, but this course has shown me how . . . how difficult and wearing it can be.'

'Nothing that's good for you is easy,' offers Stalwart.

'What about wanking?' says Dreadlock, reddening madly when he realises he's said it out loud. 'Er, yeah . . . I thought it was a good course, mostly.'

Profound feedback from the ready-meal heir. I wouldn't have expected less.

'Well, don't forget to fill-in the online course-review forms,' I say. 'And I guess that's all. Good luck with your future writing and I hope these classes will prove to be useful.'

They start packing backs and wrestling with coats. Mum offers tremulous thanks on her way out. Dreadlock salutes as he lopes. Earnest Youth self-consciously asks me if I'll sign a battered copy of my second novel (where on earth did he find a copy?). Stalwart lingers to the end and extracts an A4 brown envelope from his briefcase.

'I've had my solicitor draw up a contract regarding potential publication of the collective novel. I'd be grateful if you could read it through, sign it and return it to his address.'

'A contract?'

'One likes to do things properly. You may need to amend the four-way split.'

He settles the Panama hat on his head, nods a curt valediction and marches off down the corridor.

Prick.

THERE'S A NOTE from reception waiting for me when I get back to my desk. Avery Johns has been calling the university trying to get me. He's left a mobile number for me to call.

'Tom?' he says.

'Yes. You've been leaving messages for me at MGU.'

'Oh, yes. Yes. Tom. I was expecting you to call me.'

'Why?'

'I said I'd hook you up with my agent. And, you know, I was thinking about what you told me: about the publisher taking your address like that. I figure I owe you one. Bury the hatchet and all that.'

'You mean your people have asked you to talk to me about selling any copyright I might have on the address so you can go ahead with your CUP book deal.'

'I won't lie to you. That has come up. But it's not for me to discuss. I believe an offer will be made in due course. However, I was serious about my agent. She's going to be in Manchester next week if you want to meet her.'

'I don't know . . .'

'You don't have to sign anything. Just talk to her. Or don't. I really don't care.'

'How's life with the Dark Lady? What was she wearing after our meeting?'

'Nothing but a sheen of oil. It's an image I'll never forget.'

'Aromatic massage oil?'

'I don't know. It wasn't Extra Virgin, that's for sure. I actually slid off her at one point and hurt my wrist.'

'Well, I suppose that provided an excuse.'

'No. No. She went on top. She made me cry. I thought my heart had stopped and I was so happy when I realised I was still alive, I literally wept. She lapped my tears like—'

'Avery ... Look, I've got a supervisee waiting. I'll be at the university this time next week if your agent's in town. If not, never mind. I've got this far without one.'

'How far?'

'Bye, Avery.'

The conniving bastard – the whole agent thing is just about the copyright. How much could I get for it? Or should I just get an agent myself and go to CUP with my own proposal? They probably wouldn't take it from me anyway. It's only good if Avery wrote it.

'Was that Avery Johns on the phone?'

I turn to see Janet at the door. 'Yes. He wants me to meet his agent.'

'Great news. Tom hobnobbing with the stars. First Jerry, now you.'

'He's not a star, Janet. He's a tit. I've got to go. Supervisee.'

She dodges to one side as I scuttle down the corridor to the Vader suite, where her heavenly smell greets me.

'I'm going to miss your perfume, Kalli. Tell me the name so I can get some and spray it on my computer.'

She smiles, pristine as usual in a silvery dress. 'It's bespoke. You can't buy it.'

'Pity.'

'How about if I give you this?' She takes a white scarf from around her neck and hands it to me.

It should be warm from the heat of her skin but it isn't. The perfume, however, is powerfully locked into the silk. I fight the urge to cover my face with it, instead stuffing it into my jacket pocket ... where my fingers encounter an unexpected roughness of synthetic lace. I'm extracting the item when I realise, too late, what it is.

'Oh. Ah, I'm sorry, Kalli.'

'I'm guessing they're not your panties.'

'No. They're hers. I haven't worn this jacket for a while and ... '

'Give them to me.' She holds out her hand.

'What? Why? They're not clean.'

'I'm not going to *wear* them, idiot. I'm going to dispose of them.'

'I can do that. And should you be calling your tutor an idiot?'

'Yes. And no you can't. I bet you thought you'd already thrown them out.'

'Honestly, I thought I had ... '

'She left them for you on purpose. They're a talisman. They're why you're still having thoughts about her. As long as you have them, she has a hook in you.'

'If you say so.'

She takes the lingerie on the end of her pencil and lowers them into her bag. 'You really don't have a spiritual or supernatural fibre in your body, do you?'

'I guess not.'

'Everything is hormones and bio-electric energy, right? Brain waves and blood pressure. Man the divine endocrine system. That's why she hooked you so easily. She captured your glands. What ever happened to belief?'

'I believe in the ineffable aesthetic: the words that just come. I don't ask where they come from.'

'That's the only reason you deserve me.'

'I *don't* deserve you. I've been a useless tutor. I've learned more from you.'

'Have you? We'll see. I'm going to stay in touch with you and I'll be very disappointed if you're not writing.'

'Yes, ma'am.'

She shakes her head, smiling. 'I think the Lara Book is the best thing you've done.'

'So do I.'

'Have you won her round yet?'

'We might talk this evening. She said she'd call.'

'Would you publish? Or is it too personal?'

'No such thing as too personal if the writing's good.'

'That's the second reason you deserve me.'

'The sliver of ice?'

'The sliver of truth.'

'Do you want to discuss your writing before you go? There really isn't much point.'

'No. Let's talk about your writing.'

And we do, Kalli offering her usual laser-guided criticism and reinforcing all of my own half-formed, intuitive feelings about my work. The best kind of criticism. The only kind that works. We laugh, mock each other and swap quotes (she always winning with that photographic memory) until the hour has flashed by.

As we're standing together at the door, she leans in and brushes my cheek with her lips. A dry kiss. A cool kiss. I briefly put an arm around her slender shoulders.

'Be good,' she says, transfixing me with those glacial eyes.

'I'll try.'

Then she's gone.

At home, I keep checking to see if Skype is turned on. I've crammed Lexxi (poor Lexxi) into the cupboard under the stairs so that no hint of cleavage or blondeness can peek out to shame me. I've even tidied the room a bit – at least, the area the laptop camera can see. No need to exaggerate.

And as I wait, I'm half-watching early Aerosmith videos on YouTube and thinking about Avery's agent. The Lara Book will be finished soon. It's barely a commercial proposition, but then neither was Percy's slow-burning examination of a marriage and somebody wants to publish that one (I still haven't told them I'm not the author). Should I put the Lara Book forward for publication and watch it gnawed by the rats of the market as the masterpiece was? Or should I just print it and give it to Lara next Christmas? An appreciative audience of one is surely better than a diluted version slopped out to the general public. Isn't it?

I don't know. It seems almost blasphemous for a good book not to be read. The unread book is like the unsung song. Look at Perry and Tyler on the screen there: sweating, gurning, gyrating. They couldn't do that on their own in a room. They need the audience. A book needs a readership.

There'll be other books, of course. I've got ideas. A writer must always have ideas. I'm very interested in writing something about first-century Judaea. Lot of research involved there, though. I also quite fancy a futuristic thing like *Clockwork Orange* or *1984*. An autobiography would be a lot of fun, but not until I've made it. Made it? Ha.

Lara's call comes in and I fumble to turn off *Love in an Elevator*.

'Lara, hi. Can you hear me? Can you see me?'

'You've been cleaning.'

'Pretty much the first time since you left.'

'I thought you'd throw that vase out.'

'I've put some flowers and water in it.'

'So I see. What are they? Lilies?'

'No idea. They looked colourful and the woman said they'd last.'

'So I'm going to be in Manchester next Thursday. Mum and dad's anniversary.'

'Great.'

'And I thought we could, you know, meet for a coffee somewhere.'

'That would be wonderful.'

'How about lunchtime?'

'OK,' thinking: the no-man's land of the day. Not like a morning summit, not like an evening date. 'I'm at MGU that day, but if you come to the reception they'll call me and we can go out. I'm not teaching. Just marking.'

'I'll do that.'

'How's things? Work OK? Seen Will around?'

'I know you hate small talk, Tom. We can talk about the book if you like.'

'Thank God.'

'It's very good . . . but you know that. Very real. It's been interesting for me because . . . because there are so many things you never said. Were you really thinking those things, or is it all just retrospective fiction?'

'I was thinking them. Perhaps it's fairer to say I was feeling them.'

'But you never said. Why didn't you talk to me?'

'I . . . I just couldn't. I could have *written* it. But all of my time was going into the books.'

'Have you ever considered you should talk more? Not just to me. You seem to spend more time with people you've made up than you do with real people.'

'Yes. I'm realising it more and more.'

'You've got me.'

'Have I?'

'Yes. I'm your friend.'

'Are you wearing eye make-up?'

'From work, Tom. It's not for you. Friends, OK? You've got a lot of repair work to do.'

'I know.'

'Want to tell me about your day?'

'My blonde American supervisee has gone home.'

'Pity.'

'And one of my MA students wants me to sign a contract concerning the novel we've been working on.'

'Sounds like he's ready for the industry.'

'Yes. How about you? Tell me about your day. I know I don't know anyone you work with or even what you do, but maybe now's a good time to catch up. Just talk. Let me listen to you ... for once.'

She laughs. Pretty eyes. And she talks for the next hour about the inconsequentialities of her life, which are as fascinating to me as a new author I've discovered. Not once does she mention another guy in a way that might cause me suspicion.

Not tekkin' enny more

I'M STILL THINKING about this a week later as I'm at my pigeonhole collecting the end-of-term marking: a two-foot pile of bound student novels. Not only LUFC and Radio 4 (a low third and a high 2:2 before I even read them), but also books that Jerry's supervisees have been working on. These are complete mysteries to me, though experience shows that no student has ever understood − or often even attempted − structure in a first novel. Same issues every year: inchoate ideas badly executed, inconsistent style and tone, unfunny comedies, genre dressed up as literature, and rich evidence of multiple drafts hacked inexpertly into a hectic *mélange* just for submission. Reading them will be like passing multiple kidney stones.

Jerry clicks the door pin code and enters. 'Ah, good. You've got the scripts.'

'Yes. Really looking forward to reading them. Comfy chair, glass of wine, shotgun in the mouth.'

'That's dark, Tom.'

'Sorry. I'm actually feeling quite positive these days. In fact, let me congratulate properly on your book deal. I really mean that. You deserve it.'

'Thanks. You know it was all down to Kalli, don't you?'

'Kalli?'

'Yes. I met her last summer in Texas. Remember I told you I was in Austin? There was a big book signing at a shop there and I got talking to her. I persuaded her to take a year in Manchester and she defibrillated the writer in me I thought was long dead. I've been in touch with her since then.'

'She didn't mention a thing.'

'Well, she's discreet like that. How did you find her?'

'She's changed my whole perspective on writing. I've just finished a book that might be my best yet. Avery Johns' agent is dropping by the university today and I might try my luck.'

'Avery Johns? Well done. And good luck with it. You've realised, of course, that there's something special about her.'

'She's a special girl.'

'No, I mean ... She must have discussed the, ah, the spiritual side of what she does.'

'Oh, yeah. All that mystical stuff. Daemons and demons. The anti-muse. We laughed about it. Did she tell you anything about Mohini?'

'Discretion was her code, but I think I can guess. Where there's darkness, there's light. Where there's inspiration, there's apathy and lack of volition. Control versus impulse.'

'You *have* been talking to her, haven't you?'

Jerry shakes his head and smiles as if I don't understand. 'Look, Tom – I'm afraid there's a few bits of bad news ... '

'Fired?'

'It might not come to that. The Quality department is investigating your decision to have the MA group write a collective novel. The university may have to reimburse the students for a semester because their payment was essentially contractual. They didn't get what they paid for.'

'How did Quality find out? Are they bugging the classrooms now?'

'They know everything, Tom. Big Brother is always watching.'

'The students were very happy with my idea. They agreed unanimously.'

'It's seems one of them has made a complaint anyway.'

'Stalwart.' I'm failing his submission. Let him appeal.

'I can't say who. And, well, there's also been a couple of complaints from faculty members.'

'What? Why?'

'The sex doll offended quite a few people.'

'That was Gwynn's doing, not mine.'

'I'm sure you can argue that. And Elaine has also made a formal complaint.'

'Elaine? Who's Elaine?'

'Mature lady. She works on reception? It seems you've been requiring her to give a series of increasingly silly excuses to an old woman who's pursuing you. The most recent thing — septic scrotum? — well, it seems that was the final straw.'

'I've never seen that woman smile.'

'Smiling isn't part of the job description, Tom. I suppose she's efficient.'

'Like cancer.'

'Perhaps you'd like me to be your representative in the hearings. It's important to take them seriously.'

'I expect so.'

He shrugs. Nothing more he can do.

'Thanks, Jerry.'

Janet clicks into the room. 'Hi, guys. Oh, is that my pile of marking? Great. Really looking forward to that.' She mimes cocking a pistol, putting it to her temple and firing.

'Remember,' I say, 'that Quality is always watching. They've got a midget in that laser copier recording everything.'

'Gee, isn't MGU great?' says Janet to the copier. 'Sure do love this marking!'

'Very funny,' says Jerry. 'The spirit of Gwynn alive and well.'

'You've got a visitor, Tom,' says Janet. 'The miserable hag at reception told me to tell you. Your guest is apparently waiting in the meeting room across the way.'

'Cheers. That'll be my meal ticket courtesy of Avery Johns. Her name's Elaine, by the way, that merkin-headed woman at reception.'

The agent has hung her coat on the back of the door so I can't see through the reinforced glass. I wait briefly, wondering what kind of demeanour to adopt. Saturnine writer? Congenial writer? Busy academic pressed for time? Deranged bomb hoaxer and Avery-baiter? What's she expecting? Or is this all part of his scheming to get that copyright? I'll just go in as Tom Fynn, God help me.

It hits me as soon as the door opens: that perfume. Frankincense, sandalwood. Myrrh. She's sitting at the table wearing a black halter top with a plunging *décolletage* and a crop that reveals her midriff. Her cleavage resounds upon my retinas like a cymbal clash. Her navel is a target. Her collar bones are nunchucks to knock me unconscious. My descriptive faculties are failing me ...

'Hi, Tom.'

Those dark eyes. Those teeth. Those lips.

'What are you doing here?'

'Avery told me to come. Will you help me to come?'

She leans back in her chair. Anatomy moves beneath ensheathing fabric.

'You walked away from me, Mohini. You disappeared. You can't just come back like this.'

'Why not?'

'Because it's not how humans behave.'

'We're all just animals in the end, Tom.'

'No we're ... What are you doing? Don't ... Put that back on!'

The breasts are free. She's topless in an MGU meeting room. They are magnificent. I thrust my hands into my jacket pockets to keep them away from her and my left meets the cool silk of Kalli's scarf. Instinctively, I twist it around my hand like a boxer's strapping and some of its tassels flutter free.

'What's that?' she says, her eyes flashing darker.

'A scarf. Look, just put your top back on. We can't talk if you're—'

Her face has become distorted with outrage. 'Whose scarf?'

'Does it matter? Just get dressed for God's sake! Nothing is going to happen. It's over.'

I'm waving my hands, and with them the scarf, which spreads Kalli's scent like a censer at Mass. Mohini is backing away.

There's a knock at the door.

'Go away!' I shout.

The door opens with a gravelly muttering.

'Oh no,' the new arrival says, 'I'm not tekkin enny more of them excuses wi' yer gammy sack and yer swollen bowel. I'll 'ave me manuscrip' now, yer jumped-up little shit.'

Darts-Team Delilah.

'Oh!' she says, seeing Mohini topless, standing and enraged – apparently being threatened by me with a raised hand. 'Oh! Oh! Is it a rape?'

'No it's not a fucking rape!'

'Oh!' Delilah leans heavily against the back of a chair, then topples to the floor, where she lies inert.

'Is she dead?' says Mohini.

'Put your top on, for the love of Christ!' I say, kicking the door closed so that nobody can see this hideous *tableaux vivant*. I lean down to Delilah's mouth to see if she's breathing. She's not. She might be dead. She smells like she had cat food for lunch.

First aid. Mouth-to-mouth.

'Mohini – do you know mouth-to-mouth?'

'The kiss of life?' She pouts, still topless.

I try to remember a course MGU made me do for students who might heave Special Measures. Do I tilt the head? Something about the tongue obstructing the airway? I look down at the imploded mouth, dentures askew, lips like discarded rubber bands. Can I?

I'm pinching her nose and trying to get an airtight seal on her wrinkled chicken-and-rabbit mouth when there's another knock at the door.

'Yes?' says Mohini.

'No!' I shout, too late, as Lara appears at the crack, saying, 'The woman on reception said I could . . . '

The door stops against Delilah's legs. I'm within kissing distance of an unconscious seventy-year-old lying on the floor. There's a surpassingly beautiful Indian girl topless against the wall.

Lara turns without a word and heads back along the corridor.

'Wait! It's not what it looks like!'

I struggle to stand, then struggle to move the old woman's dead weight to open the door and get out. I glimpse Lara turning the corner to the lifts.

I race after her. The lift doors are closing as I arrive. I see her for a second though the closing gap. Her eyes lock on mine. She's shaking her head: disappointed, sorrowful. Humiliated.

'Lara … I …'

The doors clank closed.

I should run down the stairs, but there's a woman dying in my meeting room.

'Is everything OK?' says the young man who works on reception. 'I just saw you running and—'

'Call an ambulance. There's an unconscious old woman in room three.'

And a topless ex-student. No ex-girlfriend. No agent.

No deal for the masterpiece. No more money from Fenella. No hope of personal gain from Percy's book. Multiple complaints against me. My only job in jeopardy. A sex doll living under my stairs. Two weeks of marking to do.

What now?

Kalli's scarf is still wound around my hand. I lift it to my face and inhale.

I suppose I'll keep on writing.

What else can I do?

The end

Dramatis personae

OF COURSE, the end is never really the end. The storylines go on forever — just off the page. For example:

Avery Johns failed to bring out his much-anticipated next book. Instead, he took time off at a facility in California reputedly specialising in the treatment of sex addiction. The film of his earlier novel, starring Scarlett Johansson, received a critical mauling but boosted his overall book sales by around 22%. Firing his previous agent, he negotiated a six-figure advance on a three-book deal with Penguin.

Jerry's book was well received by the handful of critics who reviewed it. However, distribution problems meant that there was difficulty getting it into the shops and the marketing budget was only moderate, so ... you know. He continues to teach full time at MGU and is said to be working on another book.

Will Trewitt still works in Internal Communications in London, still hates his job, still can't lure Carol into conjugal relations and can't remember the days when he could sit and read a paper in silence. He still meets Lara occasionally around town, and has benefitted from an implausible number of competition wins.

Dreadlock Twat dropped out of the MA course, got a haircut and is now a Packaging Logistics manager at his father's ready-meal factory in the south of England. He remains partial to de weed but has shown no further interest in creative writing.

The *Fenella Ardent Chronicles* (renamed *Teach Me a Lesson!*) began on America's Hot Channel X to immediate popularity. Starring adult performer Lexxi

Cummins, the show went into a second series and saw sales of the original novels increase exponentially. Further titles by "Jed Tyler" followed, but fans claimed these books were nothing compared to the originating trilogy.

Gwynn Palmer emerged from rehab a changed man and with a new poetry collection entitled *Intoxication*. On the strength of this, and following the slow-burning acclaim for his Apothetae and Agoge address at the Las Vegas Creative Writing Conference, he was offered a professorship at UNLV. He is very happy in Sin City and has no plans to return.

Darts-Team Delilah recovered from her "funny turn" and took £500 for the Percy manuscript. She then engaged an agent, renegotiated the contract and steered the marketing for the book with various tales of Percy's life. When this was a huge success (serialised on Radio 4), she had her own story ghost-written to even greater acclaim. She lives in Blackpool, where she owns and runs a guesthouse.

Earnest Youth continues to write. He won a national short-story competition the year after the course and is planning to revisit the novel he eventually gained a first-class grade for at MGU.

LUFC's novel *Giddy Up, Our Kid* received a fail grade at MA and went on to be published by a small independent publisher in Manchester, becoming something of a cult title among readers who saw it as one of the best worst novels ever written. The endorsement on the cover reads: "This is a masterpiece" – TG Harkett. Elton John has reputedly bought the film rights.

Janet continues to work at MGU. The following year, she began an affair with a student that turned into marriage and monogamy. Her book *The Language of Film* has become a first-year set text at many universities.

RADIO 4 made another official complaint when she didn't get the first-class degree she expected. She is currently studying for another MA in Creative Writing at a different university and will continue to do so until she gets a first, until her novel is published, or until she dies. Death comes to us all; publication is rare.

Mum dropped out of the course due to familial pressures. She realised that she preferred being a reader to a writer – a realisation that will increase her happiness.

Lexxi Cummins (the doll) spent a few weeks longer under the stairs, her perineal cavity empty and her auto-grip hands holding nothing. She was later found wrapped in bin bags outside a charity shop in central Manchester and became famous there as a shop-window mannequin.

Stalwart began work on a novel that went on to achieve a low 2:2 at MGU. He appealed and threatened to sue the university, but his case was interrupted by charges of "inappropriate touching" brought against him by several members of his church's scout group. His court date is pending.

The student's collective novel was rejected by around thirty agents or publishers, eventually being uploaded to Amazon at £0.01 and selling 129 copies. Royalties were duly paid to those who requested them.

Kalli continues to be a student on different Creative Writing courses around the world. She never seems to graduate, and shows no interest in either an academic or a writing career.

Mohini's whereabouts are unknown.

Lara continues to work in London, occasionally travelling north to see her parents. Recently, she's been thinking about moving back to Manchester. Friends say she seems happier there.

HOW I WROTE THE BOOK

(Multiple spoilers)

THIS BRIEF ESSAY details the origins, plans and execution of the novel. If you decide to read the essay, I advise you to do so only after reading the book. Reading it beforehand will turn it into what I see: a patchwork of separate but loosely-stitched elements. If you're a creative writer, however, you might like to read the essay first and use the novel as a prolonged lesson. Whichever way you do it, the essay will prevent you from reading the book purely as a reader. You'll read it as a writer.

By way of a disclaimer, I cite Orwell's celebrated 1946 essay "Politics and the English Language" in which he writes that he himself is probably guilty of many of the stylistic errors he describes. *Creative Writer* is not the best novel in the history of literature, but it is the best novel I was able to write in 2014. If it's flawed, I hope you'll learn (as will I) from its flaws.

Origins

I wanted to write a book about creative writing, which I've taught at a university for a few years and which I've been attempting to master for around twenty years (resulting in a number of published, but unsuccessful, novels). My aim was to peek through the keyhole of the Creative Writing MAs that have become standard at most universities and to offer some "gossip" about what these are really like for students and lecturers. Everybody likes an inside view. I also wanted to share some experiences of being published, which very many people aspire to and so few achieve. If I could additionally make the book a sort of handbook on how to write a novel, this would marry all of my intentions

From the outset, I intended the book to be comedic, bawdy and relatively fast moving. My model in this was partially John Niven's 2008 novel *Kill Your Friends* in which the author lays bare the music industry, and partially Anthony

Burgess' character Francis Xavier Enderby, who is an unsuccessful poet and sometime lecturer across four books. The shortest of my previous novels had been 95,000 words and I wanted to experiment with something shorter (about 75,000) on the reasoning that a short book is leaner and more tantalising ... if it is any good. William Sutcliffe's excellent *Are You Experienced?* (1998) has long been one of my ideals of the short comic novel.

I also knew that the book must offer a first-person narrative perspective and that Tom would be that narrator. None of my previous six novels had used this approach because I have always been wary of first person. It can limit the portrayal of other characters and it requires a compelling voice. The so-called voice novel (Nabokov's *Lolita*, Amis' *Money*) is something I had always wanted to attempt but been afraid of. It requires a lot of authorial confidence and the ability to riff spontaneously in the character's voice. Could I do that? Have I done that? You be the judge.

The style of the book would be driven by the character-narrator: literary in influence but hopefully also easy to read. I wanted to allow myself the luxury of some word play while retaining a legitimate excuse for it. Tom is a show-off, as am I. During the writing of the book, I was careful to read mostly the kind of writers Tom would like: Nabokov, Burgess, Amis, Self and a bit of Burroughs. I think their influences are evident.

As for main characters, the storylines suggested them automatically: colleagues, students, friends. Many more would have to be created especially once I started on story and plot. It's important to stress, however, that these origins were nothing more than an idea. They were not enough for a novel. A novel requires story and structure, which comes with much greater difficulty.

Story

I had no story. I had only characters and a loose setting. Story is essential to engage the reader — it lays the breadcrumb trail throughout the novel and encourages the reader to participate by inferring, guessing, predicting, expecting, confirming and/or being surprised. Without story, there is no reason to read on to the end. Thus, story must be imposed on the material.

Ideas came slowly. What if Tom had the opportunity to publish a book by a dead student — where might that lead? What if he had written a good book and was waiting to hear about it? What if he was also writing porn to pay his rent? All of these appear in the book, but none is compelling enough on its own to drive the novel. They are minor breadcrumbs that the reader may vaguely look out for.

A stronger idea, I thought, might be if Tom was sufficiently unpopular to attract a stalker who would pursue him with ever greater antipathy: a kind of avenging force. This was another reasonable mechanism for the reader to follow, although I was quite clear I didn't want this to be a thriller and that the unmasking of the stalker was not to be the big finale. The stalking had to be merely an adjunct to the existing action. I still had no story that would help me to structure the entire book. I had only a few strands to encourage reader engagement.

The breakthrough was entirely serendipitous. I idly picked up one of my Chambers dictionaries for a quick flick (as one does) and the first word I saw was *aboulia*: "loss of willpower; inability to make decisions". That sounded like another way of describing so-called writer's block. What if, instead of there being a muse, there was an *anti-muse*: a spirit that sapped energy and prevented inspiration? What if that figure could become an actual character influencing Tom?

I've long been interested in the mythological figure of the succubus: the alluring female who visits men in their sleep, seduces them to orgasm and sucks their life force. These figures exist in the folklore of most cultures and I was drawn to the Indian incarnation known as Mohini — a name that also seemed to go with the notional surname *Aboulia*. My temptress was born. She'd be a dangerous beauty who played on Tom's existing weaknesses to bring him down. I remembered a quote from William Goldman where he mentions the demon that challenges a writer's self-belief. She would be this demon.

Almost simultaneously, I understood that an anti-muse could only be vanquished by the influence of an actual muse. This would be Kalli, named after Calliope, one of the nine muses of Greek Mythology (the muse of epic poetry). I remembered another quote, from Orwell, whose demon was a positive one driving the writer to continue – more a daemon than a demon. Structure was now becoming much clearer.

Structure

The two muses helped me to decide I would split the book in half. Tom would be brought low(er) in the first half by the lascivious influence of Mohini, all of his worst traits being encouraged until he crashed at the mid-point. This occurs almost exactly halfway at the York Festival. He meets Kalli shortly after, she having been introduced earlier by Jerry. She starts to lift him out of the pit he's in and revivifies his spirit to the point where he feels inspired to write again.

It made sense to include all of Tom's back-story in the first half of the book, partly to get it out of the way (too much looking back means we can't look forward) and partly because it meets the requirement of emphasising his failure. I decided early on that a prologue would be used to turn the first half into a kind of circle or circuit which would be completed at the mid-point. Thereafter, it was all to be (relatively) upwards.

The prologue also served the important purpose of starting off with some pace, promise and engagement. Otherwise, the book would have begun with the close analysis of the Fenella fragment: a slow start. The prologue was written at the same time as the York Festival chapter and stuck on the front. Other than that, the book was written in order. I prefer this method because it grows organically from its own roots.

It was only after I'd written about half of the book that somebody asked whether Tom would go back to Lara. She was never initially going to be a character except in the symbolic sense of what Tom gave up to get published, and as an occasional voice of caution or regret (her call after York). It occurred to me that Lara could become the "woman in the middle" between the supernatural figures of Mohini and Kalli. In winning her back, he would somehow go back to the start and be able to begin again. She would be his redemption — what he is left with after the battle of the muses.

The three-women structure alongside the Fenella/Percy/Stalker threads seemed to be enough to engage a reader, the rest being Tom's uniquely twisted way of going through life. Chapter structure would involve distributing the various story threads intermittently throughout, always leaving a gap for the reader to anticipate.

Characters

Tom is necessarily a version of me, though I am much nicer and more handsome. No real lecturer could get away with what he does, though many would ardently love to. He is, in that sense, a fantasy figure: the guy who says and does what we might wish to, and who mostly gets away with it. He is therefore also an anti-hero — an essentially bad person but one with whom we can sympathise because we feel his frustrations (especially if we're writers). As well as being a lecturer, he is also a student. He has achieved minor success, but been ruined by it. He lives to write and is the archetypal creative writer, with all the positive/negative associations of the term. His arc is from low to high, seeking redemption but ending in relative failure — the experience of most aspiring writers.

Mohini is characterised by her darkness of skin, of hair, of eyes and intent. She represents loss of control in aesthetic, moral and sexual spheres. Look again at the adjectives and similes that describe her: dark, infernal, insensate. It occurred to me as I began to write her that she could literally have been Shakespeare's Dark Lady and that she has moved through history destroying the will of writers — something Tom never really grasps, though Kalli and Jerry tell him as much. Her physicality is voluptuous, but we learn almost nothing about her mind. She's not that kind of muse.

Kalli has to be Mohini's opposite: athletic rather than shapely, pale rather than dark, cerebral rather than corporeal. She's interested in control and her relationship with Tom is on a purely intellectual plane. Descriptions reinforce her divine nature, her coolness, her intelligence. Both she and Mohini give Tom talismans (panties, scarf) and both are recognised/differentiated by their distinctive perfumes: base notes for Mohini, top notes for Kalli.

Will was created purely as a sounding board. Tom's solitary life at the keyboard meant it was difficult for me to put him into social situations where he could reveal himself in dialogue, so Will provided the requisite solution. He's there as a conduit to Tom's thoughts and concerns, as well as being a useful plot mechanism with the competition entries that lead to Christmas in London and the Avery meeting. He also allows us to see Tom as someone who does actually have friends and who is normal in some respects.

Tom's colleagues are exaggerations of university lecturers. The real thing is typically too normal to make a good character, or too-over-the top to be credible. Thus Jerry is the voice of reason to balance Tom's negativity; Janet is an ally and an additional voice to convey some truths about MA courses; Gwynn represents the occasional eccentric to be found in the Ivory Tower. I didn't decide Gwynn was the stalker until Tom went to Las Vegas. Previously, I'd been keeping my options open with LUFC, Stalwart and an unnamed self-published author. I chose Gywnn because, as I said above, I didn't want the stalking thing to be the driving narrative motivation. It had to be an arbitrary thing and Gwynn seemed to be the kind of guy who'd do it for no particular reason. Why the name Gwynn? I'd read Amis' *The Information* just before starting to plot this book and his character's name snuck in, albeit with a different spelling. No comparison is intended. All other characters (except Lara) were named spontaneously as I came to write them.

Lara's name is a sound I like. The repeated '*a*' seems open, like a sigh or a song. She doesn't give much away, and this is a symptom of Tom's first person narration. He knows more than he's saying and so we see Lara between his lines. She's an absence in him and a reflection of him.

The various MA and BA students are not based on any actual student. They do, however, combine all of the tropes and traits I've seen in the last twenty years of being a student and a teacher of creative writing. If you feel you recognise yourself in any student, I wouldn't be surprised. The students in this book represent facets of *all* creative writers, good and bad. However exaggerated some of these may seem, all are genuine traits.

Avery Johns is a generic rival established to create conflict. He's a personification of the publishing industry, but also a victim of it. I'd like to think that Mohini stays with him so long because he's breakable. She can, and does, ruin him creatively, though he continues to earn. He represents everything cynical in the market, and yet he's also something of a model to writers who want to make money. We may dislike him, but he's living the dream while Tom languishes in righteous failure.

Lexxi Cummins (the doll) was never meant to be more than an attack from the stalker, but I decided to make her a running joke when I started to wonder what Tom might do with her. Vegas was too much of a temptation and I couldn't resist putting them together in a lift.

All other characters (Suri at G-Spot, Elaine the receptionist, conference attendees, publishers *etc*) were created as I got to them. Most were required only to represent a type or provide a foil for Tom. I have no idea why I gave G-Spot Carrie a broken arm, the Beef Dreams' editor a bobble hat, Elaine a pubic scalp, or that Vegas conference delegate dungarees. Those are the first images that came to mind when I called on the characters.

Writing process

The beginning is clearly important. It must establish the narrative perspective (Tom's sardonic first person), introduce characters and the world of the story, and begin to initiate storylines prior to their overall staggered chapter structure. I would expect to do all of this within the first 10-20% of the book. Thus, by chapter three, we've met Percy, the masterpiece and all Tom's colleagues. We've also heard about Fenella, Mohini and Lara (as part of the back-story). By chapter seven, we've met the seminar students (including Mohini), Will, the Penthesilea blog, the anonymous stalker and Avery Johns. These are our major plot elements (apart from Kalli, who belongs properly to the second half and who is mentioned first in chapter thirteen). But who to start with?

I started (forgetting the prologue) with the Fenella extract, which is an insight into Tom's perspective on writing, and wrote the book strictly in order according to a plot that detailed the contents of each chapter. This was necessary in order to ensure that the various storylines were distributed evenly, leapfrogging from one to the next so that the reader would always have something to expect. In the past, I've plotted the entire book in advance, but this time I plotted only to the mid-point and plotted again when I got there, knowing that my storylines would have developed by then. This was partly because a voice novel is more unpredictable; you don't know where the voice might take you.

The plot notes tend to be vague and indecipherable to anyone who doesn't know the characters and storylines. For example, the verbatim plot notes for one of the early back-story episodes looked like this:

CHAPTER

Backstory - getting published. Vindication. Finally proved. Lifelong ambition. Partner tells him, disbelieves, meets publisher. Publication, reviews, royalties, signings. Like heroin - want more. But first hit is the best. Editing process. Other people published at same time. Better reviews. Not such good writers, but . . . Partner leaves. Get everything and lose it. chose writing . . .

With each chapter, I knew which storylines I was going to include and where these would fall in relation to the overall plot. Thereafter, it was just a matter of deciding which order the scenes would play out within chapters. I might begin a chapter with dialogue (for pace) if the previous one has been mostly Tom's interior thoughts, or I might choose a storyline that has been absent for a while, the better to bring it back into play. Sometimes it was a matter of juxtaposition. When Tom goes to London the first time, he sees the G-Spot editor before he sees the Percy editor, though it could have happened either way. Why? Because the Percy book was more important to him and perhaps to the reader, so I delayed it on purpose to build anticipation.

Plotting is the process of ordering story to ensure that it comes to the reader in an optimally engaging manner. This means promising, delaying, twisting and periodically delivering on promises. The culmination of Mohini's pursuit of Tom was initially to be a prolonged and lurid sex scene that might be nominated for the *Literary Review*'s Bad Sex Award. When I arrived at that scene, however, I realised that a long sex scene would be gratuitous and excessive even by the standards of this book. There was no way I could adequately realise the eruption of Tom's lust without falling into Fenella-style parody. My response was to leave the scene and drop memories of it into subsequent chapters, like reverberating echoes of the impact.

I had also planned for their relationship to go on a little longer, but this proved impractical in terms of overall length and pacing. If I was to write the shorter book I'd planned, I needed to control the length of storylines and so something had to happen to interrupt the affair. Having Mohini move her affections to Avery was a good solution, increasing the enmity Tom felt for that writer, raising the stakes for the imminent York Festival and permitting subsequent plot developments.

Inevitably, the writing process veers away from the plot as characters develop and structural constraints (pace, consistency, character arc) impinge. I'd originally intended Lara and Tom to engage in a long dialogue set-piece when she turns up the first time at Will's house in London. However, I knew he was going to meet Kalli the next day and that seemed like an excellent opportunity for Lara to see them, become jealous and want to get back with Tom. So the dialogue had to go in the name of narrative tension.

I'd known from the start that this wasn't going to be a thriller, so the end was always going to be tricky. In a thriller, I'd time the finale from the mid-point, accelerating storylines to terminal velocity. Tom was never going to become a big success, but he was going to reach a stage from which he might improve his life: a fizzle rather than a bang. The overarching impression I wanted to leave is that the life of the creative writer simply goes on and that the forecast is usually dim. Would this disappoint readers?

To counteract the effect, I decided to use two techniques. The first was the montage chapter: a common cinematic effect used to contract time. Until that point, the novel's chronology had unfolded relatively consistently, but my storylines (particularly the student novel and Lara Book) needed time to play out – time I didn't have. The montage allowed me to briefly speed up the action and deal with the Gwynn-stalker storyline in way that would resolve it without making it into a big deal. If there is any kind of twist here, it's a negative twist in which the whole pursuit turns out to have been drug-induced and utterly meaningless. The Iago Defence.

I also used a technique from the comedy-crime writer Carl Hiaasen, who often summarises what happened next to each of his characters, allowing the action to continue beyond the formal conclusion of the story. It's a technique I've always enjoyed as a reader and it allows for some nice ironies.

I decided very late into the novel that I would give the chapters titles. This was partly because consecutive chapter numbering offers nothing of interest to a reader and partly because a cryptic or amusing title sets the reader predicting how the chapter will deliver on it. In this, I was influenced by the chapter titles Ian Fleming used in the Bond books: "Through a Glass Darkly", "Irma Not So Douce", "The Man from Ag and Fish".

Style and themes

Simple generic prose might be compared to a melody. Its purpose is to relate story with as little overt emphasis on the language as possible. Melodic prose should be largely functional and transparent. Literary style, on the other hand, puts an opaque plane between the reader and the story, adding an extra layer of engagement – not a melody, but a symphony in which the reader can perceive many levels (brass, percussion, woodwind) combining simultaneously.

Tom being a writer, his narrative perspective should reflect some sort of style. Thus, I introduced a number of techniques intended to reveal his creative hinterland and the way he sees the world. For example, he regularly references his influences – (credit: Jackie Collins) – or stands momentarily outside his own narration to comment on sentence structure (the description of shoes in the York Festival chapter). It's a narrative perspective that's highly (self)conscious about language and its uses, often auditioning descriptive phrases to find the best. This can be seen in the description of Delilah, which plays with different tonalities in its search for the right image: *Her face is creased and gravity-ravaged. It looks like a monkey scrotum. Some orthodontic catastrophe has left her mouth pinched and shrunken: autumn's puckered windfall uncovered in a winter thaw.*

The major thematic movement in the book is associated with the transition from Mohini (insensate, impulsive) towards Kalli (controlled, responsible). Within this bipartite structure, a few other elements developed spontaneously that I was happy to follow. Tom's sense of invisibility, for example, works on a number of levels. It's his seeming lack of existence in the shops, to his publisher and on the Internet, as well as being part of the idea that the writer is often invisible behind his prose. The line between arrogance and genius is (significantly) also said to be invisible. After seeing Kalli for the first time in Vegas, Tom feels it's the audience that's invisible and he the only reality. This is the start of his recovery.

There are numerous Shakespearean elements in the book, notably from *Hamlet, Macbeth, Othello* and the sonnets. The idea of Mohini being the *actual* Dark Lady was one reason for this, as was an early realisation that Will was a kind of Horatio to Tom's Hamlet (Tom being a procrastinator who spends much of the action in a limbo between dejection and success). As a writer, he can hardly escape the reach of Shakespeare's stories, which are the genetic material of much writing in English.

Trivia

My real-life teaching of MA Creative Writing focuses almost entirely on the practical elements of research, story, plotting and structure. The thing I can't teach is the unpredictability of the actual writing process, wherein decisions are made on a whim and new storylines are engendered by the momentum of everything coming together. Such things are usually the best bits. Some examples:

Tom going to Las Vegas was never originally part of any story plan, but I woke in the night with the idea of him going there and it seemed a good solution. Vegas is a kind of fantasy other-world – a perfect place for Tom to meet Kalli and start his recovery. Many things come to me in such nocturnal interruptions, a phenomenon I explain by the writing part of the brain always working. For example, I had to grab a pencil one night and jot down the word *fissile*, which I used to replace *atomic* when describing a Christmas pudding. It's just a better and more accurate word.

Some of the book I wrote to music. I tend to be able to concentrate on writing whatever environment I'm in, and sometimes music is playing on the radio or PC or iPod. I wrote the Las Vegas conference address listening to Guns n' Roses' "Welcome to the Jungle" on repeat. Can you tell? I wrote the narrative perspective seminar listening to Red Hot Chilli Peppers' "Dani California", and the Lara section of the penultimate chapter listening to Taylor Swift's "Dear

John". Who knows whether music affects the tone of the writing? My second published novel was written listening almost exclusively to AC/DC's *Black Ice*.

Much of a novel is added piecemeal and in retrospect, often in response to prompts in a dream. I woke one night thinking it would be nice if Kalli read and responded to Tom's masterpiece, so I went back and dropped that into one of their dialogues. Just this morning, I woke with an urgent message to amend the skit on dictionaries following the present from Lara. I added a few lines accordingly.

The book took eight weeks physically to type, working to a daily target of at least 1000 words (the maximum was 3000, on this essay). This followed about three weeks of general thinking and jotting of potential character lists and storylines, and was followed by a week of editing.

The edit

I tend to write novels in a single draft, meaning that the storylines, order of scenes, word-count and chapters remain unchanged. My books do require an edit, however, and this is a systematic process of picking up various loose ends I've become aware of (and noted) as I write.

Most of the edit is concerned with imposing consistency: of storylines, of character voice, of tone, of pace. Characters tend to change over the course of a book, and Tom was more cynical and bitter until I became accustomed to his voice. He also spoke a little more formally until I introduced more contractions into his speech patterns. The edit had to make him the same at the beginning as he was at the start.

Lara became more important in the latter half. This necessitated fleshing her out a little more in the first half, filling in some context so that later scenes would have more meaning. At the same time, I had to remember that Tom is telling the story, and so we see Lara obliquely through his unwillingness to talk about her.

One good tip for editing is to read through the book a character at a time, reading only Will or only Jerry. Are their voices consistent? Do they seem to be the same person with the same kind of responses and opinions? Such things needed to be tightened.

It's the same with storylines. The plot means that I should have distributed storylines consistently, but I may have got carried away in the actual writing and lost sight of some. So I read through again story by story and ensure that Percy's book, for example, retains a regular development.

Inevitably, publishers or agents may wish to impose a further edit on the book if it is published. This edit may be designed to tailor the book to a specific market sector, or it may pick up on things the author has missed. It's amazing how some minor characters mysteriously change names or even disappear.

In summary

Books are designed to be hermetic − the reader is not supposed to notice the separate pieces and how they're put together. This is what makes reading a pleasure, but also a challenge for the aspiring writer.

As writers, we want to understand exactly how a novel is written. It doesn't help when a writer invokes the muse or speaks in nebulous terms about inspiration. If a subject is to be teachable, it must be analysable in terms of process and skills. Part of my intention in writing this book has been to strike a balance between reading as a reader and as a writer.

I hope I've succeeded to some degree. The book isn't perfect. I'm not a perfect writer. If you're a writer, I hope you enjoyed the novel for its own sake and that it's also presented a new way of reading and writing.

tom.fynn@yahoo.co.uk